O9-BTL-115

# SWORD THE MAKER'S DAUGHTER

## - BOOK ONE -

MEREDITH SHAW

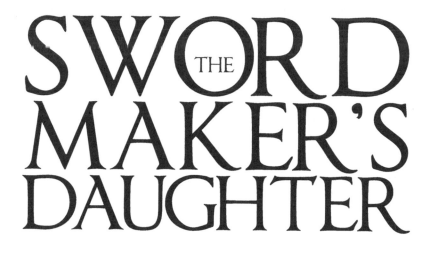

# SWORD THE MAKER'S DAUGHTER

## - BOOK ONE -

# THE POISONED PRINCE

**TATE PUBLISHING**
AND ENTERPRISES, LLC

*The Swordmaker's Daughter: Book One*
Copyright © 2014 by Meredith Shaw. All rights reserved.

No part of this publication may be reproduced, stored in a retrieval system or transmitted in any way by any means, electronic, mechanical, photocopy, recording or otherwise without the prior permission of the author except as provided by USA copyright law.

This novel is a work of fiction. Names, descriptions, entities, and incidents included in the story are products of the author's imagination. Any resemblance to actual persons, events, and entities is entirely coincidental.

The opinions expressed by the author are not necessarily those of Tate Publishing, LLC.

Published by Tate Publishing & Enterprises, LLC
127 E. Trade Center Terrace | Mustang, Oklahoma 73064 USA
1.888.361.9473 | www.tatepublishing.com

Tate Publishing is committed to excellence in the publishing industry. The company reflects the philosophy established by the founders, based on Psalm 68:11,
*"The Lord gave the word and great was the company of those who published it."*

Book design copyright © 2014 by Tate Publishing, LLC. All rights reserved.
*Cover design by Rodrigo Adolfo*
*Interior design by Jake Muelle*

Published in the United States of America

ISBN: 978-1-63063-250-2
EBook ISBN: 978-1-63185-772-0
Fiction / Fantasy / General
14.02.14

# DEDICATION

For my Lord Jesus Christ, my parents for teaching me to see the beauty in things, my brother, Matt, for helping me to see that anyone can be an artist, and my best friends, Abigail and Lexi, for always encouraging me and helping me find who I am.

# PROLOGUE

As the wind whipped through her hair, Zopporah cried out in pain.

*A lake is hardly a place to give birth*, she thought as the unbearable stab ripped through her body. Zopporah had been in labor for two days, and her husband, Läken, had never left her side. They had been peacefully rowing their small canoe in Greenwater Lake when Zopporah had first gone into labor.

Suddenly, the pain ceased. "What…What is it?" Zopporah gasped.

"It's a girl," Läken whispered. The disappointment of having the inferior sex caught him for a minute. But he shook it away and enormous pride for the small, light-haired baby in his arms filled him.

Läken rowed them back to the house and carried Zopporah to her bed so she could rest. He sat down and kissed the baby's forehead, pride once again welling up inside him.

"Zopporah," Läken said, "the child never cried." For a second, he worried. *Could she be too weak?* He thought frantically. *Wasn't it I myself that first held her when she was born?* He leaned down to listen to the short, unsure breaths of a newborn.

"Yes…" Zopporah whispered. "She's an angel, isn't she?" Zopporah looked down at the smiling baby and suddenly fell in love for a second time in her life. "She's exactly what I wanted in a child."

"What shall we name her then?" Läken asked merrily.

"Legna," Zopporah said firmly. "Something unique. Angel spelled backwards. It will give her faith in times when you are gone, defending the village."

Läken was one of the village heroes. He would learn of monsters and go on quests to destroy them. Then he would collect their spirit jewel to give energy to Aryanis, the Engjëllen's God, and the force that kept their water clean. The people of the village Engjëll had to drink the water to stay alive. Unlike normal water, the villagers could not live without it for a few days. The water was the Engjëllen's source of life. It gave them power and strength. Too much of the water would overdose them with power, and they would die from bodies too weak to hold the strength. Too little water and the Engjëllens would wither to ash. The bigger the monster Läken killed, the bigger the spirit jewel, which made more pure water.

A few days after Legna's birth, the visits from loving friends and neighbors came, all bearing meals, gifts, and love for the newest Engjëllen. Canned preserves of strawberries from their neighbors, a tonic made especially for newborn illness from the village healer, and a beautiful silk nightgown for the baby from Zopporah's closest friend, Alaqua, who was also expecting.

The time came when Alaqua gave birth to a healthy son, whom they named Traven. Zopporah brought Alaqua meals and gifts for Traven and stayed by her side during the few days after his birth, nursing her until she was stronger.

The time came when all was normal, and Läken had to return to his job as hero and energy collector.

∽

Läken roared as he dodged another of the gigantic green demon's furious blows. Rain poured down onto his face and he heard thunder rumble behind him.

"It's unbeatable!" Gidön, his shield-brother, screamed. A deep lake separated them, along with a rangun the size of a fully grown redwood tree. It was almost two hundred feet high, and its head blocked a bolt of lightning that shot down and struck a tree, burning it. Twisted, gnarled branches jutted out from the rangun's knees, elbows, and head. Mold and moss covered its body like fur, and its feet were covered with whitecap mushrooms.

Bátor, his other shieldmate, replied, "Not entirely! Aim for the mouth!" Gidön nodded in response and aimed his bow.

"I'll keep it distracted!" Läken yelled, leaping onto the creature's foot and stabbing his blade into it savagely.

The creature screeched in pain, and in response, Läken screamed, "I do not fear you!" He used his dagger and sword to climb up the back of the demon's leg, using them like one would when climbing a cliff. The rain continued to beat down on his face, drenching his hair and slipping through the slits in his armor. He continued climbing until he reached the Rangun's shoulder. His arms burned from the ascent, but he managed to pull his weapons free from the demon's matted hide. The rangun roared and turned its head to face Läken, hatred burning in its eyes.

Panting from his perilous climb, Läken whispered, "You can't win."

The rangun stared at him for some time and then he threw back his head and cackled, a horrid sound that reminded Läken of the snapping of bones.

"I will win," the rangun whispered back in a disturbing imitation of Läken's voice so accurate it sent chills down his back. The Rangun picked up Läken with two of its massive fingers. "Because I have *her* on my side." The rangun began laughing maniacally; his mouth distorting into unsettling ripples and circles that felt each sound before it was released.

"Gidön, now!" Bátor shouted. In quick succession, Gidön shot six arrows into the demon's mouth.

The laughing stopped abruptly, and the rangun stood, frozen in time. Then, it spoke its last words.

"I may not live but I can still win." With this, the demon threw Läken down on the ground and stomped on his legs with the last reserves of his strength. Läken screamed in agony as his legs were crushed. He could feel his bones being ground against each other, smashing and breaking into small pieces. Then, the rangun fell backwards as Gidön shot two more arrows into its mouth, killing it.

Läken turned to look at Gidön, but all that was left of where he once stood were wisps of purple smoke. He sat up and looked at his mangled legs, horrified by the result. All of the skin on his legs was peeled off, leaving only raw muscle. Shards of his own bones lay around him, bright white against the pools of red blood seeping from his legs. He could actually see the sharp edges of the shattered bones underneath the muscle.

Disgusted, he looked away, grimacing as another jolt of pain shot through his legs. The rain slowed until it was only a quiet drizzle, and the clouds began to move away, revealing the bright moon round as his newborn daughter's eyes. "Legna," he whispered.

"You have quite a wound there, Läken. Ketë is coming; he will bring us home."

"Bátor, if I don't make it—"

"Oh, don't say that! You are going to make it, even if I have to drag you all the way back to Engjëll myself."

"Thank you. But really, if I don't, tell Legna about me. Be a father to her. And Traven." Traven was Gidön's son, born only a few weeks after his own daughter. What had happened to Gidön,

Läken had no knowledge, only that the demon must have used some twisted form of magic to dispose of him.

"I will, I will. Now you stop worrying. It only makes the pain worse."

A screech overhead revealed Ketë, their elven partner, riding on his mount, a strange, half-bird, half-dragon creature. He broke through the clouds; his raven hair flowing freely in the wind, and he landed his steed a few yards away from Läken and Gidön.

"How bad is the damage, Ketë?" Läken gasped though he already knew the answer.

There was a pause and then Ketë responded, "Both are broken, and there is some nerve damage. Läken..."

"Spit it out! Delaying the prognosis won't help anything."

Ketë looked at him with sorrow. "My friend...this is a permanent crippling. You will never walk without support again."

Läken's heart began to race. "Never? So that means..."

"You may never wield a sword or fight in any way again...if you want to live."

Läken sat, his legs going numb with pain. He stared down at his sword, an old friend of his. Double-edged, the blade was bright white steel. The crossguard and hilt were both a deep crimson. His blade had been given to him by his mentor, Wane, fifty years ago. He had been using it ever since.

But now, he was being told he could never do what he loved again. All because of a rangun with bad sportsmanship.

"Gidön...Where is he?" Läken whispered. Aside from Bátor, Gidön was Läken's closest friend and ally.

"The rangun put a spell on him. I...I'm afraid he is lost, Läken. I'm sorry," Bátor responded.

"His son...He is fatherless..."

"Not if we act as father figures to him, guiding him."

Suddenly, Ketë whistled loudly, and a steed identicle to his own flew from the dark sky. Lifting Läken carefully, Bátor and Ketë strapped him stiffly to the creature.

"Fly, bird, to Engjëll. Do not stop for anything." Ketë stroked its head, and the creature purred.

"Aren't you coming with me?" Läken asked. He realized his question had seemed much like something someone might hear out of a child, but he didn't care. He felt too distant from his body, like his soul itself was floating away. The sound of his friends' voices were the only things keeping him from passing out.

"Head demons are invading the forest. Ketë and I are going to stop them. Trust me, this bird will get you to Engjëll before your wound hurts you much more." Bátor slapped the creature's behind and yelled "Go on, take him to Engjëll!"

Then, the bird took off into the grey sky. Läken was vaguely aware of the wind rushing across his face and cooling his wounds. There were blanks in his memories, in which he suspected he lost consciousness.

After what seemed like only minutes of flying, they landed with a *thump* in Engjëll, which Läken knew was impossible, considering they were battling in Hollïn, a nymph country. They were over a weeks travel away by land.

He heard the pounding of feet coming from all sides and voices some that he recognized and others that he didn't. He felt himself being unstrapped and then picked up by several people.

"Läken!" A familiar voice called. It was his wife, Zopporah. "Get out of my way! Move! I don't care if he's your cousin, he's my husband! That's right, now move!" Her face appeared in a tangle of dark hair, and her eyes filled with tears as she examined his legs. Their newborn daughter, Legna was on her hip, looking around at all the people, oblivious as to what was going on. Läken's mouth curled into a small smile in spite of his pain. She was such a beautiful child, with smooth skin and rosy cheeks.

"Oh, Läken!" Zopporah cried. She looked down at his face. "What have you gone and done this time?"

"I'm afraid the damage may be permanent, my dear."

Zopporah shook her head. "I knew it would come to this." She looked up at the two men carrying him. "Take him to the village healer, please. Tell him to do everything he can but not to exhaust himself over it. There are other things to do other than fight."

"I love you, Zopporah and our child. But promise me this: Do not tell Legna of the true reasons behind my crippling. I do not want her wishing for what would have been."

Zopporah nodded. "All right. But she will find out someday, Läken. There's no sense in hiding something from somebody who is just as immortal as you."

"I know," Läken whispered. The men began to carry him toward the healer's house, and he fell asleep watching his wife and newborn daughter wave to him.

# KAPARAN MEADOW

Legna woke slowly, with the sunrise, as she did every morning. She did so to enjoy the soft, serene silence of dawn, when everyone was still sleeping. None of the rattles of hammers or the chants of the produce vendors. Just silence. Her home was able to enjoy it longer for it was farthest away from the town square in a large oak tree. It was one of her favorite parts of her daily life.

"Legna!" It was her father's call, ready to start the day. She sat up and swung her feet out of the bed. She stood, night gown twirling around her feet.

*Time to start another day,* she thought, knowing the exact order it would happen. First, her father would secretly take her down to Kaparan Meadow to train with weapons. He did this because it was frowned upon for women to fight in their village, but, as her father said, "It never hurts to be ready."

Then, her mother would tell her to get something from the market, and, no matter how much she tried, she wouldn't be able to get the exact thing her mother asked for.

After this was some dead space, where she could usually go meet with one of her friends, or go read in the forest, or anything else, until her mother or her father would call her to do some errand somewhere. The chores varied from fetching more water, to helping save a little boy or girl that climbed a tree and couldn't get down. That chore had been assigned at least five times.

*Yes*, Legna thought, *ours is a simple life, but some extravagance is intertwined.*

During the night, anyone who had any questions for their high king, Aryanis, could go and ask him in his ruling place at the end of the village. Then, their Engjëllen king, Zemër, would take the village out to Kaparan Meadow and light a bonfire, where everyone would relax after a hard day's work. There would be dancing and singing, and a few older men would play mandolins and flutes. The women would share some of their baking skills in pies and cakes, and the village storytellers would tell legends of the heroes of olde.

After a few hours, the fire would be dowsed, and everyone would leave in groups, and then disperse among homes. This daily celebration of life was Legna's favorite part of the day.

She moved around her room to prepare for the day. She undressed and bathed in the tub of water in the corner of the room. She dressed in leather trousers and a white, elbow-length top for her practice time. She laid out a deerskin skirt to quickly change into for the rest of the day (women in pants was also frowned upon). She gazed into her mirror, brushing out her hair slowly. She had shoulder-length blonde hair, with deep brown eyes, and a smile that could light up the darkest of nights. Once she was finished with her hair, she strapped on her hunting knife and simple, iron sword. Then she pulled on her rabbit-hide boots and hurried down the hall to their small kitchen. She buttered some bread and cut up a peach, eating them both quickly and quietly so as not to wake her mother.

Her father limped into the room, leaning on the staff the king himself had given him. On the top, a pearl of jade melded with the wood and small emeralds circled it. In the wood, an image of a tree demon was carved. When she was younger, Legna had questioned this, wondering why her father would own such a staff. But her father had just dismissed it, saying he didn't know the king's reasons for the design.

"Are you ready?" Her father asked. Legna nodded, shoving the last piece of peach in her mouth and hopping up quickly, causing her sheath to jingle.

Her father shushed her and motioned to the door. They crept out into the fresh, morning air. They kept behind the treeline, trying to stay undetected from other early risers. When they finally reached the edge of the village, Legna broke out into a run to their practice spot in the beautiful meadow as she did every morning. Läken stayed behind because of his injury, and anyone who spotted him was much more likely to believe he was only going on a walk than young Legna.

Legna counted the types of wildflowers on the way there as she did every morning. Tigerlilies, lavender, foxgloves, tea roses, poppies, daisies, baby's breath, bluebells, zinnias, pansies, and peonies covered the ground everywhere, overwhelming the air with a floral scent.

She covered ground quickly and finally leapt into their hiding place behind four boulders. Here, logs were set up in crosses with sacks of cotton stretched over the tops and red targets painted onto them. Knicks and gashes from many of Legna's successful blows covered them. A hay-stuffed circle of burlap was supported by thinner logs in the corner. This target was for archery and knife-throwing.

Legna was in this place so much its target dummies had become like friends to her, ironically enough.

There was a noise behind her, and she turned to find her father climbing behind the boulders.

"I'm getting too old for this," Läken mumbled as he stumbled into the clearing.

"Come on, Father, what should I do first?" Legna asked cheerily.

"Archery," her father responded. Legna sighed, despite the fact that she knew he would say archery. It was the same everyday.

But, nonetheless, archery was her weakest point, and she didn't love it as much as melee.

She picked up the long bow that leaned against the archery target and walked back to the spot she always shot from. She drew back, aiming at the bull's-eye, and, holding her breath, released. The arrow went slightly too high and hit the ring above the center.

"Good!" Läken exclamed. "Better than last time. Just relax, and aim a little lower."

Legna nodded and strung another arrow, pulling back but keeping her muscles looser. She aimed slightly below the center and released once again. This time, the arrow found its mark perfectly, hitting the bull's-eye. With newfound confidence, she quickly shot two more arrows, both hitting the center circle next to her second arrow.

"Wonderful! That's enough archery, get your knives." She retrieved three throwing knives from under the target and then once again returned to her spot. "Fingers and wrists tight, arms loose," her father said.

Taking her father's advice, she closed one eye and aimed at the head of the crosses. She pulled her hand back and threw it. It spun cleanly through the air and planted itself deep into the cotton. She walked to a spot in front of the next target and, still walking, threw it perfectly. She did this once more, running this time and then she collected her knives and threw each squatting, every one finding its mark. It was the result of ten years of hard training. She had been throwing, shooting, and handling swords since she was six. The practice had payed off.

"Now, your swordsmanship." Her favorite part. She unsheathed her sword, holding it upright in front of her. She stationed herself so she was facing one of the dummies and held her small sword in her right hand.

"Begin!" her father said. She paused for a moment before going into a fantastic frenzy of backhand cuts, overhand cuts, jabs, thrusts, and sideslashes before smacking its head with the flat of her blade and cutting straight through the bottom of the log, causing the target to topple over altogether.

"Whoops," Legna said, sheathing her sword. Her father scratched his head and shuffled over to the dummy, kneeling to look at it.

After several long moments, her father said, "I think you killed him."

Legna smiled uneasily. "Sorry, I didn't mean to break it."

Her father stopped her. "It took you ten years to kill one. And you've finally done it! That means you're progressing!"

"Oh. Thank you." Legna was suddenly upset because, had she known before, she could have broken one years ago and "progressed" earlier.

"Ah, don't look so sad, Legna. This means you're strong enough to kill an orc with three blows. You could go to war!"

"Three blows, huh?" She thought it was a good idea. A woman going to war? No one had heard of such a thing. Not in Engjëll, at least. But she would love to put orcs back in their place.

"That's enough practice for today. Go see your mother. She probably needs something."

Legna sighed. She knew her mother would ask her to go to town. She climbed out from behind the boulders and saw a short, squat figure in the distance. All Engjëllens were tall, and mostly slender. No one had the strange, small build she saw right now.

"Father?" She asked as he walked into the meadow. "What is that?" She pointed to the figure, now moving toward them.

"An orc?" Her father mumbled to himself.

Legna panicked. "What did you say, Father? An orc?" She said desperately. The figure was now only one hundred yards away, and Legna could see its features. It was, indeed, an orc. With a fat green face and long, white tusks protruding from its mouth, it was unmistakeable.

"Legna, get back to the village."

"No, I won't leave you to die."

"Who says I'll die?"

"I'm still not leaving."

"Fine, then. But I'd better see some of your training come out when this thing tries to maul you."

"You have my word." The orc started running toward them, swinging its short sword in circles above its head. There was only one word to describe this—awkward. He snorted and ran faster until he almost crashed into Legna. He stopped and swung his sword at her neck, but she ducked, causing him to trip over her. He landed flat on his back, and Legna plunged her sword into his gut, disembowling him as she pulled out her sword. He groaned and sat up, weak and dying.

"Should I kill him?" Legna had never been in an actual fight; she wasn't sure whether to kill him or let him die slowly.

"If you want to be kind. Or if you just want extra practice."

Legna looked at the gruesome sight. "Hm. For extra practice." And she cut off his head. As she watched his head slide off his neck, she wondered why killing something didn't bother her. It was strange how easily she had done it, how her mind worked to kill.

"Personally, I would have left him to die," Läken said. "But it was your first true fight, and you fared excellently." He leaned closer to her. "But, if I were you, I wouldn't tell your mother." He winked and Legna nodded.

"Father, why don't I feel strange, you know … killing like that?"

"What makes you say that?"

"I just feel like I should … I don't know, be surprised or scared or something. It felt too easy."

"Legna, that's how all Engjëllens feel. We were made to kill those things. It's in our blood. It's in your blood."

"I have the blood of a killer?"

"No, my dear, you have the blood of a warrior. If you had the blood of a killer, I would probably be dead, and you would be celebrating with your orcish friends. You see, Engjëllens have been destroying evil since the dawn of time."

"Then why isn't evil gone?"

Läken sighed. "Because orcs breed like rabbits, and we signed a blasted treaty last year. Now, shall we return home?"

"Of course, Father."

Then they walked, arm in arm, back to their village.

# CHOSEN

Läken left for a meeting with the king, and Legna went back to her home to change into her more "appropriate" clothing. Once she snuck into her room and put on her skirt, she walked plainly back into the kitchen, where her mother was stirring pineapple jam.

"Oh, Legna you're up. Would you go to the market and buy some elephant heart plums?"

"Yes, Mother."

"They're the green kind."

Legna sighed. "Yes, Mother." They had had this conversation many times before.

"And, could you get some manna?" Her mother called as Legna turned to leave.

"Of course." Manna was Engjëllen sweet bread, considered a rare delicacy in the other provinces of Zerùa, and was apparently so wholesome that it was once sent down to the mortal world, Giza, to a group of nomads favored by Aryanis when they had no other food. It was the only food with traces of spirit jewels inside.

Legna walked to the market slowly, enjoying her hometown. Roses curled around every support beam, roses of every color. Joy and laughter was prominent everywhere, a perfect day. Everyday was a perfect day. Bards dotted the streets, and they would sing to whoever happened to pass by. Couples would receive love songs and soldiers would hear war ballads. Each bard had a unique, beautiful voice, and every song they sang was original. They strummed mandolins or harps and blew on pan flutes and ocarinas.

She found the many produce vendors and looked for the plums her mother had asked for. Each vendor she came across, she asked, "Elephant heart plums? Anyone? Elephant hearts?" She received mostly shakes of the head and, in one case, she was offered a piece of an actual elephant heart from a butcher, over hearing elephant heart and getting the wrong impression.

It was no use. There were no green plums. She found large purple plums, so she picked out six, figuring it was the same. Then, she headed to the bakery to pick up the manna bread. She liked the village baker, a quiet old man named Malin. His small bakery had been there since Engjëll was first built, and for generations, his family had provided beautiful cakes, bread, and cookies. This was where the first Engjëllen manna was baked, and the only place that you could get real manna. Many of the other provinces attempted to duplicate it but to no avail. They did not have the true recipe and never would.

Malin was kind to everyone and rarely spoke his mind. When Legna was younger, she had asked him why he was so quiet. He had responded with, "Nothing is truly worth saying unless you think about it for a very long time and find nothing wrong with it." He was a wise man whom Legna respected, and she had always thought that his appearance added to his character. A long white beard curled to his shoulders, and he wore a burlap apron over his white shirt that was always covered in flour and jam. A spoon was strapped to his belt, like a knife on a warrior. He was a bit pudgy, as a good baker should be, and a cherry wood pipe was always balanced between his lips.

The little children loved him because at night, during their celebration, he would gather all of them, give them a ginger cookie freshly baked, and tell them stories of Engjëllen history. They were stories of heroes and princesses, demons, and dragons. Once in a while, Legna would stop to listen, and Malin would offer her a cookie too. She would begin to decline but would look into those dear, old eyes and find herself accepting.

"Hello, Malin!" Legna said cheerily.

"Mornin', Legna. What'll it be today?" Malin answered.

"Oh, just a loaf of manna."

"Sure thing. We just finished cooking a batch this morning. I'll go and get a fresh loaf."

"Thank you, Malin." Malin nodded and walked back to the kitchen. After a few minutes, he returned with the bread wrapped in brown cloth.

"Thanks so much," Legna said when he handed her the package.

"Legna," Malin said, "I wanted to talk to you about something."

"What is it?" Legna asked.

"I was walking in Kaparan Meadow this morning, and I witnessed something quite strange."

"What do you mean?"

"I saw a young blonde girl, fighting an orc with her father."

"Oh…You saw that?" Legna said.

"I did. But don't worry, I won't tell your secret."

"Thank you, Malin. I owe you. I've been training with my father for years, and no one has caught us." As she said this, Elanya, the village tailor, entered the bakery. Dressed in a purple gown and too much jewelry, Elanya showed her love for clothes in her everyday lifestyle. She piled her black hair atop her head in a fanciful fashion, stringing pearls and ribbons throughout the tower.

"We can continue this conversation later," Malin whispered. "Meet me upstairs as soon as possible; I have something to show you." Legna nodded.

"Hello, Malin, how are you this fine day?" Elanya said.

"I'm doing well, Elanya, how are you?" Malin answered.

"Oh, fine, fine, just came for some scones for a few guests I'm having this afternoon." Elanya looked at Legna disapprovingly. "Legna, you have a tear in your skirt, child. Come by my shop tomorrow, I'll fix it for you. You can't be running around like a street rat, now, can you?"

Legna smiled and said, "Thank you, Elanya. I appreciate it." Legna liked Elanya well enough, but her views on a woman's duties were very different from Legna's, as Elanya was very against women having anything to do with war. "If you don't mind me asking, Elanya, who are your guests?"

"Some old friends from the Elvish Isle. They will be at the Celebration tonight if you want to meet them." Malin handed her a bag of scones. "Mm, thank you, Malin. This will make afternoon tea so much better. Well, I'm off to a fitting for the king! See you both tonight!"

"Good-bye, Elanya," Malin and Legna said. Once the door closed, Malin said, "You take those plums and that bread home and then come back here. I really do think you'll enjoy this."

"All right, I'll be back in twenty minutes." Legna left the bakery and walked back onto the busy streets of Engjëll. She ran through the crowds, navigating her way expertly. Her house was on the outskirts of Engjëll, closer to the farms than the market square. The trip felt long and mindless, but as she rushed into the kitchen, her excitement returned and she quickly threw down the food.

"Legna? Is that you?" Her mother called from her room.

Legna sighed. "Yes, mother."

"Where are you going?"

"Malin told me he wanted to show me something. I don't think I'll be long. You know, it's only Malin."

"Did you get the plums, dear?"

"Yes, but they didn't have elephant heart plums, so I just got the purple kind."

Her mother sighed in exasperation. "All right. Be careful on the way back."

"I will," Legna called as she ran back out the door. Once again, she made her way back to the bakery. She finally arrived and burst into the room. No one was there except for Malin. "I'm back," Legna said.

Malin nodded and said, "I can see that."

"So, what did you want to show me?"

Malin placed a sign on the display case, reading "Be Back Soon," and motioned for her to follow him. He walked up the stairs to his living quarters, Legna trailing him. He unlocked a door and swung it open, revealing a room full of wooden boxes.

"What is this place?" Legna asked.

"This is my hobby," Malin responded. He pushed the top off of one box and pulled out a shiny, red case. He opened the case and pulled out a throwing knife, holding it carefully in his right hand.

"Knives?" Legna asked.

Malin shook his head. "Weapons. Magical weapons."

"That knife is magical?" Legna questioned. Malin looked at her, and then threw the knife at an empty box. At first, nothing happened. But then, slowly, the box began to burn. The flames spread until the box was only a pile of ashes.

"Wow," Legna said. "I've never seen anything like that!"

"Not many have. The king wants to keep these as . . . last resorts. So, he hid them in the most unlikely place possible—the bakery. At the time, it was my father who ran the bakery, so I didn't know until he was ready to hand the bakery over to me. Every decade, the keeper of these fine weapons may choose one hero to bless." Malin smiled at Legna.

"Who is your hero?" Legna asked.

Malin sighed. "Why it's you, of course! I bless you with either a magical knife or magical bow from my collection. Your choice.

But, you may only use it if your need is desperate in the face of evil."

Legna was speechless. All she could do was stare at Malin. Finally, words came back to her, and she said, "Thank you so much, Malin. This is incredible!"

Malin nodded and responded with, "Now go on, and choose your weapon." Legna wandered around, looking at the boxes. They were all labeled in the language of the nymphs. "ದುರ್ಬಲಗೊಳಿಸು ಬಿಲ್ಲು (Paralyze bow)." "ಮಂಜುಗಡ್ಡೆ ಚಾಕು (Ice knife). As she was looking, one title caught her attention. "ಬಿಲ್ಲು ಆಫ್ ಬೆಳಕು (Bow of Light)." She pushed back the top and peered inside. A beautiful bow made of what appeared to be ivory sparkled against the dim light in the room. The face of a nymph was carved into it, beautiful with long, flowing hair. Above her was the sun, and below her was the moon. A strange silver bowstring set next to it along with a quiver full of golden arrows.

"Malin," Legna said, "What is this?"

"That's our newest weapon. The Bow of Light is probably the nymphs' most advanced accomplishment. The arrows never run out as long as you use them correctly, and whatever you hit explodes, killing everything around it. It's dangerous but extremely effective in most cases."

"What do you mean by 'most cases'?" Legna asked.

"Well, the Bow of Light does not work against Engjëllens or any other of Aryanis' people. The arrows just float through. And it will be revoked, if it is the hands of the hero who shot the arrow. But, once the arrow has edged its way into a valid target, and exploded ... well, let's hope you aren't too close when that happens."

"Oh," Legna said. She thought for a minute. Although archery was not her strength, she did not own a bow. And if she was to be Malin's champion, the weapon in front of her was a good way to start.

"I suppose I will take this then," Legna said. The bow was so beautiful, and although she doubted she would ever use it, she did not want to let Malin down.

"All right, then get down on one knee." Legna did as she was told. Malin picked up a butter paddle from nearby and twisted the bottom. Legna started to question, but Malin shushed her. He pulled the paddle apart, revealing a blade underneath. The round, spoon-like part he was holding began to shift and change, rearranging itself until it became a hilt. The paddle had transformed into a cutlass.

"How did you—" Legna started, but Malin held up a hand to stop her.

"The Naïfonians made it for me as a gift for a service I did for them long ago," Malin responded.

"What did you do?" Legna asked. She was truly curious as to what the sweet old baker of Engjëll could have done for the lizard-like Naïfonians.

"I helped gather their senators when three hooligan heroes thought they were demons," Malin muttered. Legna nodded, thinking if she had ever heard stories about this. Malin's voice startled her. "Let us get on with the proceedings!" He touched the sword to her shoulder. "Do you, Legna Glowston, vow to protect this village and world in its darkest times, and to follow Aryanis, our king, with undying faith?"

"I do," Legna responded. This was all happening so fast, and she wasn't sure what would happen once she took the oath. But she vowed, nonetheless, considering she would sacrifice herself for Aryanis anyway.

"Then say these words, in Aryanis's own language. *Ma vannun fealty meie küla ja meie maailm Zerúa, et ma kasutan seda andi vööri valgus ainult hüvanguks Aryanis rahvas.*" This meant "I swear fealty to our village and our world of Zerúa that I will use this gift of the Bow of Light only for the good of Aryanis's people."

Legna repeated these words, and Malin rested his sword on the other shoulder. "*Igavesti, ma võitlen verega sõjamees, armu ja õiguse, slaying tahes deemonid minu tee* (Forevermore, I will fight with the blood of a warrior, with grace and justice, slaying any demons in my path)."

Once Legna swore this, Malin shifted the blade to her head. "*Ma teen oma esivanemate uhke, Meistrite enne mind peab naeratada mõtlesin mina. Ma püüdlema tipptaseme, ükskõik asjaoluks. Ja meie kõige tumedatel aegadel, räägin jõud tekivad. Tõuse!* (I shall do my ancestors proud; the champions before me shall smile at the thought of me. I shall strive for excellence, no matter the circumstance. And in our darkest times, I shall tell the forces to arise. Arise!)." As he said these words, loud banging was heard outside, and Legna picked up traces of the orcish language. "Quickly, Legna, say it! My sword must be touching you for the vow to be complete."

"Um, *Ma teen oma esivanemate uhke, Meistrite enne mind peab naeratada mõtlesin mina.*" Another bang sounded. The orcs were in the bakery. Legna could feel it.

"Keep going, Legna, hurry!" Malin exclaimed.

Legna closed her eyes. They were coming up the stairs. "*Ma püüdlema tipptaseme, ükskõik asjaoluks. Ja meie kõige tumedatel aegadel, räägin jõud tekivad.*" They were at the top now. There were three. Even with her eyes closed, she could tell.

"One more word, Legna, hurry!" Malin urged.

"*Tõuse,*" Legna whispered. She heard an arrow rush past her ear, barely missing, and opened her eyes just in time to watch it pierce Malin's chest.

"Now go," Malin whispered to her.

Legna realized what had happened, and, grabbing the bow from the velvet lined box and fitting an arrow to the string, she shot an orc square in the forehead. She blocked her eyes as the orc erupted into an explosion of bright light, consuming the orc next to it. Only one was left: The orc who had shot the arrow.

Legna ripped her sword free from its sheath. She charged the orc, ripping his bow from his hands and stomping it to pieces before impaling him with her sword.

She rushed back to Malin, noticing he was still breathing. "Malin? Malin, can you speak?"

Malin wheezed before saying, "You…cannot tell…anyone about this until…they need…to recognize you…as champion. You are…my champion. Prove me…right…Legna."

"You're talking like you are going to die. You're going to survive! I will make sure of it!" Legna said desperately.

Malin shook his head. "I'm over…nine hundred years old…Legna. I…I can't do…much good here…anymore."

"Of course you can! You have kept this secret for years, running this bakery like it's your only job, keeping us fed and protected at the same time. We still need that. We still need you."

Malin smiled and shook his head. "You must…destroy…them."

"Them? Who? What do you mean?" Legna pleaded.

Malin ignored the question. "You must…stop…*her*…" After this, his eyes glazed over, and he fell limp. But a smile of satisfaction was frozen on his lips. Legna heard a noise behind her. Malin's son, Garren, stood there, mouth open.

Legna stared back at him, too weak to speak. Garren was a good friend of hers, even if he was three years older. He walked to his father's dead body and knelt down beside Legna. Garren was too shocked for words and too sorrowful for crying. Legna put her arm around him, and he put his arm around her. Then, the tears came.

And they sat there, crying together until it was time for the Celebration to begin.

# THE CELEBRATION

Four hours later, Garren and Legna gathered themselves and prepared to leave for the Celebration. Legna picked up the bow she was given and slung it across her back, carefully putting on the quiver.

"I'll kill them all," Garren muttered as he trudged down the stairs. "Every last one of them."

Legna considered telling Garren about the oath she swore, but Malin had told her not to breathe a word to anyone until absolutely necessary. Garren was the new keeper of the weapons. Surely, he should know that she was chosen. "Malin gave me this bow. He told me I was his champion."

"I noticed. A woman has never been chosen. Crazy old man, he never followed the rules. I personally think women should be left out of these affairs. They should stay home, start a family." Garren reached the last stair and suddenly sat down. He put his head in his hands, weeping. Garren had fairer skin with tousled brown hair and bright blue eyes. He wore a green shirt tucked into brown cotton trousers with an apron on top, just like his father. He had the scruffy beginnings of a beard on his chin. Legna noticed some scars on his fingers, probably from his knife slipping while cooking or baking.

"I just wish it didn't happen this way." Garren sobbed.

"It's all right, Garren. We must get to the Celebration. They will be waiting for us." Legna sat down next to him and put her arm around his shoulders. "Your father would want you to continue on, no matter the circumstance," she added gently. He looked up at her, eyes full of tears, looking like a disoriented child.

"Yes," he said, pulling himself up. "Let's go." He walked warily out of the bakery and into the street, but a thick stream of people stopped him. Everyone had begun to proceed to the meadow. Legna grabbed his hand and held it tight.

"Come on, Garren. We still have life with us." Together, they joined the crowd and were swept away.

They followed the others mindlessly, having made the journey millions of times before. Once they had gotten away from the crowd, into Kaparan Meadow, Legna stopped. Garren, still holding her hand tightly, was jerked backwards.

"What's wrong, Legna?" He asked.

"This is where it happened," Legna responded. She could see the body from a distance.

"Where what happened?" Garren looked at her strangely.

"It's where I first killed," Legna whispered. "I feel so distant from it...like it was another part of normal life. It was just this morning, too. But it was so strange how easy killing was. I lost my mind and just relied upon instincts."

"If you hadn't killed, my father wouldn't have chosen you as his champion. You really deserve the title, Legna, don't forget it." He put his other hand on her face. "Even if everyone else does."

Tears came to her eyes. She felt as if she never wanted to leave. Then, she kissed him, quickly, so no one else could have seen. When she drew back, Garren smiled at her. Suddenly, the night didn't seem as bad.

"We're going to be all right, Garren. We'll get through this," Legna promised. Then they proceeded on, in a thoughtful silence. They finally saw the bonfire ahead, but they were in no hurry.

They slowly walked to the conspicuous light and music came to their ears.

As they came into view of the other villagers, the king announced in his deep voice, as he did every celebration, "Garren and Legna have arrived!" And cheers erupted.

"I must go tell them about my father," Garren said firmly.

"I'm going with you," Legna said.

"No," Garren said, turning to face her. "This isn't your burden to bear."

"Of course it is!" Legna exclaimed. "I was there when he passed. I gave a vow of fealty. And I won't let you do this alone."

Suddenly, Legna heard a shout behind her. "Legna!" She turned to see her best friend, Traven running toward her.

"Traven," Legna said. Traven had reddish-brown hair that came to his ear. He had intense green eyes and a cheerful look about him that made the darkest of days bright. Freckles covered his handsome face, blending together to make for a tan complexion. He was tall and somewhat muscular. His hands were calloused from working in the forges all his life. He wore a white shirt and comfortable, cotton pants. Normally, he wore no shoes, going barefoot.

Traven looked down at Garren's and Legna's hands and then at their expressions. His eyebrows knit together as he said, "What's wrong?"

"You'll see in a minute," Garren answered. They walked to the king and Garren said, "I need to make an announcement about something. It's urgent."

The king nodded and motioned in front of him. Legna looked at the crowd and noticed with interest the two richly dressed elves standing in the back, listening to Elanya, looking incredibly bored.

"People of Engjëll," Garren began, "there has been a tragedy this day!" The people muttered and whispered among themselves, and then Garren held up his hand for quiet. "Those murderers, those filthy, lying fleabags called orcs! They have done something unthinkable; unbearably horrifying."

"What have they done, Garren?" someone in the audience shouted.

"They've killed him. They've killed my father." The audience stirred, chattering noisily.

"They've killed Malin!" Legna shouted, getting their attention again. "Somehow, they got into the village without our knowing, and now Malin is dead. Dead!"

"Impossible," a woman in the audience screamed. Legna turned to her. It was Nimba, Malin's sister. "They could not have gotten through our defenses! You lie!" This stirred up shouts from the rest of the crowd.

"Quiet!" Legna cried. "It is not a lie! I was there when he died; he was shot with an Orcish arrow! I killed the very orc who committed the crime!" *Oh no*, Legna thought. No one but her father knew she could fight.

The king stood, and said, "That is against the treaty. They are to harm no Engjëllen."

"Well apparently, there is no more treaty," Garren answered. "You cannot control the impulse of evil with a mere agreement. They do what they please, when they please."

The king rubbed his head and then said, "Our warlord will think this over later. For now, let us get on with the festivities." There was a small pause and then the music and chatter started back up again.

"How can they just ignore it like this?" Garren whispered to Legna.

"Maybe the king has too much on his mind." Legna paused, glancing over at the elves. Garren was looking in their direction, also. "Would you like to meet them?" she asked.

Garren nodded. "Anything to take my mind off of things. Do you speak elvish?"

"Yes, my mother made me learn all the native languages of Zerúa," Legna responded. "I'm just going to speak with Traven. I'm sure he's interested, too."

Legna searched through the crowds until she bumped right into Traven. "I was just looking for you," Legna said.

"I was looking for you, too," Traven replied. "I can't believe it! Malin can't be dead!"

"Yes," Legna said. "Neither can I."

"Were you really there? You know, when he passed?" Traven whispered.

"Yes. It was terrible. He told me there was nothing more in this world that he could do, that he was nine hundred years old."

Traven nodded and then glanced at Legna's new weapon. "Where did that come from?"

"If I tell you, you must promise to tell no one."

"I promise."

She pulled him to the side, where no one was watching or listening. "Malin gave it to me. The bakers of Engjëll have long kept a secret room where they store all the magical weapons. Every decade, the baker chooses a champion and gives them a magical weapon from his collection. But this is highly secretive, and the champion is supposed to tell no one who they are, unless they are in desperation."

"Incredible! Why you?" Traven asked.

"Malin discovered our little secret … My father and I. He saw me training, I guess." Legna fingered the smooth, silver string attached to her bow, and decided to avoid the subject of the orc.

"I almost forgot why I was looking for you!" Legna exclaimed. "There are two elvish ambassadors here, and Garren and I were going to go meet them. Want to come?"

"Elves? Of course! But I wanted to ask you something about Garren."

"What about him?" Legna replied.

"Do you … Are you in love with him?"

Legna turned bright red. "Of course not, he's three years older than me. What makes you think that?"

"Well…I don't know how to say this, but…it's obvious that you adore him." Traven said bluntly, raising his eyebrows.

"Well, you know, I'm only…Ah, be quiet. It's nothing but a little crush; it will pass."

Traven raised his eyebrows a little higher but did not question further. "Let's go meet the elves, shall we?"

"Yes, let's." Legna and Traven made their way back to where Garren was standing, and Garren waved to them.

"Ready?" He asked.

Seizing his hand, she said, "Whenever you are." She saw Traven roll his eyes but ignored him.

The three strolled over to the Elves, who, upon seeing them, smiled. One was a female with wavy, silver hair, and stunning yellow eyes. She wore a long green dress and carried a thin sword on her back. She wore an emerald and gold tiara and red war paint was striped onto her cheeks and curved out in a flame-like design from the tips of her eyes.

The second was a man with long black hair and deep brown eyes. He held a black long bow in his hand and a quiver was strapped to his back. He wore a dignified maroon cloak and a ruby circlet on his head. Both had the significant pointed ears of an elf, and they were slightly taller than the Engjëllens.

"*Én vagyok Legna. Te itt nagykövetek?*" Legna said to the Elves.

"What did you say?" Garren whispered.

"I said that my name is Legna, and I asked if they were the new ambassadors," Legna whispered back.

"*Üdvözlet. Örömmel látom, hogy egy lány a te korodban ismeri a nyelvet* (Greetings. I am impressed that a girl of your age knows our language.)."

"But there is no need for it," the male elf continued on in Engjëllen. "As ambassadors, we are required to know all languages of Zerúa. I am Ketë, and this is my companion, Kalaila."

"I am Legna, and these are my friends, Garren and Traven."

"Yes ... I am sorry to hear of your father, Garren. I knew Malin, and he was quite a man. What I truly do not understand is why you are so young while your father was almost one thousand years old," Ketë said.

"When my father met my mother, whom is no longer with us, he could not get her father's permission for marriage until he had proven his worth. He courted her for almost 200 years until her father finally agreed. Thank goodness Aryanis gifted us with immortality; otherwise, I probably wouldn't exist. My parents decided they didn't want a child until they were too old to be sent off to war, so my father would never have to abandon me. As you may know, in Engjëll, once a man reaches the age of 800, they are not required to fight unless they so choose. My father waited until he was exactly 920 to have me so as to make sure that even if they rose the age to 900, he still wouldn't have to go." Garren cast his eyes down. "And yet, even when we thought we had gained peace with the orcs, my father was still killed by an orcish arrow."

"Yes ... war is a cold, terrible thing. Once again, we offer our condolences," Kalaila purred. Legna looked harder at Kalaila and realized that she was not much older than Garren; she only looked a mature age because of the makeup and war-paint on her face.

"So, is there a reason you are in Engjëll right now?" Traven asked.

"We are on our way to Naïfon to pick up some supplies for our queen. She is traveling to the Szent Sziget or Holy Island as you call it, as she does every year, and she needs the special boat the Naïfonians designed to make it through the roaring waters surrounding the island," Ketë answered.

Legna nodded. The Holy Island was where Aryanis's palace was, and each year, the royalty of Zerúa were granted entrance for a time of meeting.

"Why do you stay with Elanya instead of in the ambassador's quarters at the palace?" Garren asked.

"Elanya is a good friend of ours. And she's the best tailor in Zerúa. We had soiled and torn clothing that needed mending, and we wanted it done by a master in the craft. She offered us her home, so we accepted."

"Ketë?" Legna asked. "Do you believe that we will go to war again against the orcs?"

Ketë shrugged, with a sympathetic smile. "That all depends on the warlords of the countries. They will consult with the high king to make the final decision. We shall spread word of the betrayal to Naïfon and then to our own country. If they believe war is at hand, so be it. We do not fear death."

Legna nodded. "I only hope the orcs pay for what they have done to Malin. And everything else they have committed. I hope they are shown no mercy."

"Don't we all?" Kalaila said; her voice quiet. "The orcs and their cousins, the demons, killed my brother in a battle. Shot him with six arrows, they did. But he kept fighting. He fought like that for over an hour, bleeding to death."

A silence followed, sad and heavy with questions.

"Night has fallen. People are leaving this celebration, remembering your news, Master Garren," Ketë said. "They are still raw from the news as you are." He paused, knitting his eyebrows together and stared at Garren, shaking his head. "I see nothing but grief coming from your heart. Grief of a fallen loved one."

Garren averted his gaze, wiping away any tears in his eyes.

"Master Garren, you are not the one who must be strong in this. He was your father, and the hurt is too new. No man should be afraid of sadness," Kalaila said.

"I'm not afraid of my sadness. I just prefer not to show it in public." Garren looked at the men and women leaving. "I'm going home. It's late."

"It is. I'm going to rest too if you don't mind. It was an honor to meet both of you," Legna said, bowing slightly.

"I will accompany. We are all tired, I think," Traven added.

"Lamtumirë. Good-bye, Legna, Traven, Garren. Lamtumirë. We will meet again, whether it is as allies on the battlefield, or friends in a village. We will meet again," Ketë said.

"Lamtumirë, friends," Legna called as she walked away, letting go of Garren's hand and leaving him behind in the meadow to go home. Traven followed her, but she took no notice. She just wanted sleep.

"Legna, wait!" Garren's voice sounded behind them. Legna turned and watched as Garren brushed past Traven and ran to catch up with her. "Would you like an escort home?"

"I have Traven," Legna said. She was avoiding being eager for Garren's attention after Traven's comments.

"Oh. I thought maybe you would like my company, but if Traven is all you need, I understand." Garren began to turn away.

"Wait!" Legna grabbed onto Garren's arm, pulling him back. "I would love your company. I just thought you wouldn't want to bother going a half mile in the wrong direction just to walk me home," Legna said.

"I don't mind. The walk back will give me time to think. And, I want to avoid sleeping alone in my empty house for as long as possible." They began to walk.

There was a long silence. "I'm so sorry I couldn't stop them. Malin's death was my fault," Legna said; her voice barely a whisper. "I'm so sorry."

Garren stopped, shaking his head. "No," he whispered back. "It's not your fault. No one but Aryanis himself could have stopped them. Do not blame yourself for the orcs' treachery. I don't." He began walking again.

"I just needed to say it, is all. I wouldn't have felt right if I had not apologized. Thank you for your kindness. It takes a strong spirit to blame no one but the culprit for a crime committed against you. Most creatures would have cursed the world, and all in it. But you stay upright. Our race never ceases to amaze."

"Such a large truth, spoken by such a young woman." The small cluster of large trees containing Legna and Traven's homes came into view.

"You know what they say, don't you? The young are the ones who shape the future. Do not underestimate those who are younger or smaller than you. Not everything is as it seems."

"I meant no offense. I was not insulting your age, just noting how ... mature you are."

Legna didn't answer for a long time. Finally, she said, "I want to change the world somehow, Garren. Even in a small way. I want to be the champion your father believed he saw in me."

They arrived at Legna's house and stopped in front of it. "I have no doubt that you will be. No doubt at all." Garren held both of Legna's hands, facing her. "Make your difference, Legna. Put your heart into it. But I am here for your stability. Whatever you do, I'll be waiting here at home for you, ready to start a new life. Whatever you do, think of me."

"I already do," Legna replied. They stood there for a few moments, reveling in the moment. Then, Legna glanced at her father in the window, watching them.

"Good night, Garren. I will see you tomorrow." She let go of his hands.

"Good night." Garren did nothing at first and then stooped down and kissed her on the cheek. "In case they come for me too," he said. Then he trotted away, back to the market square.

Legna touched her cheek. "If they do, I'll go to war," she whispered to herself. Then, she opened the door to her home.

Once inside, she sat down near the fire to warm herself. She stared into the leaping flames, watching orange, yellow, white, and red dance before her eyes.

Her father spoke behind her, jolting her back into existence. "He's a good one, Legna."

"What do you mean?" Legna asked. She kept her gaze locked onto the fire.

"Garren. I think he's a good man."

"That's nice. But we're only friends, nothing more."

"Well, then you had better tell him that." Läken sat down next to her, placing his staff by his side. "You are almost of marrying age, Legna. You are our only child. Your mother can have no more."

Legna was silent for a while. "I don't know if I want to marry Garren."

Läken looked at her, "I'm not saying you have to marry Garren. But if he were to ask you, I would not oppose."

"I don't know I want to marry at all." Legna took her gaze away from the fire. "Not yet, at least. Not while I'm young, and I can still make a difference in the world."

"Is that what you told him? Before you came in?"

"I told him I wanted to be a champion."

"What did he say?"

"He told me to think of him in whatever I do. But that I always have a home with him."

The room fell quiet. Nothing was audible but the crackling of the fire. Legna was glad for the silence. It gave her a break from life, from decisions she didn't want to make.

"He loves you, Legna. There are many other men that have taken a shine to you. But Garren truly seems to love you. Do you love him, also?" Läken's words posed a question she had been asking herself for a few months, but been unable to answer.

"I don't know. When we are speaking, I feel as if I do. But when we are apart, I feel confused, like I'm not sure what to think."

"What of Traven?"

Legna looked at him, confused. "What of him?"

"What does he think? You trust his judgment. Have you asked him?"

"About Garren? Or about marriage?" Legna asked.

"Garren." Läken threw a stick in the fire.

"I haven't asked him anything. He only pointed out how much I seem to adore Garren." Legna paused for a long time, looking back at the fire. "I think we would be too young. I want to be older, more mature before I choose a husband."

Läken stroked his greying beard. "Life is difficult, Legna. If you ask me, sixteen is only a child compared to the ages of the others in our race. So is nineteen. You are both children, yet you have already witnessed death. Already heard the last words of someone you were fond of. Already killed for those you love."

Legna's eyes began to tear in spite of herself. "You must kill her," Malin had said. Then, it had been like she was staring at a statue.

Läken noticed Legna's sudden emotion. "I'm sorry, angel. He hasn't asked you. You don't need to make any decisions right now. I have been too blunt with you. Don't worry, you will be fine." He put his arms around Legna. "We will all be fine."

"What did the king want with you? What was the meeting about this morning?" Legna asked, changing the subject.

"The elves have sighted demons in the West Wood. That is right in between the largest and the smallest of the elven villages, Mär-Linna and Oarányi. Lahti, fire demons, were seen. Disgusting creatures."

"Why would they need to tell *you* that?" Legna asked. Her father was nothing but a sword maker.

"In case I need to make more weapons. These are dangerous times, Legna, I won't lie."

A sudden wave of fatigue washed over Legna. She could hardly keep her eyes open. "I suppose I won't be of any help if I get no rest tonight. I need to sleep."

"Yes, of course, sleep. You deserve rest. Today's events were not good for the mind of a child."

"Good night, Father." Legna sauntered to her room. She opened the door and spotted a flower on her bed. A beautiful black rose with a note attached to it, "I'm sorry for the terrible day you've had. I'll always be there for you. —Traven"

Legna held the rose, smelling its light aroma. Traven was the best friend Legna had, and she knew he would never betray her. She loved him like a brother.

She added the black rose to a bouquet of wildflowers a little girl had picked for her a few days earlier.

"When I grow up"—the little girl had said, handing Legna the flowers—"I want to be just like you, Legna."

"Thank you," Legna had said. "They are beautiful. But when you grow up, I hope you are your own person. I hope you are beautiful and the best you can be, regardless of everyone around you."

"That's exactly what I want to do," the little girl had replied. "That's why I said I want to be just like you!"

*It's incredible how a child can make such a difference in your day and not even know it*, Legna thought. She looked back at the rose, like a shadow standing alone in a field of bright sunlight. Like an orc standing free in a wave of Engjëllens.

Legna looked away to her nightgown, folded on her end table. She undressed and slipped it on, enjoying the feel of such a soft fabric against her skin. She brushed out her hair and washed her face in her water basin. Then, she turned and fell into bed, pulling the covers tight under her chin.

A few minutes later, Legna recognized the distinct feeling when you are in between consciousness and sleep, when you think eccentric and ingenious thoughts, but do not remember them.

It was in this state when she thought, *What if I were to marry Traven?*

But then, just as quickly as the thought had come, it was lost in her slumber.

# BLOOD MOON

Legna awoke with an aching head. She touched her cheeks, realizing they were wet. She had been crying in her sleep. *How odd*, she thought. She only had small recollections of her dreams, scenes of war and Malin's whispered words. "You must stop her." What did that mean?

Legna wasn't sure who "her" was, or how "she" was supposed to be stopped. She looked outside and realized it was still dark. She got out of bed and slipped out of her nightgown and into an elegant orange dress—the first thing she touched in her closet. She quietly walked past her parent's bedroom, to the kitchen, and then out the door.

Her bare feet hit the cobblestone path outside and a chill jarred her legs. She wrapped her arms around herself. *Why is it so cold?* she thought. Ignoring the strange combination of a low temperature and chirping crickets, she slinked around the houses, weaving her way through until she reached Traven's home. She looked up at the moon. It was tinted red.

*There must have been a battle. Blood has been shed. I wonder where?* Once she thought this question over, she felt foolish. Malin's blood was shed, along with four orcs. To Legna, it was strange to think that the majority killed was because of her. Not without cause, of course. The orcs were murderers, thieves, and millions of other unspeakable things. But to Legna, it still felt wrong that it didn't feel wrong to kill.

She looked at Traven's home; a simple cottage with a golden thatched roof and white walls with a small, green door in the front. Flowers were in the window, illuminated in the moonlight. They were tinted shades of red.

Legna looked away from this second reminder of the events of the day before. The mementos were unwelcomed and unappreciated. Shaking her head to clear her mind of the distractions, Legna slowly crept to the back of the cottage, to the window where Traven's room was.

She peered in and noticed Traven sitting at his desk, a small candle burning next to him. He appeared to be doing nothing but staring straight ahead, a thoughtful expression on his face.

"What are you doing?" Legna whispered, pulling herself through the open window.

Traven's gaze hardly shifted as he said, "I couldn't sleep. I've been having nightmares."

"I want to thank you for the rose you gave me. You always know what to do when someone else is feeling low."

Traven nodded. "They're frightened, Legna. I can feel it."

"What do you mean? Who?" Legna asked, frustrated that everyone seemed to be speaking in riddles lately.

"Everyone," Traven responded. "Our king, our parents, the elvish ambassadors. Everyone."

"What would they be frightened for? Engjëll is safe, now."

Traven shook his head, turning to face her. "The Orcs are rising. They are plotting against us, and I believe they are aligning themselves with the Demons. Together, they could overpower Engjëll."

"How do you know this? Who told you?" Legna asked, slightly shaken.

"My nightmares show me things, Legna. They are powerful. I think Aryanis is giving them to me. I just know that they are too real to ignore. Our race must go to war, no matter the cost."

Legna leaned back against the wall. Changing the subject, she said, "There is a blood moon tonight. Even it knows what I've done."

Traven stood up suddenly, staring straight at Legna. "Stop talking like you've done something terrible! Those Orcs deserved every ounce of pain you gave them. Every Orc does. They murder, they cheat, they treat crime like it's a game they must win. They had no reason to kill Malin, which gave you a reason to kill them. No one is angry at you for wielding a sword that defeats evil. I believe Aryanis was smiling at your bravery, despite the grief he must have had. What you did was right. Do not believe any differently."

Legna was quiet for a long time. "My father is speaking of marriage already. It frightens me."

"Marriage? You're sixteen! You should be off, pursuing what you love the most! Besides, who would you marry? Garren?"

Legna looked away. "That's what my father is hoping for." Legna laughed bitterly. "Could you ever picture me married to a baker?" She slid down the wall until she was seated on the floor.

"Growing pains. We all have them. You don't see anyone telling me I have to get married! Why should it be any different for women? I think you should marry whomever you want, when the time is right." He sat down next to her and put his arm around her shoulders. "When the person is right."

She looked at him, watching his bright green eyes. They gazed solidly back at her. Impulsively, she leaned forward and kissed his cheek.

"We won't be able to do this anymore, you know," Legna said.

"What do you mean? Are you saying we can't be friends?"

"No, Traven…We won't be able to be children anymore. No more climbing into each other's windows at insane hours of the night. No more carefree days spent entirely together. It will cease to look innocent as we age, as we marry. Our intentions may be pure, simply to talk as two old friends, but it will become unseemly to the public."

Traven cast his eyes down. "Then we should go."

Legna laughed. "Go where? You mean run away? What would we do, live in the forest?" She caught his eye and held his gaze. "We're growing up, Traven. We can't run away from that. It's just a new adventure we have to face."

Traven slid his hand over hers for comfort. "Can we at least face it together?"

Legna smiled and held his hand tightly. "I'll always be here if you need a friend." Legna looked out at the first hints of dawn, blooming like a new flower bud in spring. "I should leave. My father will wonder why I'm not there to practice with him."

"I understand. I'll see you later, right?" Traven asked. He stood and then offered Legna his hand.

"Of course." She hoisted herself back through the window. Then she looked back. "Thank you so much for the rose, Traven. It really cheered me up."

"Oh, think nothing of it. The old gardener, Marina gave it to me as I passed by. She said it was the last of the summer. It reminded me of you."

A hint of a smile appeared on Legna's face. "It was sweet of you." She turned and sprinted back to her own home, slipping in the door and dropping into one of the chairs positioned around the table. She thought about what Traven had said, about the Orcs rising against the inhabitants of Zerúa.

A sound from the hall behind her startled her. Läken walked from his bedroom, fully dressed. "I'm sorry, Legna, but I cannot practice with you today. The king has invited me to meet with the warlord and discuss the problem with the Orcs. You understand, don't you?"

"Of course, Father." She stood, and Läken inspected her orange gown.

"Were you truly expecting to train in that?"

Legna looked down at her clothing and laughed. "No, I was visiting Traven late last night, and I was too tired at the time to think about what I was wearing."

"Why did you visit Traven so late at night?"

"I couldn't sleep," Legna replied simply, making it obvious she did not wish to discuss the topics of their conversation.

"I see." Her father studied her, picking her apart, and he seemed to settle on the answer he was looking for. "Well, I must be going. Tell your mother when she wakes up where I am, will you?"

"Yes, Father." Läken waved to Legna and slowly shambled out the door.

Legna was too tired to go back to her bed. Instead, she dropped her head into her arms and fell asleep there, dreaming of nothing.

When she awoke, her mother was bustling about the kitchen.

"Ah," her mother said, turning to look at Legna. "She has stirred. What prince did you go to see this night?" Zopporah asked, motioning to her dress.

"The dress?" Legna laughed. "It's a long story." Legna yawned and looked out the window. She was surprised to see that the sun had fully risen. She had been asleep for quite some time.

Her mother nodded and sat down across from her, gently grasping her hand. "You're such a beautiful girl, Legna. I'm so proud of you." Zopporah looked down at the tablecloth and then back at Legna. "Garren stopped by this morning. He was asking for you, to see how you were. He's quite the man, Legna." Zopporah smiled and Legna smiled back, nodding.

"Garren is a very good man, that is true."

"He's got a stable trade, he's well off, ready to start a family. He's pretty good looking, too, don't you think?"

"Yes," Legna said, looking out the window wistfully. "He is very handsome."

Zopporah caught her eyes. "I think he's the best suitor for marriage, Legna."

Legna was silent, taken aback by her mother's bluntness. "Mother…"

"He could teach you to bake, he would be a loving spouse, I could teach you to prepare spirit jewels; it would be a match made by Aryanis. He provides the food and you provide the water. Can't you see what courting him would accomplish?"

"Mother!" Legna said sharply. Her mother looked at her sternly and Legna softened her tone. "I'm sorry it's just…You're trying to plan my future. Garren is a good man, and I could see myself loving him. But he wants a family right now, a woman that can keep a house and doesn't wish she was on the battlefield. I want to go to *war,* Mother. I want to fight."

"Legna Glowston, I will hear no more of this nonsense! You will find no better man than what you are being offered. He can give you a stable life; he can provide for you! I want you to forget about all those silly dreams of war. Women don't fight. Plain and simple."

"Maybe this woman will," Legna said, setting her jaw firmly and looking her mother in the eyes with an irrevocable stare of stubbornness.

Zopporah sighed, giving up for the moment. "Go change and then I want you to go fishing. We are low on trout."

"Yes, Mother." Legna stood from her seat, stretching her stiff legs. She shuffled back to her own room, still drowsy from lack of sleep. She threw on a blue blouse and brown cotton pants. Deciding to go barefoot, she traced her steps back through the door and then to Traven's cottage. This time, she used the front door.

Alaqua, Traven's mother, kept a fairly neat home. A small kitchen bolstered the front of the home as with Legna's home. Then, there was an atrium, the most magnificent part of the house. Judging from the outside of the home, you would not expect the room. A deep hollow in the middle of the room was surrounded by white railings made of smooth wood, forming a circular balcony. Round tables and chairs were set around the hollow, and the ceiling was covered in ferns and flowers, a feat accomplished by Marina, the oldest woman and the best gardener in Engjëll. Paintings of the many wonders of nature covered the walls. There was a close-up portrait of a daisy, a howling wolf, a mammoth redwood tree, and many others, all painted by Alaqua herself, for she was the artist in the village. Many of her sculptures of wildlife were set around the room, looking as lifelike as possible. But the true grandeur of the room came from the chasm in the middle. From far away, you could not see its contents. But, leaning against the railing, you could look down and see that the ditch was filled with beautiful, sparkling jewels, poking out at every angle. Amethyst, pink quartz, and slivers of diamond threw beautiful, rosy colors onto the ceiling and Alaqua's sculptures, tinting the ferns pink atop of their green hues and bringing the carvings to life as they danced and leapt from figure to figure.

Legna had visited the atrium since the day she was born, but the room's sumptuousness still amazed her. She walked through the atrium, slowly, admiring the artwork. She reached the doorway on the other side of the room more quickly than she liked, but she continued to go nonetheless. She reached Traven's room and knocked on the wooden door heavily. She heard a grunt and then a muddled "come in."

She opened the door and found Traven pulling on a pair of boots, eyes drooping from too little sleep.

"I'm going fishing. Want to come?" Legna asked. "Sounds easy enough," Traven replied. He finished lacing his boot and stood. They walked back through the atrium, and Legna silently marveled at its beauty. They reached the kitchen, and then they were out the door.

The walk to Greenwater Lake was short, only a few minutes from the village. When they got there, they found wooden fishing rods in the small shed nearby, and they dug up some worms from the shore of the lake. They pushed their canoe into the water and jumped in it, gaining control with the paddles. Riding out to the center of the lake, they each put a worm onto their hook and cast their lines into the water.

And neither felt a bite for hours.

# DECLARING WAR

King Zëmer rubbed his temples. Neör, his warlord, had been presenting the reasons why they should go to war, and Lana, his arbitrator, had been giving her reasons of why they should keep the peace. Meanwhile, the ex-hero and blade smith Läken sat silently in a chair, occasionally commenting.

"Your Majesty! The Orcs have killed one of our people, even more, a defenseless old *baker*, going against the treaty which specifically claims that murder on either side would ignite war! Furthermore, I have gathered from Läken that an Orc coming from the direction of the Forest of Engjëll attacked him and his daughter in the Kaparan Meadow. Now you see that I was right in saying the treaty should not have been made! The Orcs are evil, devious creatures guilty of every crime imaginable! You and I both know that the Orcs are just Elves that have been twisted into disgusting, depraved things. Everything good about the Elves they were derived from just melted away! Why do you delay the inevitable?"

"War is not inevitable, Neör!" Lana retorted. "We only need to handle this in a rational way." The woman was tall and thin, with long black hair down to her knees, which she usually pinned up. But today it hung loosely, getting in her face whenever possible.

"And how do you expect we handle it, Lana? Are we just going to let the Orcs defy the treaty? Are we going to let them get away with things they would hang us for? That's not keeping the peace, that's being afraid of justice! Let us not be spineless fools and make a difference for Engjëll!"

"Wanting peace is not being spineless. It is only logical to avoid war. Have you lost all sense of logic?" Lana asked.

"No, logic would be to get rid of those heathens called Orcs! And then we can march right into Mëkator and slay every Demon it has to offer while we're at it!" Neör stopped, jutting out a finger toward Lana. "What are you, a spy? Are you turning to a Demon, Lana? Is that why you're striving for peace with the Orcs?"

"Why you little—"

"Enough!" Zemër roared. Both Lana and Neör shrunk back into their seats, casting their eyes down. Zemër saw what was happening. There was an evil stirring between his court leaders, an unnatural wedge in between their sanity and their actions. "I want neither you to speak again until I say you may. Am I understood?"

Both nodded, not removing their gaze from the floor. They resembled two little children getting rebuked by their elders.

"Good. Now, amidst your yelling, I came to a decision. In my mind, I asked Aryanis if he agreed, and he replied that it was the best decision for Zerúa. We are going to war as we did in earlier years." Zemër noticed a twitch of Neör's lips. "Do not think I have sided with either of you. I came to this decision without any of your 'reasoning' if that's what you call it. Läken, I know you have not been as active in your forge as before the treaty, but I need you to prepare us for a war. Swords, battle-axes, maces, crossbows. Give us all you have."

"Yes, sire."

"And get every apprentice to help you, including that girl of yours."

"I shall."

"Leave, then. Do what you do best."

Läken stood and bowed, an awkward thing for a man completely dependent on a cane. Then he shuffled out of the room.

Zemër looked down at Lana and Neör. "I will deal with you two later. Back to your quarters." They scrambled up out of their chairs and out the door, closing it with a muted *thud*.

He was so tired. So tired his eyes threatened to drop into sleep. He lay his head down on the table. *I'll only rest my eyes for a few minutes.*

He slept for an hour.

# THE SPHERE

"Legna! I feel a bite!" Traven exclaimed. The tug was very strong.

"Well, pull it up then! You might have lost it already!" Legna scolded. "A large waste of our time," she muttered to herself, "sending us to catch trout."

Traven looked at the blonde girl sitting beside him, and he shook his head.

Suddenly, he was pulled under the water by his fishing line; it had been too strong for him. Legna began to laugh and then Traven pulled her under. She pushed Traven playfully, but he seemed frozen in the water, staring into the darkness. Legna followed his gaze and saw the strangest thing she had ever laid her eyes on. A purple, black and blue sphere floated in the middle of the lake. Even the fish seemed to stare at its haunting beauty. Legna lost the need to breathe. She felt as though all she wanted was this strange phenomenon of a sphere. As she drifted closer, she could see that it was sucking in water, almost filtering it. But what came out was not clean water. It was green slime that reminded her slightly of the mold she had found on their goat cheese a few summers ago.

A fish bumped Legna's arm, and she remembered to breathe. When she tried, she sucked in water, and she remembered that she was in Greenwater Lake, and she was drowning.

Traven was nowhere in the water, and Legna lost all feeling in her arms and legs. She wilted like a daffodil in June and then she felt a strong hand pulling her from the water.

She looked up and saw her father, his cane at his side, and she coughed up some lake water. She was alive.

"Legna! Legna, can you hear me?" Her father cried frantically.

Legna coughed some more and sputtered, "Yes, I'm fine. But I saw the strangest thing in the-"

"We can talk later. Right now, I need to go and take inventory of weapons. When you're feeling a little drier, I need you to go down to the forges and make a few weapons. It doesn't matter what kind—swords, daggers, axes—we just need weapons. With the war beginning again, I need your help in the forges more than ever. Make as many as you can before the sun goes down," Läken said.

"Yes, Father," Legna whispered.

"That's my angel. I'll be back as soon as I can to help in the forges. Stay out of trouble."

Legna laughed weakly and said, "No promises." Läken smiled, stood, and started back to the village.

Traven looked at Legna while Läken hobbled away. "Did you see that thing down there?"

"Yes," She breathed. So she had not been hallucinating!

"Good, I'm not the only one. Let's talk about it later. I need to dry off."

Legna nodded. Traven stood up uneasily and ran back to his house, red hair glinting in the sun.

Läken was still trying to get up the hill. "Wait, Father," Legna called as she ran to hug him. "I love you."

"I love you too."

As Legna watched him go, she realized how much older her father looked. She could see his grey roots and stooped back. She was lost in thought when her mother's call startled her back into reality.

"Legna! Legna, my dear, come here!" Her mother sounded distressed.

As Legna made her way back to the market square of her small village, she surveyed the many thatched-roof cottages and trees that housed the Engjëllens. Groups of her friends waved to her, laughing and talking. A group of men played string instruments in an intoxicating, soothing melody. Women danced and sang beside them, powerful lyrics of days to come:

> Praise Aryanis for days ahead!
> When Mëkator will fall and the Demons are dead!
> Fire will cease and rain will come!
> At the snap of his fingers, all will be done.
> We have been trialed, tested, we have passed.
> Wisdom, strength, and courage gained fast!
> Now a hero among us rises to fight,
> Restoring our land to its past state of light.
> As darkness comes, he'll have no fear.
> All evil will cower whenever he's near!
> Blood will be shed with a touch of his blade!
> Igonian Diamond will even be slayed!
> Humble beginnings will prove to progress
> incredible bravery, exceptional finesse!
> Elements slain, he'll be lifted higher.
> Water, ice, plant, and fire.
> But all will be done once he's finished his task,
> Evil no longer will bear a mask.
> The trails will be lined with roses and berries!
> We will all be filled with making so merry.
> Aryanis again will wear the crown.
> At the hands of a hero all evil fell down.

As the song ended, Legna ducked into her own family's oak tree and felt the cozy warmth of a fire. Here her mother stood, smashing spirit jewels to be given to Aryanis. Zopporah was one of the three only beings alive who knew how to correctly prepare spirit jewels for energy. These spirit jewels were tinted with green and red.

"What is it, Mother? Is something wrong?" Legna asked.

"Well, yes, I suppose you could say that. Why are you all wet? Where's Traven?" Zopporah asked, wringing her hands. A worried look was on her face.

"I fell into the lake…Traven went to dry off a little. Father told me to go down to the forge once I wasn't soaked through to help with some of the smithing." Legna pulled off a boot and grimaced as she turned it over, spilling water everywhere.

"I'll let you go as soon as I show you something. Come with me," Zopporah said.

Zopporah left her work and walked out of the kitchen to the bedroom. Legna followed her and found her standing beside the bed, holding something small and red. It squirmed a bit, but Zopporah kept a firm hold on it.

"Legna, I would like you to meet someone I found while you were fishing." Zopporah held up the little red thing. It was a dragon. Its scales sparkled in the afternoon light; its forked tongue flitting in and out of its intimidating mouth. Spikes rose from its back, tail, and chin. It had black eyes that twinkled with curiosity.

It took Legna a few seconds to register. But then she panicked. She backed away and said, "Mother! Where did you find a dragon? Do you know how dangerous that thing is?"

Zopporah cuddled the hatchling. "He doesn't seem very dangerous to me. He took a liking to me when I found him on our doorstep. Here, hold him. See if he likes you." Zopporah placed the dragon in Legna's arms. The dragon looked up at Legna and smiled. Legna smiled back. But a little voice in the back of her head screamed at her. *No! He's a dragon! He might be cute now, but soon, he'll betray you. He'll eat you. He's not to be trusted. What do you even know about dragons?* Legna pushed the voice aside and told Zopporah, "He's wonderful! Do you think we could train him?"

"He likes you. And if we could train him, it would be of huge advantage to our armies. All of the Demons, trolls, and Orcs in the world couldn't take down a dragon. So what do you say?" Zopporah asked.

"Yes…" Legna trailed off in a dream of dragons, soaring through the skies on a fire breathing beast. It was right up her alley. Suddenly, she remembered her father's request. "Mother, I have to—"

"Of course. Go ahead," Zopporah said. She winked to Legna and shooed her out. "Go, and be careful."

"Wait, Mother," Legna wanted to tell Zopporah about the strange sphere she saw in the lake, but she had already closed the door.

Legna shrugged and ran toward the forge. She would tell her mother later. As she neared closer, she could hear some of the clanging of the swords. She ran into the forest and found the set of vines hiding the cave that held the forges. She pulled them back and plunged into the dimly lit cave.

# MALREI AND THE SWORD

L egna heard the voices before she saw the shadows as she stumbled along the tunnel leading to the forge. The language sounded too ancient to be Orcish or the grumbles of trolls and zombies. It was like nothing she had ever heard before. She sneaked along the damp wall of the forge and saw shadows that looked like they were changing to different shapes constantly. She peeked around the corner and saw rippling sea green figures. Their only solid-looking body part was their long fangs. Green tendrils of steam curled off their bodies. Otherwise, they looked like waves on the stormiest of days.

"Farrages. *Sea Demons*," Legna whispered to herself. She looked around the forge to see the nearest weapon, but she knew it was no hope. No one but the bravest of heroes ever killed a Farrage, needless say four at the same time. She saw an iron sword still cooling in a barrel. In one swift move, she reached over, grabbed the sword, and charged at the Farrages.

In one second, the Farrages's expressions changed from surprised, to confused, to indignant. The biggest Farrage smirked and bared his fangs.

"Stupid girl; we will tear you to pieces!" It snarled. Legna dodged its reach for her and stabbed the Farrage in the stomach. It looked at her with hatred and dissolved into foam. The other three demons looked genuinely baffled.

The next Farrage that attacked her was so short; it couldn't have been full grown. It pulled out a spear dripping with dark green liquid. It smiled and rasped, "Poison from the deepest depths of Mëkator...soon will cause your death." It stabbed at her arm, but she deflected and caught the tip of its spear with the flat of her blade. She twisted the poisonous spear out of its hands and sliced through its neck. The Farrage let out a horrible cry and dissolved. The last two Farrages scowled at her.

"You have killed our captain and his offspring. Now you must meet our king." The Farrage grinned, and the two vanished, leaving nothing but some sea foam and the smell of seaweed.

"Your king?" Legna squeaked. She listened, but there was nothing but heavy silence. Then, a small rumbling shook her feet. The tremors became increasingly intense until they knocked Legna to the ground. A large spout of water exploded out of the floor. The water started to collect, and form a distinctly large being. The creature seemed to attract all the liquid in the room to its body. The water in the barrels all around Legna splashed out of their containment to join forces with this huge creature. It had glistening red eyes and yellow teeth, and stood about twenty feet tall. It wore a crown of shark carcasses and seaweed. Like the Farrages, it was made of stormy, green waves. It roared at Legna and admired himself in a wall of reflective rock.

"Ah, 'tis good to see myself again," the Farrage king rumbled. Its voice sounded like rocks grinding against each other. "I was starting to think I would be trapped in Mëkator forever." It looked at Legna. "You have conjured me! You have done a great deed for the Farrage race. For this I shall make your death quick and painless. Thank you." It said.

Legna stared at it and said, "You thank me by killing me? It wasn't even I who conjured you. But it is I who will send you back to whatever hell you crawled out of." She raised her sword and plunged it into the king's foot. The sword bent backwards and Legna looked at it in disbelief.

"You stabbed me. And I offered to kill you quickly, too! There is no *known* way to kill me, child. Anyone who knows is dead or insane. You are neither, I suspect. My skin is made of igonian diamond. It is the hardest substance in the universe. The only sword that can kill me was destroyed centuries ago," the king scoffed.

"You're Malrei. The demon king from the old legends," Legna murmured.

"Indeed." Malrei gloated. He smiled grotesquely at her and roared. Huge droplets of spit landed on her face.

She wiped the spit off her face and glared at Malrei. *Well, if I'm going to die soon, I might as well do it with style.* Legna thought. So she took a chance. She remembered her father talking of everyone having their flaws and that some lead to the death. So, she decided to find Malrei's flaw...other than being unhygienic. Malrei seemed very prideful, so if she could just cut down his huge ego...

"You're disgusting," Legna said.

"Excuse me?" Legna could tell Malrei wasn't very bright.

"You; you're the most disgusting creature on the planet. I've never seen or smelled anything so horrible." She prompted.

"You should watch your words, girl. It's never good to anger the being in charge of your death." Malrei warned.

"You've never won a battle. You were always defeated. You were banished to Mëkator because you were irritating, not threatening. You're the most pathetic monster I have ever seen." Legna taunted.

"I was sent to Mëkator because I destroyed an entire city. It was a punishment." Malrei shot back.

Legna tried one more insult. "Would a real monster have been caught and punished? Face the facts. You are weak. You're not even fit to be called a monster, much less the king of sea demons."

Her insult worked. "That is it, girl. I will cut each part of you to pieces, starting with that loose tongue of yours." Malrei lunged for Legna and knocked her against a wall. She turned to look for a weapon and spotted a large, black sword. She jerked one way, causing Malrei to reach for her and then she ran to the sword. She grabbed hold of it and ran for Malrei. He smiled and swatted at her, but she stabbed his hand. She expected the sword to deflect his hand, but instead, it cut the hand off at the wrist, a mix of sea foam and sea weed squirting from the wound. Legna and Malrei stared in disbelief.

"But...how is it possible? I destroyed that sword! What witchcraft is this?" Malrei bellowed. Legna had no answer. She had no idea why the sword that could destroy Malrei was in her father's forge. But she wasn't about to show her confusion to Malrei.

"My father reforged it, and now I will kill you with it." Legna said confidently. She sliced him through the leg and he fell. She jumped onto the leg that was still intact and ran to his stomach; all the while dodging Malrei's grasping hand. She tripped along his stomach and landed with her sword skewered through where Malrei's heart should have been. He let out a horrible screech, and Legna was engulfed with sea foam. She opened her eyes and found herself face-to-face with a shark carcass. She let out a muted yelp and backed out of the suffocating pile of foam. A bright light made her turn her head away, and when she looked back, a huge blue-green spirit jewel floated above the foam.

"Legna, some Orcs attacked! We won the battle, and I killed five of them!" Traven ran in. When he saw the sharks, foam, and spirit jewel, his eyes widened.

"What happened?" Traven asked.

"I just killed the King of the Farrages with one the most powerful weapons in the world. I think." Legna said.

"Excuse me? Are you all right?"

"I'm fine. I just have one question."

"What?"

"How do you collect a spirit jewel?"

# AFTERMATH

"You sure do know how to stir up trouble. Why didn't you come and get one of the men? We could have handled the Farrages just as well as you did," Traven said as he stuffed the jewel into his bag.

"Traven, if the men had handled it, it wouldn't have been near as impressive, now would it? You've got to let me have a little bit of enjoyment in my life. Father has already refused to give me the forge when he passes, just because I'm not a male. He knows that I'm the best swords master in the village. So why not let me kill a few Demons now and then? It's better than catching trout, that's for sure.

"Now, onto another subject, you said you killed five Orcs?" Legna asked, impressed. Traven had always enjoyed fighting but had never been part of a war.

"Zemëroj killed more."

"Zemëroj is about as smart as his sword hilt. The *only* ability he has is to kill things with an axe. You are far more intelligent than that fool. And if you ask me, intelligence makes a better warrior than even a strong arm."

Traven laughed and smiled at Legna. She always knew how to make him feel confident about himself. And she was right. Zemëroj was not as bright as his father, the brilliant Zemër, king of Engjëll. The intelligent genes of both his mother and father had skipped a generation, making him incredibly slow-minded and extremely temperamental. Zemëroj was the first in the humble village of Engjëll to completely lose his temper with a negotiating king from their neighboring country, Naïfon. Traven thought of how badly Zemëroj was punished for scaring off Naïfon's king. A flogging on his backside certainly was not enough to control his temper forever, but it calmed him for a small amount of time.

As the two friends walked out of the cave, Traven thought back to what Legna had said about her father's reluctance to let her inherit his forge.

"Legna...I'm sorry about the forge. I know you really love it. Maybe I can convince your father to give it to me when he passes. Then I can give it to you, and we can work in it together. I love the forge too, but no one is quite as attached to it as you are. I don't believe that your father is foolish at all. Otherwise, I would be worried he would will it to someone...unworthy." Traven said.

"Oh, Traven, I know he would give you the forge if you asked him! He has thought of you as a son ever since..." Legna stopped herself. She knew that the topic of Traven's father was delicate. Gidön, Traven's father, had gone missing on a quest when Traven was very small. Legna looked at Traven. He was looking at the ground, tears on the corners of his eyes.

"I'm sorry Traven. Sometimes, I wish I could cut my tongue out."

Traven looked up and forced a smile. "It's fine, Legna. You meant no harm."

They walked in silence for a few minutes and then they came to Legna's oversized oak tree she called her home. She opened the door and started to walk in, but she paused.

"Traven, about that...thing down there," she said.

"Yes?" Traven answered.

"It was beautiful. I felt like I could look at it forever"

They stood, silent, thinking about their experience with the purple sphere. Zopporah came, stirring something in a bowl.

"Children, come in! You're letting the evening chill into the house." Traven and Legna stepped into the tree. "Are you staying for dinner, Traven? We're having chicken, if you would like to join us."

"Thank you, but I really shouldn't leave my mother to dine alone. She has been so depressed lately; I just couldn't forgive myself if I skipped dinner with her," Traven said.

"You should invite her to come! She must need to get out! If there's one thing I know about your mother, it's that she needs time with her friends. Now you run and fetch her, and don't you dilly dally, boy!" Zopporah commanded.

"Yes, ma'am!" Traven sprinted out the door to bring his mother.

Zopporah turned and began to cut strawberries.

"How is the dragon?" Legna asked.

"Oh, he's doing pretty well."

Legna looked at the bundle of red sleeping in their home. She again thought of all the things her family could be capable of. She thought of her strange day and remembered that she hadn't told anybody but Traven about her encounter with the Farrages or Malrei.

"Mother ... I have to talk to you and Father. Some very peculiar things have happened today. Where is Father?"

"He's out tending the orchard." Zopporah looked at her daughter's dirty, worried face. "What is it, Legna? What happened?"

"I was almost killed by four Farrages and their king," Legna answered.

"Well, I appreciate your straight-forwardness," Zopporah said, taken aback.

Legna continued on, "And I saw the strangest thing under the water in Greenwater Lake. It was purple and black, and when I looked at it, I no longer felt the need to breathe." Legna's voice began to fade, "All I wanted was to hold it, or touch it, or…something. Do you have any idea what it was?"

"No…but it does not sound good at all. Go tell your father. He might understand," Zopporah said. Legna nodded and walked out the back doorway to their small orchard and found her father picking guavas.

"Father, I have a lot to tell you, and I'm afraid that it's not good news." Legna shifted nervously from one foot to the other.

Läken plucked a guava off the tree and bit into it. "This isn't about that dragon, is it? I told your mother that keeping a dragon as a pet is never a good idea." He smiled, and Legna knew he loved the dragon as much as Zopporah.

"No, the dragon is fine. It's quite nice, actually." Legna responded with a forced smile.

"Hm. Now, what is it that you were going to tell me?"

"It's two things. The Farrages found the forge. They were trying to invade, I guess. But I killed two of them. Then, they sent their king, Malrei, to kill me. But you would have been so proud of me, Father! I killed him! I killed Malrei!"

"You killed Malrei? But…how did you do it? That so-called all powerful sword has been destroyed for years." Läken glanced down at the sword by her side, and his eyebrows shifted into arches. "You really do have it! Where in Engjëll could you find something like that?"

"I found it in your forge, Father," Legna answered.

"I had constructed you a sword for your seventeenth birthday. I wanted to make it special, so I went searching for some different materials to use. I found some black steel, and I sprinkled some ash into it. I know there was a third component…Ah, half a spirit jewel from a fire demon. It glowed quite well and gave a beautiful effect."

"Father, I haven't heard of any Farrages attacking lately. Were there any in the battle?" Legna asked.

"No, as far as I know the Orcs and the Farrages have never been two races that worked together. I do not think the Farrages are part of this war. They mainly keep to themselves and drown a few people every once in a while. For them to try and invade is different. They must have wanted something from my forge; the sword, perhaps?"

"No, Malrei was too surprised that I had the sword to be looking for it. It had to be something else. Maybe they were just trying to rob your forges."

"No, Farrages are disgusting murderers, but they aren't random thieves. They had to be looking for something. I will have to bring this to the king. If the Farrages get involved with the war, unspeakable things could happen. Was there something else you wanted to tell me?" Läken asked.

"Yes. When I fell into the lake this morning...I was drowning because I saw something down there. It was taking our water and replacing it with something...green," Legna said.

"Did Traven see it?"

"Yes."

"Was this thing purple? And so beautiful you couldn't take your eyes off of it?" Läken asked.

"Yes!"

"I know exactly what it is."

"What is it?"

"A very, very bad sign."

"Why? What was it doing in our lake?"

"Legna, sit down. Traven is coming for dinner, right?"

"Yes, he should be here any second."

"I need to talk to both of you. Our village is in a lot of danger. Since both of you saw it, both of you will get its story."

"It was so beautiful, Father."

"Sometimes, my dear daughter, things that are beautiful are the worst type of evil."

Traven came behind Läken and said, "I gave the jewel to your mother." Traven saw Legna, and Läken's expressions and froze. "You told him?"

Läken nodded and said, "Sit. We need to talk."

# SECRETS OF THE
# LAST HERO

Once Legna and Traven were sitting under a pomegranate tree, Läken began his story.

"That sphere you two saw…it is called Korrtar, and it is the most evil creature in Zerúa. It usually takes the form of a stunning woman, so most people refer to it as a "she." You both know that we worship the king of kings, Aryanis. Well, a long time ago, Korrtar was not wicked but was actually part of a race called the Ederra, Aryanis's favored people. They were gorgeous beings, like nothing anyone had ever seen. They lived at the top of the world, and they were a people related to our very own. I suppose you could say we were derived from the Ederra. They were peaceful and very secluded. We did not bother them, and they did not bother us. But Korrtar wanted more than what she had in her race. She wanted power, a chance to rule the world. She would step over anyone to be equal to Aryanis. Aryanis had a close relationship to Korrtar; I suppose you could say Korrtar was his apprentice. When Korrtar realized how powerful Aryanis was, she was prepared to take Aryanis's place. There was only one problem; Aryanis was far too strong for Korrtar. Therefore, Aryanis cast Korrtar to Mëkator and cut off any communications between Korrtar and her people. She was to live alone, in the barren wasteland of Mëkator.

"During this time, there were a lot more Engjëllens in this world. We populated many villages, guarding them from Korrtar. We were called heroes, angels. I'm sure you have heard of the legends." Läken looked at his daughter, and she nodded.

"Father, this Korrtar you speak of was never mentioned in the legends. The heroes fought demons, orcs, trolls. That was their job, to keep the villages safe," Legna said.

"For a time, there were no Demons. There were only Orcs and trolls. The Demons used to be heroes. But Korrtar corrupted them. She got into their minds and found their deepest desires. She gave each group of Demons an element to manipulate, Ice, Water, Fire, and Plants. She offered them infinite power and a chance to rule their element of the world with it. They could not resist. Each was given a king to govern them, one of which you have killed." Läken smiled at Legna and glanced down at her sword. "For a while, the Demons were given equal power as Korrtar. But slowly, Korrtar took their power away until they were her servants. At one point, some of the Demons begged Korrtar to turn them back to heroes, but they were beyond the point of redemption by then. They were trapped as peasants of Mëkator."

"Father, how on earth do you know so much about Demons?" Legna asked.

"Because, I ..." Läken paused and looked at Legna and Traven's troubled faces. He felt horrible for hiding his past. "I used to be a hero of Engjëll. I was crippled while fighting a tree demon. I withheld this from you, Legna, and I regret it. I didn't want you to feel bitter against me for being crippled and not out fighting with everyone else. I was forced to become a sword maker to help the village and pay our tributes. I know I told you my crippling was caused by an avalanche in the forge, but it wasn't."

"You were a hero? You fought Demons everyday? That's amazing! I mean, you're a great blacksmith and everything, but to

say you were of the last generation of heroes? That's incredible!"
Traven said. Then he looked over at Legna and found tears
slipping from her eyes.

Legna choked out, "Father...I would not have been bitter
toward you. You had no choice to quit. You...You would have
died if you continued on with your heroic ways. I am proud
of you."

"Legna, don't cry. Your father just wanted you to grow up in
knowing he's always there," Traven said. He put his arm around
Legna and said, "What did Korrtar want with our water?"

"I think she wanted the power from the spirit jewels. And
if someone doesn't stop her soon, we are all going to die,"
Läken replied.

All three sat in silence for a few minutes until Legna spoke.
"Father, what happened to all of the heroes? Where do we get our
spirit jewels from now?"

"In this dark time, we only have a few heroes. They remain
anonymous always so the Orcs will never know." Läken got up.
"I must consult the king about this. We need to choose who is
going to stop Korrtar. Someone who is unafraid of death. But we
will do it tomorrow. It's late, and none of us can think straight."

Legna nodded. Soon after, Traven and his mother left, and
Legna walked to her bedroom and cuddled up with a wool
blanket. She realized that her sword was still in the sheath on her
waist, but she was too tired to take it off. She closed her eyes and
fell into a fitful, nightmare filled sleep.

# BEGINNINGTOANADVENTURE

*In her nightmare, Legna was unable to move. A black, faceless form appeared to be standing guard of her. It occasionally poked her with its spear and produced a cold, soulless laugh. In the distance, she saw prisoners in rope bonds and people being hanged. There were screams of tortured beings. Then the hanged bodies, the prisoners, and the screams were gone. Legna was standing on a tiny, square platform above a deep abyss. Then, she heard a voice.*

*"Run, girl. Dance for me. Entertain me. You will never destroy me. I am invincible. So run, child." The voice was raspy and seemed to be dripping evil.*

*Legna heard a thump behind her. She turned around and saw a hideous monster with twelve black eyes and claws that were dripping blood. She opened her mouth to scream, but she couldn't. She ran to the edge of the platform and looked across the chasm to see if there was refuge on the other side. There was nowhere to go, just endless darkness.*

*The voice cackled and said, "You either jump to your death or you'll be ripped to shreds. You can decide." Legna looked down at the abyss and thought about which way would be less painful. Then she jumped. She fell for a time that seemed like forever. Then, as she felt she would die from the pressure, she awoke in a cold sweat.*

She could smell eggs from their Elven chickens cooking. She felt relieved, but the screams of the tortured and the roar of the monster echoed in her mind. She thought of all the other nightmares in her lifetime and thought none could surpass the cold voice that had told her to run. She hoped none of these nightmares would ever come true. The old women in the village had told her stories when she was younger, of Engjëllens who were driven mad by their nightmares.

"Nightmares attack us. Do not let them control you, young one. You can make them bend to your will. Anything can happen." They would tell her.

*That dream won't come true. That doesn't happen. They were just old ladies trying to entertain a young child*, Legna thought.

She walked into their kitchen and hugged her father. She saw the yolks of the eggs, and she despised them for their happy yellow color at such a desolate time.

Zopporah smiled, "Eggs for your breakfast!"

"Thank you, Mother." Legna took a bite of the scrambled eggs and smiled. "They taste wonderful."

Zopporah nodded. She smiled at Legna and gestured to the eggs. "Eat, girl. Everyone was told to attend the meeting, so we may all know who the last hero will be."

After the meal, Legna walked to Traven's house. They had agreed to go together for both were interested to see who would take on the task. As they approached the village square, they noticed the massive circle of men surrounding the King.

"All the candidates, I suppose," Traven whispered to Legna. Men of every size and shape, all carrying a weapon, shifted and chattered nervously. Legna studied the men, and then noticed Garren there, in a group with the other nineteen-year-old boys. He caught her gaze, but she looked away, at Traven.

"Who do you think it will be?" Legna asked.

"I don't know. I hope it's someone unlikely, though. Someone nobody will suspect."

"So you don't want Zemëroj to go?"

"That would be a perfect example."

"So, aren't you eligible to be chosen? You are of age, and you are male."

"Come on, Legna, you know they won't pick me. I'm ordinary, not a warrior."

"You just said you wanted it to be someone unexpected."

The King began to speak. "Shh, the King is talking," Traven said.

"People of Engjëll! A great evil has been unleashed! Korrtar herself has left her palace in Mëkator and come to poison our minds!" He pointed to a barrel, which was promptly tipped over by a servant, displaying green slime. Gasps swept through the crowd.

"Who will step forth to silence this evil? Who will defend their people from Korrtar's wrath?"

None stepped forward. Legna grasped the hilt of her new sword and stroked her Bow of Light.

*Someone unlikely.*

"Will none of you fight for those you love? Will you sit by and watch as your race dies off because no one had the heart to step forth?"

If someone else stepped forward, she would have to give up her sword. She would make no difference in her world.

*Someone nobody suspects.*

"I will do it!" Zemëroj cried. The King looked at him.

"No, son," King Zemër said. "You know the laws. Aryanis forbids any of royal blood to enter Mëkator, otherwise, I would be happy to let you go."

A look of disgust entered Zemëroj's eyes. "Well," he said in a venomous voice, "maybe it's time for the laws to change."

A gasp rippled through the crowds like a breeze through the grass and then everything was silent. No one broke the laws, for they were a creed that was unquestionable. Aryanis was all knowing, and one simply did not question him. To think of it was insanity.

A look of concern passed through Zemër's eyes, and in a careful voice, he said, "Son, you don't need to do this to prove yourself. You've already shown you're more than fit for the throne. But we cannot go against Aryanis."

Zemëroj looked at him with complete contempt and, taking his axe, threw it down and stalked out of the town square, muttering to himself.

Sighing with the thought of the talk he would now have to have with his son, Zemër seemed to put it out of mind for the moment and said, "You would not want to be called cowards, would you? Where is the time of heroes? Of Engjëllens who leapt at the chance to save their people?"

If someone else was chosen, she couldn't be Malin's hero. Malin's life would have been taken for nothing.

*Someone fearless.*

She knew what she had to do.

"I will do it," Legna said quietly, pushing through the crowd of men. Each looked at her with the same face a woman would have if she had seen a two-headed mouse.

"Who said that? Was that a child? Is a young one besting the bravery of my finest men?" Zemër asked.

Finally, Legna reached the front of the crowd. "Not quite a child, sire, but close enough. I will do it. I have already wielded the sword that killed Malrei. And I—" Legna stopped, fingering the Bow once again. If she didn't make her point, someone else would be picked. She couldn't let that happen.

"Right before he was killed, Malin gave me this bow and appointed me his champion. I feel like I would be failing you all if I let someone else go and do what I was chosen to do." Legna stopped, looking around at all the men that surrounded her. She felt out of place, uncomfortable. Commotion to her left distracted her. A red head appeared in the crowd, and then Traven's face broke through to the front. He pushed one last time into the middle of the circle, and then drew his sword.

"I support Legna in this. I would follow her to Mëkator and back if that's what she wanted of me!" Traven yelled. Legna smiled at him and then her smile vanished and she looked back at the King.

A long silence frightened Legna. She started to doubt her judgment, until she heard a familiar voice cry, "As would I. I would jump into an abyss full of Demons if Legna told me to, Your Majesty." Garren smiled at Legna, and Legna smiled back.

"A woman doing a man's job is unheard of in Engjëll." The King looked at Legna, boring into her with a stare that tempted her to squirm. But she held her ground, staring back at him.

"How old are you, child?" Zemër asked.

"Sixteen," Legna responded. The crowd around her roared with laughter.

"I have two who would willingly follow me to their deaths." Legna continued to stare at the King until the crowd settled into an uneasy silence. "Are you aware that I have been training to fight since I was almost six? Test me if you must. But I am capable of more than it seems." The King watched her as she drew her sword, proposing a challenge.

"This is a fight you cannot win, child. Do not challenge me," Zemër said. His eyes flickered dangerously.

"I don't have to win," Legna said. "Only make an impression."

Zemër shook his head. "You already have. Legna, I accept your proposal. I grant you permission to go on this quest. And I want you to leave today."

Legna's eyes widened. "Today?"

"You, the one with the red hair. It's Traven, am I correct?"

"Yes, sire, it is Traven."

"You will accompany her. Make sure she is safe."

"Me? I can hardly hold my own in battle," Traven responded.

"This is no battle, boy. This is larger, much different than battle. You will go with Legna, and you will both come back alive."

Garren looked at Zemër. "I'm going, too," he said firmly.

"No," Zemër said. He lowered his voice. "You must keep watch over the weapons."

"But, My King …" Garren pleaded.

"Garren," Legna said. Garren turned to face her. "I'm going to be fine. Just please protect the weapons."

"I … I just want you to be safe." Garren took her hand. "I don't want to lose you too. I love you. And women shouldn't be fighting. It's not right that it's come to this."

"I know. And I love you." She saw Traven look away, uncomfortable. "But we are both young. I have found my purpose for now. Find yours while I am gone. We are both but children; we have seen too few years to know what love is. And if a woman wants to fight, I say let her," she said with a fire in her voice. She hugged him, burying her face into his shoulder. She was scared despite her evidential confidence. She wasn't sure what had come over her to volunteer like she did.

She withdrew from the embrace and smiled at Garren. "I'll see you in a little bit."

"Right."

Legna walked away through the crowd to her gaping parents.

Legna's mother put a hand on her shoulder and said, "Are you sure about this?"

"Yes," Legna replied. "I can't back out now."

Zopporah nodded and handed Legna a silver locket in the shape of a heart. "This locket has been passed down for generations in our family. Believe it or not, you were not the first heroine in our lineage. Your great-great-great grandmother was just as strong as you are. The locket will keep you safe in your time of darkness. Use it wisely for it will only be useful once you truly need it." Zopporah hugged her daughter and wiped away a tear. She coaxed the dragon she had found out from his hiding place behind her, gently pushing him over to Legna. "I hope he serves you well. His name is Aspör, Elvish for fierce. I will pack him some food in each of your bags."

"Thank you, Mother. I didn't think you would understand my calling. I love you."

Zopporah managed a faint smile. "I will always love you, my daughter. I am so proud of you." Zopporah kissed Legna on the head and then hurried away to gather food for Traven and Legna. As soon as she had departed, the King approached them.

"I want to give you these." King Zemër handed them each a vile of shimmering purple liquid. "It is the innards of a spirit jewel from the Head Demons of Korrtar. One drop is equivalent to a pail of our water. Use it carefully." He smiled at them and put his hand on Legna's shoulder. "You are smart and talented. Do not let Korrtar tempt you. The whole village thanks you for your bravery." He smiled and walked away.

"Come now, Legna, Traven, Aspör. Let us wait for your mother by the forest, so you may depart as soon as she gives you your supplies." Läken led them to the outskirts of the forest. Along the way, Legna received many thanks from multiple villagers. The little girl who had given her the wildflowers earlier whispered to her, "Now I know I want to be just like you." Then she skipped away.

When they got to the brilliant, bright forest, Legna gasped. The small waterfalls that surrounded the forest were streaked with green. They stood gaping at the forest until Zopporah returned with two sackcloth bags filled with food, water, and dried firethorn flowers for Aspör.

"We do not have much time. Go and take my blessing." Läken kissed Legna's head and hugged Traven. "Traven, I want you to know that I have always thought of you as a son. I love both of you. Be safe, please. And get in no more trouble than necessary." He turned them toward the forest and told them to stay down and move quickly. Then he watched as his daughter, leading a red dragon, and her best friend walked calmly and fearlessly into the forest.

# THE BEJEWELED APPLE

Legna and Traven stayed away from roads and moved as quickly as possible. Neither of them had ever been outside of Engjëll, so Läken had explained to them their route. First, they were to make it through the Wilderness of Windör. Then, they would go through multiple Elven villages on the Elvish Isle. After they did all this, they will have finally made it to Mëkator. Legna ran this through her head and tried to trace the route on the very few maps she had seen. It was no use. The maps had all been different, and some did not include the Elvish Isles or Mëkator. She took in a deep breath and thought of how far they had walked so far. They could still see the rows and rows of raspberry bushes in the local farms of Engjëll.

Both Legna and Traven had been quiet for a while, and it became eerily silent. The regular sound of birds chirping and squirrels quarreling had stilled, to the point where the only sound was the padding of the friends' feet and Aspör's deep breathing. It was as if the animals of the forest sensed Korrtar's presence.

Legna looked around at the streams of sunlight coming through the branches of the silver and gold trees that bore shimmering apples and pears. She picked off a silver apple and bit into it, and sparkling white juice dripped down her chin. The apple's juice reminded her of ivory, and she smiled when she thought back to the time in Kaparan Meadow, when she had seen a baby mammoth stuck knee deep in some mud. She had panicked at first, thinking that it might charge her, but then she had realized that the poor thing was trapped. She worked with the colossal creature, pouring some water in the holes and using a dagger to scoop the mud away. Eventually, she had gotten it out of the mud. The mammoth had then done something that surprised her to this day. It had taken her with its trunk, and held her, almost hugged her. She felt its cold ivory tusks against her hair. Then, it had stomped away.

She was so lost in her daydream, that she didn't notice the group of Rangun that had gathered in a clearing in the trees until she bumped into Traven.

The Rangun were dark green and brown and were covered in moss. They seemed confused, like they were arguing. A particularly fuzzy Rangun made an exasperated face and pointed toward a silver pear tree. Another shook his head and threw his arms up in the air.

"What are they doing?" Traven whispered.

"It looks like they're arguing. They're confused about something, maybe which direction they must go. Maybe they want something, but they're not sure where it is. Either way, they are blocking our path. And that will not do." She put her hand on her sword.

"Legna. We really shouldn't cause any more trouble than necessary. What are you doing?" Traven asked.

"Causing trouble." With this, Legna stood and received the attention of the Ranguns.

"Hey!" One of them grunted. "It's one of the little white shrimp. It might know where the fruit is."

"White shrimp?" Legna asked incredulously. She knew that Demons had strange perceptions of Engjëllens, but she needed something to stall them.

"Your race...they glow white. You have a halo around you. I can sense another, one that glows very brightly...And compared to us you are the size of a bread crumb, at the most," a large Rangun answered. Upon recognition, Traven stepped out of the bushes with Aspör by his side.

"Okay...So, what are you doing in the forest of Engjëll?" Legna asked. She suppressed her fear, making her voice casual and indifferent.

"Looking for the bejeweled fruit, the one that your people guard. We need it for...well, let's just say that you help us find it, or you die."

"Bejeweled fruit? What are you talking about?" Legna asked. Then it hit her. Once, there was an Engjëllen hero named Bátor that was bravely fighting an army of head demons, with only an Elf by his side. He was struck down by a huge Demon, and he barely had any life left in him. In order to save him, the Elf quickly changed him to an ordinary fruit, but his impeccably humble and sinless spirit shone through to make a kaleidoscope of beautiful jewels encrusting the simple apple. The Elf hid the fruit, and its location had been passed down in Engjëllen history. Legna knew it was hidden in a small, dead elm tree in the center of the woods. The log was so unnoticeable; it was near impossible for anyone outside of the Engjëllen culture to find. Fortunately, the Elf later crafted a duplicate, and hid it in a more obvious place. The apple contained the power of the greatest hero that ever lived. The Ranguns were probably trying to get it to Korrtar.

"Sure, I'll take you to the fruit. On one condition." Legna said.

"Well, what is it?" The Rangun licked his lips in anticipation, and Legna grimaced at his green, slimy tongue. It was as if all he drank was algae.

"You let us go and never come back to our forest ever again." Legna said.

The Rangun had a rare look of deep, painful thought on his face. Legna could almost hear the gears in his dead, zombie-like mind turning as he thought through Legna's proposition. "All right," he finally said. "But no tricks. If I find out that you are fooling us, I will slaughter you personally."

"Can I just have a moment to speak to my fellow companion?" Traven asked.

"Remember the slaughtering ... No funny business," a Rangun said.

Traven pulled Legna aside and whispered, "What are you doing? You can't just show them where the fruit is!"

"Calm down, I have a plan. We might double back, but it won't take long. We show them where the decoy is. Then, they'll leave." Legna sheathed her sword.

"How do you know that they will listen to us? They might get the fruit and then kill us. You cannot trust Demons."

"If they come at us, we will simply kill them. Ranguns aren't as smart as Farrages. If I could kill three of them, I can kill a few Ranguns."

"I hope you are right, Legna." Traven glanced at the Rangun nervously.

"Have I ever failed you?" Legna said sarcastically.

"I have to think about that..." Traven said. Legna scowled at him.

"All right you two, enough talking. The sooner you show us the fruit, the sooner we will leave." A crafty smile spread across the Rangun's face; his features resembling a green, scaly snake. He pulled them up and pushed them along with the tip of his spear. "Show us where to go, white one."

Legna pointed into the woods, toward a large, majestic oak tree. It seemed to rise above the other trees, like the golden pear trees were bowing to it. She knew that the imitation apple was lying just inside the hole in the middle of the tree.

"That tree. It...It's in there." Legna faked reluctance; like she was unsure she wanted to show them the location of the "fruit." Her drama worked, and the Ranguns pushed each other as they greedily ran to the tree. The largest Rangun stuck his hand into the hollowed out part, and pulled out a beautiful, rainbow colored apple. He turned it over in his hands, studying it. After several uncomfortable minutes, he glanced over at Legna and Traven as if just remembering that they were there. He carefully placed the fruit into a ripped burlap sack. Then, he said two words: "Kill them."

Legna and Traven drew their swords, and the Ranguns advanced on them. One lunged at Legna, but she easily sidestepped his attack and kicked him in the knee. He fell, and he was decapitated by her sword. Next to her, Traven stabbed the extremely fuzzy Rangun in the chest. There were five more left, and Legna began to see a problem developing. The Ranguns backed them up against a large maple tree, and Legna stabbed one in the stomach. It fell, and a small sapling appeared in the ground, a small green spirit jewel floating above it.

"Well, this comes as no shock to me. Who was it that told the over ambitious girl that drug him into this that we shouldn't cause trouble?" Traven said.

"Traven, this *really* is not the time for this." Legna said. She blocked another thrust by a smaller Rangun and sliced right through his shoulders. The top half of his body fell on her, and she could still smell the foul, earthy odor of his breath. She threw him off of her and another sapling sprouted up.

She made a face but regained her composure quickly. Traven gouged out the eyes of another Rangun, blinding him. He screamed a shrill, horrible screech. Traven stabbed him in the neck and pushed him aside. Only one Rangun remained, and it happened to be the holder of the apple. The Rangun cackled and slapped Legna's sword aside with his crudely forged hammer. He raised his hammer and swung it at Legna, but Traven jumped in front of her and caught it with his sword. They froze for a moment, like time itself had stopped. The second it seemed Traven would overpower the Rangun, the Rangun kicked Traven in the stomach and shoved him aside. He raised his hammer once again, but a sudden look of pain took his deformed face. Legna was confused at first, but then she watched as flames engulfed his body. She listened as he shrieked in terror and watched him wither to ash, as if he took on hundreds of years of decaying in five seconds. When he was reduced to a pile of rubble, Legna tore her eyes from it to see the cause of his death. There, amidst the smoke, was Aspör. He had grown from Legna's knee, to her waist. Legna and Traven stared, open-mouthed, at Aspör. Not only did he get bigger, but he had malted from red to silver, shimmering scales. And there, leaning on his back, was a man, white-faced and shivering.

# BÁTOR

The man attempted to stand, but he fell over again. Legna ran to his side and leaned him against her shoulder. A large scar ran down his cheek, and he had greying brown hair. His beard was neatly trimmed but covered the entire bottom half of his face like a blanket. He had a large nose and curious, brown eyes. He was tall and muscular, the ideal picture of a hero. Traven looked at Legna questioningly, but Legna had no explanation.

"Sir? Sir, are you all right?" Legna pointed to her pack. Traven brought it to her and she took out some water. "What are you doing out here in the forest? Are you part of our village?" Legna asked.

"What? No…I'm not sure. My life seems like a blur…I- I'm not sure what I'm doing here. The last thing I remember is the Elf…He was leaning above me, working his ancient magic and then dark, cold emptiness. I could hear my own breathing and occasionally hear the rustling in the trees, maybe a bird chirping." He took a sip from Legna's canteen and panted.

"Wait, what? What are you—" Legna stopped and her eyes widened. "Bátor? Is that your name?"

"Yes…Yes, I believe that it once was my name. I don't think I have an identity anymore, though. My existence is only a distant memory to all living things." Bátor rubbed his head and slowly stood up. "What are you two young ones doing out this far into the forest?"

Legna and Traven looked at each other. "We are…We are on a quest. We are heroes. I thought that was the decoy that we showed them," Legna said to Traven.

"Someone must have switched them," Traven replied

"So what is this quest about?" Bátor asked, his loud voice overpowering his younger rescuers'.

"We were sent to defeat Korrtar," Legna said in a diminished tone.

Bátor chuckled. "And who, exactly, sent a sixteen-year-old girl to save the world? What gives you the power to do this, little one?"

Legna noticed her sword still lying on the ground where the Rangun had knocked it aside. She walked over and picked it up, wiping the dirt off of it as she strode back to Bátor.

Bátor smiled as she displayed her beautiful, glowing sword. "The Sword of Power. I haven't seen that sword in centuries. You have proven your worth, little one. How did you reforge it?"

"I didn't. My father did. It was a birthday present, but…well, you can see." Legna studied it and noticed the extreme detail of the blade. The white, glowing swirls imprinted from the fire spirit jewels were glaring brighter than ever. The sharp, black metal made from ash glinted in the sunlight. The inscription of an ancient language was carved into the blade and the handle. A ring of crystal surrounded the area in which the blade and the handle met. At the bottom, a luminescent cross was engraved, shining like a star.

"Sir, this is an overwhelming predicament that Traven and I have fallen into," Legna said.

"Yes. It is quite a rare thing, little one, that someone of your age would wield so much power. The dragon, where did he come from?" Bátor smiled in a father-like way, gesturing to the silver beast that was contentedly dozing in a sun patch, smoke tendrils twirling out of his nostrils.

"I'm not sure. Aspör is his name. He was a gift from my mother, who found him on her doorstep just a day earlier," Legna said.

"Interesting." Bátor stroked his grizzly chin inquisitively. "Dragons are not known to leave their young alone. They are rather maternal creatures, believe it or not. Almost like a bear and her cubs. You are very lucky, though. Dragons like this oversized lizard probably would have run away by now if he didn't think you were special." Bátor stretched, the color returning to his face. "So, you are going on a quest?" Legna and Traven nodded, still in awe of the once-dead legend standing before them. Bátor leaned toward them and said quietly, "I believe it is high time for a new adventure."

"You don't look very healthy right now. Maybe you should go back to Engjëll and rest. They would be ecstatic to see you." Legna leaned down and picked up one of the dark green spirit jewels. Her fingers tingled from the power.

"I am forgotten there, little one. I am nothing but a record in books. I disappeared when I was a young man. As you know, we Engjëllens live for centuries, for age matters not to us. We fear no sickness, only the glint of a stronger opponent's blade. The best thing for me to do is travel to the Elven villages. I would love to learn their magic, for it was something I inquired from an old friend many times. He was never able to tell me, though. He said I wasn't ready. I decided that he was probably right, and eventually, I gave up asking. But, I still have some years left in me, and I don't want to retire yet!"

Legna was silent for a little bit, but then she dared to ask the one eternal question, one she could never take back. "Would you like to go with us?"

Bátor lit up at the hints of a new quest. A playful fire danced in his eyes, and Legna realized that he was still rather young, no matter how long he had been shut up in his life-preserving cage. He took a deep breath, like he was relieved he could continue with his calling. He smiled, and calmly said, "Yes. I would love to come with you. But having me along would put you in much danger. Korrtar is not foolish. She will know that her Demons failed to do her wishes, and she will find the cause of the Demon's unusual incompetence. Are you sure you would like me to come along?"

Legna pondered this. Bátor would be able to teach them multiple things regarding legends, sword fighting, and even magic. He was a famous hero, but he was almost like a Demon magnet. Something inside of Legna mustered up the courage and said, "Of course you can come. My name is Legna, by the way, and this is Traven."

They walked a mile more in silence. The afternoon sun was relentless, but the sparkling branches of the silver apple trees guarded their backs. As they walked farther and farther away from Engjëll, the trees became larger, and they stopped bearing silver apples. Instead, there were bright green limes and sunset oranges. An occasional oak tree or elm tree looked awkward and tall compared to the groves of citrus trees, but they provided sufficient shade.

Bátor broke the silence abruptly, "Let me see your sword."

Legna unsheathed her blade and handed it gingerly to Bátor, who took it firmly and flipped it through the air a few times.

"This is truly an incredible blade. Who was your father, again?"

"Läken Glowston. Did you know him?"

Bátor looked down at the sword once more and then his head shot up in alarm. "You? You're Läken's daughter? I was there when you were a newborn! How old are you child?"

"Sixteen," Legna responded, a bit surprised by his last statement.

"Sixteen years," Bátor mumbled to himself. "I was trapped in a stupid piece of rotting fruit for sixteen years." Then, he handed back Legna's sword and looked at Traven. "And yours," he said, holding out his hand.

Traven pulled his simple, yet elegant sword out of its sheath. Words were inscribed into his blade, also, but these were in their own tongue. *Grace and sophistication are only ornaments. Never forget who you are. —Gidön*

Bátor looked carefully at the sword. "This is a beautiful blade also."

After many more painful minutes of silence, Bátor said, "Gidön was a good, wise man. He was a close friend of mine. Where did this inscription come from?" He asked, pointing at the runes.

Traven's face dropped. "Gidön was my…my father. He went missing when I was very, very young. He gave the sword to my mother, Alaqua, to give to me. You knew him?"

"Knew him? He was my best friend! What a rascal, your father. He always wanted to do daring things, like jump from a roof into Greenwater Lake. Once he straightened out, though, he was an unbelievable warrior and hero. Even more than that, he was an incredible friend. Be proud of your father, my boy. He was special. I sense that this trait has been passed on to you. You have an amazing bloodline. You are the result of many brave heroes."

Traven smiled and Bátor talked of the many adventures that he, Gidön, and Läken had encountered. He told of the time that they discovered a courtyard of pure crystal trees, shrubs, and animals. "They glittered like a rainbow. Every color imaginable was trapped inside their bodies. The animals moved and the trees swayed in the breeze, too. Gidön wanted to take home a small, crystal mouse, but as soon as he slipped it into his pocket, the ceiling came down on us, and all of the animals escaped. From then on, we promised to never steal anything. It was a good thing too because that place was the Akulls' (ice demons') fortress. We became public enemy number one amongst the Akulls. We had no way of knowing that the crystal animals were some of the Senators of Naïfon, being held captive by the Akulls. When they were released, we thought we had started some sort of animal apocalypse. We ran all over the Demon Isle, trying to catch the animals. The Akulls were hot on our trail, and we had to kill quite a lot. Have you ever seen an Akull?" Legna and Traven shook their heads. The Akulls mainly stayed in Mëkator, so Legna and Traven didn't encounter them in Engjëll. "They're horrible creatures. They put a chill right down your back. Other than the Head Demons, the Akulls are the largest Demons, so they are the hardest to kill. They are white and scaly, but hair pokes out of places, too. They have a face like a possessed monkey and a body like a white dragon.

"Anyway, it wasn't until we had spent a week catching crystal emu that someone contacted us to tell us the animals weren't dangerous. Well, you can only imagine how stupid we felt! It's kind of comical, now that it's over, but we were so embarrassed that we had spent days caging up the royalty of our neighboring country." Bátor had a tear in his eye as he thought of the many fond memories he had of Gidön and Läken.

They walked another five miles before the sun dipped down below the hills. Legna tied Aspör to a tree and fed him a few fire flowers. She stroked him and talked to him, telling him about the strange happenings of the day and how proud she was that he had saved them. He looked at her, drinking in every word. She wondered if he understood as his tongue flitted in and out of his mouth. Then, Bátor startled her.

"How good are you with that sword? You have it, but now you must use it!" He pulled his sword out of its sheath and took a fighting stance. Legna looked him over and then decided she had nothing to lose. She drew her sword and prepared herself for a fight. Bátor lunged for her side, but she easily deflected his blow.

"Good," he said. He faked a swing to her head, but then put the point to her unguarded stomach. "You must think of the unpredictable. Eventually, the unpredictable will become the predictable, and the predictable will become the unpredictable. Let nothing surprise you. Anything is possible." Once again he went for her head, but Legna predicted the unpredictable. She faked a block toward his sword but guarded her stomach. The clash of metal rang through the forest.

"Start a fire," Bátor mumbled to Traven. "It's going to get cold." With this Bátor spun, breaking the hold of her sword. Legna deflected many more of Bátor's coordinated swings. But several minutes later, when she caught his sword with her own, she began to get cocky. He twisted her sword out of her hands and put his own blade to her neck.

"The predictable, my dear, just became the unpredictable." He took the point away from her and sheathed his sword. Then he pointed to Traven and said, "You are next."

"Me?" Traven asked, unsure.

"Yes. But not until tomorrow evening for we walked far today, and we need the energy. Sleep, young ones, and may your dreams be protected." Bátor lay down on his blanket and fell asleep almost instantly. Aspör stirred in his slumber, kicking his legs, and softly roared. His head jerked up, and he looked around sleepily before settling his head back onto the ground and resuming his quiet snoring.

"Legna," Traven said, sitting down on his red, fuzzy blanket. "I feel like something's been following us. I can feel it watching me."

"I'm sure you're just nervous. The woods can be—" A rustling interrupted her. "What was that?" Legna looked at Traven and he gave her an I-told-you-so look. There was a salmonberry bush nearby, and Legna could see a dark figure behind it.

"There is something behind the bush over there," she whispered. They stalked over to it and Legna put a finger to her lips. They were right behind it when she plunged her hand forward and grabbed it by the neck. In a smooth, swift movement of her arm, she drew her sword and placed it on the intruder's Adam's apple. "Move one muscle and I will slice your neck," she whispered to whatever-it-was. Suddenly, the man twisted out of her grip and rolled, pinning her down and pressing his sword to Legna's throat with frightening strength.

"I'm sorry," he cried. "I had to follow. No one paid attention so I followed. I wanted to help. I'm sorry. I don't want to hurt you."

Bátor's voice came, "Legna, are you all right?" He came carrying a torch, which lit up a man's face, and who they saw made Legna gasp. The tanned, chiseled face of Zemëroj the prince posed above her, tears streaming down his face and his lip curled in an odd snarl.

# TRANSFORMATION

"**M**y prince, what are you doing here?" Legna asked, looking into his deep, blue eyes. He released her from his grip; his eyes apologizing for any pain he caused. He stood and helped her up, stalking to the fire.

"I wanted to help and show that our High King might just be incorrect," Zemëroj said in a deep voice. He had golden hair and muscles fit for the finest of warriors. His cheekbones and perfect features were lit up in the firelight, but there was something strange about his eyes. They never stayed still; they were always flitting from one thing to another as if he was expecting an attack at any moment.

Legna looked at him carefully. Something was not right, and she could not place what it was. "Zemëroj, there's no sense in disobeying Aryanis." As soon as she said their High King's name, Zemëroj flinched, and for a moment, it seemed he was a different person. His face seemed more shadowed; his eyes black and vacant. It was gone almost as soon as it came, but as Legna caught Traven's eye, she knew he had seen it too. She knew now that something had gone horribly wrong.

"Well maybe," the prince said in a voice like a serpent, "Aryanis doesn't have to know."

The three companions stared at him in silence, and even Aspör sat up in shock.

"I don't think that's how it works," Traven said slowly, trying to stay respectful.

"Aryanis isn't so powerful. If he was he would just go to Mëkator himself."

Dead silence. What on earth had happened?

After a long, uncomfortable pause, Bátor spoke up. "We should decide this in the morning. It's too late. You should stay for the night, at least, son."

A pleased smile graced Zemëroj's face. "That sounds perfect."

Traven sighed with fatigue. He threw a rolled up blanket at Zemëroj and retreated to his own.

As Legna smoothed her own blanket, preparing for sleep, she feared the type of dreams she would have. As she lay down, she squeezed her eyes shut and hoped that whatever gave dreams would give her a break.

As she slowly drifted into sleep, she could hear an owl relentlessly hooting. Strange images flickered in and out of her mind, threatening to turn into nightmares. She pushed them aside and thought of her father, open arms and laughing. She then allowed herself to be pulled into a deep, engulfing sleep.

Her dream was simple, yet heart wrenching. She stood in a land she did not know, with white sand everywhere and no trees. Everything was incredibly flat and boring, and there seemed to be no life other than herself. She could hear the roar of the ocean in the distance, but from which direction, she was unsure. Where she was standing, she could see the full moon perfectly, shrouded in green mist. It looked like the sun had been swallowed by darkness. She looked up at the stars and saw that they spelled the words, "He's gone."

❦

A sound was heard, awaking Zemëroj with a start. He looked around and saw that Legna, Traven, and Bátor were still asleep.

He got up and silently searched the small clearing in which they were camped. Nothing seemed to be there, so he ventured slightly into the woods. There, beside a crepe myrtle tree, was a dark, hooded figure holding a thin scythe. It turned its face toward Zemëroj, showing nothing under the hood but darkness. Zemëroj froze with his heart pounding. The hooded creature eerily walked toward him. It sheathed its scythe and put its arms up in surrender. The being pulled off its hood, showing the face of a beautiful woman, with a few wrinkles displaying her age.

He relaxed a bit and crept cautiously to her.

She spoke, revealing a smooth, buttery tone in her feminine voice. "What is a fine young man doing out in the forest this late at night?"

"I was about to ask a similar question to you," Zemëroj said.

"My reasons are my business, but I'm curious toward yours. Why are you here?" She asked.

"Well, I wanted to go on a quest with my friends, but I'm not allowed to," Zemëroj mumbled. He kicked an acorn, making a mouse skitter out of the shadows.

"A quest?" she said inquisitively. "What kind of quest is this?"

He kicked another acorn. "I don't know. I just know that I'm sick of not being picked for the special things."

"You don't know what the quest was for, but you want to go on it anyway?"

Zemëroj squinted at her. "Are you part of our village, or—"
She put a finger to his lips.

"What is it you want, Zemëroj?" His eyes widened at the use of his name. "For your true love to love you back? To be talented at everything you do? Tell me your greatest desires, child. I will make everything perfect. Just close your eyes and think. Think of what you need." She put her hand on his forehead, probing his mind for his desires. His fear and absolute pain were impossible to conceal. He thought of Traven's warnings to go back to Engjëll and wished immeasurably that he had listened. He remembered

Legna's eyes brimming with tears as she tried to explain why he shouldn't have come. And all that time, all he could do was think of his own reputation. Above all feelings he felt ashamed and wished to once again receive the esteem that he used to have among his people.

"Ah, you would like respect in the eyes of your family? You would like glory and honor? A chance to change the world?"

Yes!" Zemëroj exclaimed, a wild sensation rising in his chest. "I'll do anything. Anything!"

"You shall receive these, my child. You will receive this and more!" Suddenly, purple and blue sparks erupted from her fingertips and surrounded him, swirling around him and encasing him in an inescapable cage, lifting him off the ground as he struggled against them. She cackled evilly as everything slowly blurred out of his vision.

⁂

When he awoke, he was in a dark cave. He was sitting on a throne made of black velvet and dark wood. Beside him, a cold, stone throne loomed high, making his chair look like it was crafted for a dwarf. He felt strangely different as if he suddenly understood everything. He glanced down at his hands and was surprised to find them gnarled and charcoal black. He was dressed in a purple robe made of silk that he did not own. He heard a thud behind him and saw the woman standing there, now clothed in a purple gown and an amethyst crown on her head.

"Look here, my pet has awoken. You were asleep for quite some time, but it was worth it! You are now respected, and you know everything." The woman smiled cleverly.

"I…I don't know where I am or who you are." He glanced back down at his hand again. "For that matter, I'm not sure who I am!"

"Oh, of course. Welcome to your kingdom, my dear. I am your queen." She displayed her sparkly crown. "And you, on the other hand, are Zemëroj, my lord."

"Queen? What happened?" He rubbed his head, and was disturbed to find that skin flakes fell from his forehead.

"You asked for respect from your family," She replied simply.

He interrupted her statement with a sharp tone, "Where are they, then?"

Korrtar raised her arms and lights illuminated a courtyard far below, with many Demons bustling about. Some were clipping black and purple roses, and three were attempting to fix a fountain that was made of black onyx.

"Zemëroj! Meet your new family!" She said. All of the Demons turned to look at him, and he felt an odd sense of belonging, like he felt at home. He timidly waved, and the Demons heartily waved back, erupting into bursts of cheers.

"They respect you! Everything you do is perfect in their eyes!" She said excitedly.

He rose from his throne and said, "I am ready to serve you, my queen." He knelt before her.

She watched him, delighted, and then she winked and yelled to the cheering crowd of gardener Demons, "All hail the new Prince of Mëkator!" The cheers increased until the noise was deafening.

A strange realization came to him. If this was Mëkator, he had just sworn fealty to none other than Korrtar herself. A part of his mind protested this, creating a battle that gave him a bracing headache. He could feel the side against Korrtar slowly subsiding though, seemingly listening to what the darker side had to say.

She put an arm around his shoulder and told him to go rest. A fire Demon came to them upon her request and led him to his exquisite room. A huge canopy bed took up one corner of the sanctuary with a large wardrobe and a mirror. He rushed to the mirror and found to his slight shock that his skin was now pitch black and weathered with many wrinkles. He had undergone a complete transformation. He shrugged, accepting his superb new lifestyle, and searched the wardrobe for nightclothes. A silk nightshirt caught his attention and he slipped it on. He settled onto the soft bed and fell into a deep, peaceful sleep.

# FINDING HORSES ... AND OTHER THINGS

Legna's other dreams were pointless and made no sense. One just had large, colorful sparks dancing throughout the dark abyss of her mind, randomly flickering. They illuminated thoughts long forgotten by Legna and memories so insignificant they seemed to cower in the looming shadows of other, more imprinted memories. It was a strange experience to be had, and it made Legna uncomfortable.

Her next dream was of a mirror. The face in the mirror wasn't hers, though. It was blackened, charred like it had been burnt and scooped out of a fireplace, and it had no hair. Her hands were bloody and scarred, and her clothes torn horribly. She stretched her arms above her head, and the creature in the mirror did the same. She touched her hands, and again she was mimicked. The face bore what looked like fangs and leapt out of the mirror, waking her up.

Legna looked at Traven and Bátor, who were still peacefully snoozing. The morning sun was sluggishly rising above the distant mountains of Windör. She realized that it must be a right time to start on their journey, so she shook Traven to wake him. Traven sat up, startled. He rubbed his head, pushing back his red hair and revealing a bloody gash left from the Rangun's hammer.

Bátor woke and sleepily rose. "We must move. If Korrtar doesn't know of you now, she is not the same evil I remember battling when I was younger. There will be Demons soon, more than before. Roll up your blankets, wake Aspör, and eat breakfast before they arrive."

"Wait," Legna said, "where's Zemëroj?" She looked at his empty blanket with curiosity.

"He must have come to his senses and went home. I'm glad of it; I most certainly did not want to convince him to go back." Traven said, folding his blanket quickly and deftly. "I expect he would be well on his way by now, no need to worry." He seemed to be reassuring himself.

"Give the dragon some food, and let's go. We can't afford to lose ground. We traveled about eleven miles yesterday, but it's not enough," Bátor said. Legna threw a flower to Aspör and slung her bag across her back.

"We can't travel any faster on foot, though. Unless we run the whole way," Traven said.

"I know that, boy. We need to get horses somewhere," Bátor said. He pushed Traven along a deer trail between some blackberry bushes as Legna led Aspör through a thicket.

"There's no civilization until the Elvish Isles, and we have to cut through the Wilderness of Windör to get there," Legna said.

Bátor grunted and said, "There has to be somewhere in the Wilderness that some creatures live. Hasn't Engjëll explored Windör by now? It can't be completely uninhabited."

"We have never had a purpose to take a deep interest in Windör, I suppose. But you're right, Bátor. How do we know it isn't? We might as well try," Traven said.

Legna stopped her knee-deep wade in the thorn brush as her ears picked up the strange syllables of Orcish.

"Orcs," She said quietly.

Traven stopped and turned to her. "What?" He asked.

"There are Orcs nearby. Don't you hear them?" Legna said.

Bátor listened and widened his eyes. "I'm not so worried about the Orcs. It's the other creature I hear."

"What other creature?" Legna said, straining to hear.

"Horses!" Bátor said excitedly.

"It's coming from the southwest. Let's continue to move, we are already going that direction," Legna said. They walked a mile and a half longer until the babbling sounds of Orcish became unmistakable.

There were about fifteen Orcs, and they seemed to be a military camp. Legna saw horses with wide, frightened eyes. Hiding behind some bushes, the three companions watched quietly as the Orcs tried to contain a large, slimy animal with green scales and extremely sharp teeth. It's long neck and seal-like flippers displayed an aquatic background of sorts, but the animal was strange and unfamiliar.

"What is that?" Legna asked.

"It's a Shasute. They are endangered, hunted for their hard scales. Being rather aggressive animals, I wouldn't say that's a bad thing. But considering that the Orcs have one, we might want to fight for it," Bátor said. Legna grimaced as one of the Orcs wiped its slobbery mouth with its hand. The Orcs were simply sickening creatures, and they smelled like rotting carnage.

Legna looked to her right and saw three more Orcs taunting four nymphs in a cage. Each nymph was small and delicate, about three feet tall, with the smart look of a trickster in its eye. Wings protruded from their backs. One was a woman, with long black hair and piercing black eyes. Half of a nut the size of Legna's head acted as her cap, and she wore a leaf-crafted dress. Two others were men, each with chestnut brown hair and wooden shoes. They wore pants made from dyed spider silk and small linen shirts. The last nymph was smaller and looked younger. She had blonde hair and wore a similar knee-high dress as the older nymph. A golden amulet with an emerald in the middle hung from her neck, and she wore a silver tiara. Small, shimmering threads were strung into her dress, sparkling silver. Each nymph had a look of pain on their face, and scars were visible on their backs and arms.

"Tell me where it is!" one of the Orcs shouted. The blonde nymph kept her unchanging look of dignity and poise straight. The Orcs shook the cage and whipped them. Legna was suddenly grateful her mother had made her learn Orcish. "I said tell me! If I have to ask one more time, I will kill you each personally! Now tell me where it is!" They all kept silent, staring straight ahead. Legna was gaining the uttermost respect for these resilient nymphs.

"We have to help them," she said suddenly.

"I agree, but are you sure we can take on eighteen Orcs at once? We're not sure of our limits yet." Traven said.

"Then we should test them until we find the boundary."

Traven nodded grimly and said, "Should we just charge, or …"

Bátor smiled and murmured, "I say, there's no time like the present!" He sprung from the bushes and ran for the Orcs guarding the Shasute. Giving off a war cry like a baritone banshee, he startled the Orcs into dropping their clubs. Legna and Traven drew their swords and followed his lead, running for the group of brutes. The Orcs put their hands up in surrender and backed away. As sly as a fox, one of the Orcs unhooked the latch to the Shasute's cage, releasing the beast. It roared and looked around hungrily.

"Retreat!" An Orc yelled. They ran, leaving their horses and the nymphs behind.

*That's one thing about Orcs*, Legna thought, *they can be extremely smart at one point, and incredibly stupid at another.*

The Shasute waddled out of its cage, and Legna heard a roar behind her. Here Aspör stood, proud and tall, ready to attack. The Shasute made some strange, bobbing motions with its head. Then, with a loud and undistinguishable sound, it sprayed greenish slime all over Legna. The realization that she had just been sneezed on by a sea monster made Legna nauseous.

Legna, Traven, and Bátor approached the creature cautiously, trying to figure out its intentions. It snapped its teeth aggressively and looked menacingly at each one of them, considering who to eat first. Then, suddenly, the Shasute slapped Legna with its tail, taking her by surprise and knocking her ten feet away. Traven dodged its next attack on him and cut its tail off. It yelped loudly and snapped at Traven in anger. Traven deftly parried its blow, and pushed it back further into the forest. It let out a high pitched screech of frustration, and swung its neck at Traven as fast as possible. Traven easily sidestepped this and Bátor stabbed one of its flippers. It squealed again, snapping viciously at Legna, who had rejoined the fight and barely missing her stomach. Swinging at its neck and knocking Legna down, it roared mercilessly.

It licked its lips hungrily and began to rise to its full height to finish Legna off as Traven sprinted and jumped, landing on the beast's back with a *thump*. He thrust his sword into the Shasute's back, and it went completely still. Traven dropped wearily from its back and cleaned his sword with a cloth he pulled from his pocket.

They heard a sound behind them, like someone shrieking. "Lotus! Lotus, get up! Help will come soon! You must live!" Hysterical sobbing was reduced to pathetic whimpers. "No. No. They went too far this time, Anais. She's not going to live. Not after the whipping, the poison. There's no way. There's just no way."

*The nymphs! We forgot the nymphs!* Legna thought frantically. There was a large hill separating the nymphs, and their current position that made it impossible to see the other side of the camp, so Legna assumed the nymphs missed their attack on the Orcs entirely.

She sprinted over the hill without a word to find the pretty blonde nymph lying on her side; the color drained from her face. Her sparkling tiara had fallen off, and the largest diamond had fallen out. She was disturbingly still, and the older nymph was sobbing quietly into the blonde's hair.

# STRANGE MAGIC

"Hello," Legna said softly, startling the sobbing nymph. The nymph stood suddenly; her palm glowing slightly with a pinkish hue. She looked upset, ferocious, and destroyed all at once.

"Please, have mercy! Do no more to her! She is beyond return now! She can tell you nothing!" The nymph collapsed in a heap, wailing. "She's only a child! Take me instead! Take me instead!"

"Don't worry; I'm not going to hurt you. I just want to help you." Legna unlatched the cage, and the male nymphs dutifully led the woman out of the cage. As the woman walked, she dragged the blonde with her.

"Come, Lotus, you must get up!" the woman begged Lotus quietly. Lotus sleepily opened her eyes and stood on her own for a second, but she fell instantly.

"Who are you?" The raven-haired nymph asked with a hard, bitter tone in her voice.

As Legna introduced herself, Traven and Bátor came over the hill, leading three horses. Each was large, as they should be to carry an Orc, and two were a chestnut brown. The other was pure white.

"You are an Engjëllen?" The nymph's voice had a melodic purr to it, and it had a slight accent that was unfamiliar to Legna.

"Yes, all of us are," Legna said. Aspör lumbered over the hill, and the nymph cried out at the sight of him, cradling Lotus's head on her shoulder. She cried harder than before; the pink glow growing stronger, now not only coming from her palm, but from her fingers. Legna watched her hands closely; one hand on her sword's hilt.

The nymph whispered some words in an inaudible language between her sobs. Suddenly, the nymph stood. She placed her palm face-up and a beautiful pink light shone above her hand. She thrust the light forward, filling Legna's soul. A deep burning started within Legna, making every stray thought gather together, an uprising of memories. She remembered the strange dream she had experienced before and realized that the grouping memories were illuminated by the sparks in her dream.

Searing pain ripped into her very being, scouring each trace of memories she possessed. She lost sight. She lost feeling. She knew what it felt like to die inside. She was aware that she fell. She was aware that there were familiar voices in her head, and she eventually recognized them as belonging to Traven and Bátor. She could taste sound, hear scents. She could touch true terror. She could see music. Nothing was right. Everything was right. She loved the sensation, and she hated it. Then it stopped. It stopped suddenly, too suddenly. Legna felt truly enlightened, as if many heavy burdens were lifted from her.

Her sight returned. She no longer felt the burning. She could no longer see into her own mind. But she could see into the nymph's mind. Legna knew that this nymph's name was Wisteria, and she was the guardian of Princess Lotus, the princess of a large tribe of nymphs called the Hollïn and the ambassador for their king. The Hollïn were Aryanis's most faithful tribe of nymphs. Because of this, they were chosen to be the strongest tribe in magic. Legna was able to abstract the knowledge from the nymph's mind that the order of Aryanis's people was chosen as follows: The Ederra were the head of his creatures. Because the

Ederra could no longer reach the planet of Zerúa, the Engjëllens, called Bellaphim in Ederra, were gifted with strong leadership and fighting skills, so they were made the guardians of the inhabitants of Zerúa. Then came the Elves, Terraphim, who were made nimble, clever, and one with nature. They protected the less intelligent life forms of Zerúa, such as plants and animals. Next in order were the Naïfonians, Opiphim, whom were talented in mechanics and weaponry. Last to be selected were the nymphs, Magephim, and because of this, were given magical talents that the other races could only obtain through instruction of a nymph.

She knew that Wisteria would give her life for precious Princess Lotus. She knew that as a child, Wisteria believed that any lessons her old professor would teach her not pertaining to magic were useless. She knew that Wisteria despised toadstools and adored raspberries. Most of all, Legna knew that Wisteria was an absolute stranger in every way. Yet, she understood Wisteria. Wisteria was part of her, and she was part of Wisteria.

Then, it stopped. Legna couldn't see into the nymph's mind anymore. She came out of her trance and back to consciousness. Her head was in Wisteria's lap, and both her right and left hand were held by a different person. Traven occupied the right, and Princess Lotus, who had regained her composure, held the left.

"You are awake. I thought I had killed you," Wisteria said. "I suppose in the adrenaline rising moment I went too far…I apologize for my quick actions." The nymph brushed wisps of blonde hair from Legna's face.

Legna was only able to mutter something about toadstools and magic before falling back into darkness.

# THE KING'S WAR

King Zemër paced restlessly across the marble floor of his bedroom. It had been two days since his son disappeared, and he was in desperate need of an explanation. Considering the facts, King Zemër already understood that Zemëroj had most likely tried to go with Legna and Traven. But no matter how much it made sense, he could not, *would not* except the fact that his son was a complete fool. He had planned to deem Zemëroj the new general of the ranks for the war as a surprise. But then he had been defiant, disobeying everything they lived for. He could not even think of a punishment large enough for this insolence.

*We have waited too long... I will send a messenger to fetch him. If he is unharmed and sane, he won't be for long,* the king thought. He looked around at his surroundings as he made it a habit to stand in an area and attempt to absorb every miniscule detail possible.

He saw the canopy bed in which he slept, with emerald green sheets that had beautiful floriated patterns woven carefully into them. He admired the swirling patterns of brown and black in the grey marble below his feet. The walls were stone and would be dreary had Engjëll's best artisans not painted a colorful phantasmagoria of murals, all intertwined within each other, as if each event depicted was happening at the same time. The strangest thing about the mural was that it shifted and changed with the events of the present. Although he suspected a nymph's magic, King Zemër was unsure of how the mural worked.

The next thing he noticed in his room was the chip in his bureau that was created by the Orc that attempted to murder him in his sleep. It had been quite a fight, and King Zemër had been just a young lad, a boy of nineteen. He had just taken over the throne, and he was not heavily guarded, for the war had not yet begun. Later, his carpenter had offered to make him a new bureau, but Zemër refused, saying the nick in the ebony wood was just another memento of his kingship. "If my heir wants it gone, so be it. It will mean nothing to them," he had said. "But as long as I live, that will be a medal for when I first crossed blades with an Orc."

The bureau was a gift from the Elves, another reason in itself to keep it. Its dark nooks were carved into exquisite pictures of acorns and leaves. When all its drawers were closed, it formed the picture of a wide-eyed fawn, innocent and waiting for its mother to return to its side.

On the other side of the room was a window. Its windowsill was covered with morning glories, petunias, and the rare black lily. Each black lily contrasted with its snow white stamen. Zemër touched the stamen, silky white pollen coming off onto his hands.

On a small desk in one corner of the room, scrolls and poems he had written were in neat stacks across it.

When he realized that his observance had come to an end, he reluctantly rang the tinny bell attached to his wall to call his footman. Instantly, he heard footsteps from outside his door. Then came a knock, deep and echoing on the heavy, wooden door.

"Come in," Zemër said, not stopping his troubled tone. The door opened, and a young man about the age of fifteen in the formal footman's uniform appeared. This confused Zemër, for it was not his usual footman. *This man must have just started at the castle,* Zemër thought.

"You called, Your Highness?" the man asked tentatively.

"Yes, please summon a messenger and send him into the forest to find the party containing a maiden named Legna and her guardian, Traven. I fear they may have information on my lost son." Zemër stroked his beard, examining this new worker.

"Yes, sir." The man turned to leave, but Zemër called out to him.

"Wait, son. What is your name?"

"Lenard, sir," the footman answered cautiously.

"Lenard, is it? Well, tell me, Lenard, how is it that you have obtained a position in my court without my knowledge?"

Lenard looked genuinely surprised. "I was not aware you did not know of my presence in your home, Your Highness. I am your butler, Eagis's son, and I came to take the family job." Lenard shuffled his feet nervously.

"I see. Now, boy, tell me why I am not looking upon the face of my Eagis, and instead indulging my energy into this conversation."

"Eagis, my father, that is, was poisoned by an Orc." Lenard stopped to sniffle. "They snuck into Engjëll and slipped something into his drink. The healer doesn't think he will live."

"Why was I unaware of this also?" At this point, Zemër was talking more to himself than to Lenard. "Why not just declare the war over and leave me out of the peace negotiation meeting?"

Lenard's lip began to quiver, so Zemër stopped his ranting long enough to take pity on the boy. "I am sorry to upset you, boy. I just wish everyone that made my life as it was when I was young would just stay put. First my wife, then my son, and now my beloved butler," Zemër mumbled. "I am sorry about your father, Lenard. Now, be off with my instructions."

Lenard nodded and walked out the door, closing it behind him. Zemër chuckled in spite of himself, remembering when he took the throne. He had prepared for years, but had been astonished the day of his coronation, insisting that he wasn't ready. But his wise old tutor had told him that even if he wasn't, he couldn't reject the throne. There was no other heir, and Zemër's father had died and left Zemër, his only son, all of his estate. Therefore, there was no use whining that he wasn't ready, because no matter what, it was happening. And even if he made the world totter precariously under his kingship, he had no choice but to accept the throne and apply what he had learned.

Zemër heard a knock on his door, and he quietly groaned, for he was in no need of another visitor. He plastered a smile on and said, "Enter."

Once again, the door opened, but this time his messenger appeared. "Sir, I have a problem with your request." Zemër put his head in his hands.

"What is the problem now?" He asked with a hint of irritation.

"How am I supposed to reach Legna and Traven? They have two days head start on us, and our horses aren't fast enough to catch up to them. We certainly can't go on foot."

"I don't care how you must strain your abilities. You *will* reach them and you *will* find out what happened to my son." Zemër was beginning to raise his voice. "Do I make myself absolutely clear?"

The messenger cowered in Zemër's presence. Zemër rose from his throne. "What are you doing still standing here? *Get out that door and find my son!*" The messenger scurried out the door and didn't bother to close it. Zemër was angry that he had to use such blunt actions to control his workers, and he felt bad for bellowing so. But, unfortunately, it was the only way to get what he wanted.

He saw the face of his head general, Neör, appear at the door. The tall, strong man bowed and said, "Your Highness, I have come to discuss war tactics for infiltration of the Orc camps."

"But..." Zemër began to protest, but then he remembered that his personal life and his kingship should not intermix, and the fact that his son was missing should not interfere with the citizens of Engjëll. "Of course, Neör. It's always a pleasure working with you. Come, let us discuss tactics. It will get my mind off of...things." He gestured toward the door leading to his study. "Shall we take this to my study? We may receive better solitude to consider this wretched war." Neör nodded, and they both walked into the extravagant study. Each wall was made of a huge bookcase, stuffed full with books and scrolls of every size, color, and genre. There were epics, poems, and history scrolls. The ceiling formed a gigantic dome, and if you were looking at it from the air, you could see that it looked just like a small, colorful planet. In the middle of everything, there was a single, magnificent desk with an everlasting lamp purchased from the nymphs. On his desk was a map of the entire world of Zerúa, detailed with every land feature penciled in. Zemër sat down heavily onto the desk's wooden chair, and Neör sat across from him.

Zemër stared down at his hands, and looked at the lines accumulating on the back. *I'm too old for this type of stress*, he thought.

Neör pointed to the Wilderness of Windör and said, "We know that the Orcs are scattered throughout Windör without any solid protection."

"Correct," Zemër responded flatly. He felt guilty for his uninterested reaction, but he was in no mood to repeat things that he already understood.

"And if we spread throughout Windör, we may be able to exterminate said Orcs. But, we have never ventured very far into the Wilderness; therefore, many men might be lost. Another problem is that the Orcs have blockaded the entrance to the Orcish Isle, making it almost impossible for us to attack their king."

"Also correct."

"But, if we raid enough of the camps in Windör and let a few Orcs stay alive so they can retreat back to the king to send out more troops, we may be able to keep repeating the process and eventually drive all of the troops from the Orcish Isle, making it penetrable. Then, we can lead a raid and defeat the Orcs!" Neör seemed very proud of his plan of action, and Zemër, once again, felt guilty for being uninterested.

But he kept a reassuring smile on his face and said, "That is a good idea, but how could we navigate Windör if we have never explored it?"

Neör took on a grave expression. "That is the flaw," he said, "our warriors would have to sacrifice everything, even more than they have to protect Engjëll. I don't think it is the most congenial strategy, but it will have to work for there is no other way." Neör wiped his brow and looked at Zemër and said, "Listen, I know that as your servant, I have no right to speak to you this way. But as a friend, I say that you need to rest. Zemëroj brought whatever it is upon himself, and you needn't worry."

"Nonsense; I am fine. Do you think that the great kings of old became great by 'resting' when they were a little tired?"

"Yes. In order to rule, you have to be energetic and a good, healthy example to your people. You cannot be a sickly, worried mess."

"Why are you saying this?"

"My king, have you seen yourself? Your health is deteriorating. You are as white as a lamb's wool. You must get outside, feel the sun on your face, and relax somehow. You cannot stay held up in your study until your son returns."

"How dare you," the king began to say when he stopped himself. Neör was right. He was letting Zemëroj get to his head and his health. "I'm sorry, Neör. You're correct; it isn't healthy for me to stay in this dusty old castle all day." With this, he stood and picked up his cloak, which was hanging on the back of his chair. "Shall we continue our discussion tomorrow?"

Neör smiled. "Yes, you're Highness. Tomorrow it is." They shook hands and Zemër strode briskly out of the study. He passed the mural and stopped dead in his tracks. There, on the lifelike wall, was a picture of his son, with his mouth open in a scream, and surrounded by purple smoke and blue sparks. And next to him was a fair woman, her face curled in a maniacal laugh as she took a strangle hold over his son's psyche.

Everything stopped. The flies stopped buzzing, the birds stopped chirping, and Zemër did not hear Neör approach him from behind.

"What is it, Your Majesty?" Neör asked.

"Korrtar," Zemër whispered.

"Excuse me?" Neör responded. Zemër did not hear him. Instead, he walked, quite like a zombie, out of the room and down the corridors, wandering aimlessly until he reached an exit. As soon as he reached his courtyard, he came back to reality. From here he sprinted. He sprinted to the place in their village known as Aryanis's Keep. He slid back the ancient door and walked inside, the door closing behind him and enveloping him in darkness.

# THE LIGHT OF TRUTH

When Legna awoke, it was dark and she could only make out a distinct figure by her side. When a distant fire caught the color of his red hair, Legna knew it was Traven.

"Traven?" Legna said tentatively.

"You're awake?" Traven said. Then, louder, he called, "She's awake!" She could hear feet rushing to where she was as she sat up. She still felt weak and couldn't stand.

"I…What happened? I felt…so…strange." Legna struggled to get the words out.

"I'll let Wisteria explain that. For now, you just rest. You need strength so we can keep going tomorrow."

Wisteria approached, light as a feather on her lavender wings, and Lotus, a soft smile touching her lips. Wisteria smiled and murmured, "Child. I promise to explain everything if you eat something." She handed Legna a biscuit, and Legna eagerly bit into it. "Good. Now, where to start? Ah, yes I am the king's diplomat and these"—she motioned to the two nymphs—"are Anais and Judd, my guards. Princess Lotus and I were traveling to Naïfon to get a special contraption requested by the King of Hollïn. Apparently, it was supposed to turn spirit jewels into something, I don't know. Anyway, we were going to stop in Engjëll to refill our supplies. So, naturally, we went through the

Forest of Engjëll. And, as we were passing the border between Windör and Engjëll, we found that we were being followed by none other than a camp of Orcs!

"We tried to move faster, to outrun them to Engjëll, but they had horses, and we were weak from the long journey anyway. So they captured us, torturing us and asking us where the Solas na Fírinne was. They carried with them a Shasute. They poisoned us, whipped us, and starved us. But to no avail. We were not about to give up the secrets of our race to a lowly, filthy Orc! This went on for a week, and then you rescued us. Thank you, by the way. Anyway, here we are!" Wisteria looked happily at Legna.

"Yes, I see that. Now, if you don't mind me sounding ignorant, what is the...Solas na Fírinne?" Legna asked

"Oh, you didn't contract that information from my memories?" Legna shook her head. Wisteria continued on, saying, "The Solas na Fírinne is the special light gifted unto the nymphs that allows its bearer to know if someone is telling the truth or not. In your language, it is called the Light of Truth. But I believe our language just makes it sound much more exciting. If it turns out that the interrogated one is being honest, then the nymph wielding it has the choice to allow the victim to see into their mind, in apology for violating the privacy of the victim. I believe you experienced this, didn't you?" Legna nodded, rubbing her head to stall the massive headache that was transpiring in her temples.

"Not to be...disrespectful, Wisteria, but what do you think I could possibly be?" Legna said with a hint of sarcasm, but still gently.

"Well, you could have been Korrtar, or, maybe a..." Wisteria faltered as she realized how blinded she had been by her fear. Legna had the unmistakable features of an Engjëllen. She was too short to be an elf, and she obviously wasn't an Orc. Zombies were mindless, merciless beings and trolls were large and ugly. Demons had a fire of hate consistently burning in their eyes, and Legna was the absolute, complete opposite of the foul brutes. She obviously wasn't a nymph, and the scaled, lizard-like characteristics of the Naïfonians were the most distinctly different of any of Aryanis's people.

Legna's fair, smooth skin and ever-present white glow was shared with no other race. Wisteria sighed. For once, she could think of no excuse for her actions. They were pointless and imprudent. The most difficult part of her realization was confessing it to the three heroes watching her every move.

"Nothing; you couldn't have been anything else but an Engjëllen. While it is possible for Korrtar to bend her appearance to look like an Engjëllen, she can never erase the sense of impending malice that fills every fiber of her putrid existence." Wisteria nodded in conclusion, pleased with her description of Korrtar.

Legna smiled, seeing a genuine heart in Wisteria. She liked the older woman and could see that if she had the time, she would have enjoyed getting to know the mysterious diplomat. But, nonetheless, she had a mission that could not be swayed by personal matters, as did Wisteria.

"Now that I understand," Legna said. "I must leave. Engjëll's welfare depends on it." She tried to stand but was pushed back down by Wisteria and Bátor, whom had just come from the fire.

"Traven told you. You need rest, not more stress. We can press on tomorrow," Bátor said gently. Legna wanted to protest but found she didn't have the strength.

"Here, Legna put your arms around my shoulders, and I'll take you to the fire where it's warmer," Traven said. She did and Traven supported her, leading her to the small campfire. Aspör was curled up, dozing. Wisteria's guards, Anais and Judd were sitting on logs arranged around the fire, carving pieces of wood into long rods, engraving intricate pictures of war into them with daggers. They had grown, so they could meet eye-to-eye with Bátor, and their wings were gone, giving them a similar appearance to an Engjëllen. She could see the blonde nymph lying down on a blanket, resting.

As soon as she had settled down on her own log, she asked the two male nymphs, "What are you carving?"

Anais smiled and said, "The bottom of a sword hilt. This is a skill that most nymph boys learn when they are very young, and the only way we find fit to pass idle time." Anais was older than Judd, she could see, not only by his facial features, but by the weary look in his eyes. But he also had something else there: Just a hint of kindness and a look of humble wisdom.

"Oh, Anais, you're making us sound so boring!" Judd exclaimed. Judd, Legna concluded, must only be a few years older than herself. He had a younger, more playful look in his eyes.

"Now, listen, Legna, this is only what we do at night if we have time. At least that's true for me, old Anais over there is always carving something," Judd said, looking at Anais to make sure his comments were irritating enough to receive a reaction. Anais only raised an eyebrow. Disappointed, Judd continued on to say, "No we have tournaments all of which I am the champion," Judd bragged.

"Are you, Judd? How impressive," Legna said rather flatly. Judd noticed that he wasn't making an impression, and he glanced to Anais for support.

Anais sighed, deciding to humor the boy if impressing Legna was really so important. "It's true," Anais said. "The rascal does have quite a knack for athletics."

"Oh, you're an athlete. How are you with a sword? I would love to duel sometime," Legna said boldly. She understood what Judd was trying to do, and she knew it wasn't going to work. She had never been enthralled by incredibly athletic people. They were just people, and they weren't any better or any worse than the people who weren't athletes.

Something in her voice made Judd nervous about accepting any challenge from the fair Engjëllen "Well, I couldn't fight a girl. It wouldn't be a fair fight!" he said.

"You're absolutely right, Judd. For it to be a fair fight you would have to be at least six feet taller, and you would need to try and eat me. Aryanis knows that's the only thing I've ever fought."

Traven, who had been watching the conversation, laughed. "Legna, for it to be a fair fight, he would need to magically turn into the king of sea demons."

Legna chuckled in return. "Goodness, no! I wouldn't be able to stand the smell! That horrid creature smelled worse than the stables after a month with no cleaning. That's the reason I almost lost!"

"You fought Malrei? What happened?" Judd asked, intrigued by this bit of information.

"Let's just say...I'm sure he's sorry that he told me his only weakness," Legna said, pulling out her sword and lopping the branch off of a nearby tree. Traven put his arm around Legna's shoulders, afraid she was over exerting herself for her current state. Legna took the hint and sheathed her sword. Then, tired, she laid her head on Traven's shoulder. She was glad he had come with her. Otherwise, she would be lonely, or possibly dead.

"I believe that the girl has the right idea," Anais said. "Let us sleep, so we may rise early and continue on our separate ways."

❧

The next morning, Legna woke first. Hints of a brisk breeze whispered of the changing of seasons. She could see the dark mountains of Windör on the horizon and she figured it would only be another day before they reached the border. Aspör was curled up next to her, his head resting on her leg.

She reached over to shake Traven awake, but stopped. She decided to take Aspör out into the forest, for a short walk. She lightly touched Aspör, for fear of startling him. He slowly opened his eyes and looked at Legna accusingly.

"Sorry," Legna said, "I figured I would walk to regain my sense of balance, and thought you might want to come too." She had no idea if he could actually understand her, but he seemed to have a positive reaction. He stood and leaned back on his hind legs and put his front feet on her shoulders. Then, he licked her.

And so, they set out into the woods. Dawn was just beginning when they slipped into the forest line. And as they walked through, they could hear noises like never before. It was a cacophony of sparrows, robins, cardinals, and thrushes. They were directing their cries at Aspör, casting him away from their trees. Aspör grumbled in reply, deep in his throat.

They neared a clearing, but Legna groaned inwardly as she saw two huge trolls fighting over a sparkling piece of metal. Trolls were incredibly stupid and single-minded and usually retreated in cowardice to their abodes underground.

The trolls were at least eight feet tall, and they were covered head to toe with dirt and grass. Maggots wiggled on every inch of their bodies, and one of them had three heads.

Trolls normally stayed underground, waiting for an innocent passerby to approach, and then they would lunge out of the ground and feast on their victim. This worked well for them, because the top of their giant heads were completely flat and could be instantly covered with whatever foliage or earth was in the area. At the time, the troll's heads were covered in rocks, ferns, and moss.

If the trolls weren't dangerous, the fight would have been comical. One troll swung a punch, but he missed; his fist whistling past the other troll's three faces. The troll who was almost hit laughed at his opponent's embarrassing miss, only to kick in between the other's legs in his attempt to bring him down.

The first troll looked down at his legs, realizing what the second had tried to do. Then, he shoved his hand forward, bending the other troll's middle neck backward.

That was too much for Legna. She stifled her giggle, but the trolls heard it anyway.

"Eh, looky 'ere, Chud, we got ourselves a wee li'l girl," the ugly, vile troll with three heads hollered.

"With a nasty li'l poker too, Stag," Chud said, gesturing to Legna's sword. Their accents were foreign and difficult to understand, with unnatural breaks in words that should flow.

Stag laughed dumbly, then stopped abruptly, scowling at Legna. "Why don't you look scared, maggot?"

Legna did feel scared. In fact, she was terrified. But she realized that she found the trolls as amusing as she did frightening, so she had been able to keep a blank face the entire time they had been talking to her.

Before she could answer, Chud noticed Aspör and said, "Wha' is tha', Stag? Is it a lizard, or a really ugly dog?" Stag laughed at the dim-witted humor, but by the way that Chud looked confused, and then joined in on the laughter, Legna knew that he had been posing an actual question. It was, of course, an illegitimate question, but still a genuine question.

Aspör understood that he was being insulted, and a deep growling started in the back of his throat. Before Stag knew it, his head was on fire; the flames spreading quickly. He batted at it and only succeeded in spreading it to his lower body and limbs. Soon, all that was left was a pile of ashes and a brown spirit jewel.

And of course, in all seriousness, Chud had to have said, "Wow! I di'n't know dogs could breathe fire!" Unfortunately, his interest just brought his demise. Aspör decided that burning him was boring and instead took to tearing him limb from limb and then sitting back and grinning without finishing him off.

"Aspör!" Legna cried, trying to conceal a smile. "You cannot be that cruel! You shouldn't just leave him to die!"

"No, no!" Chud gasped quietly. "You shoul'n't kill poor Chud like tha'!"

"Right, we shouldn't kill poor Chud like *that*." Chud smiled weakly as he thought Legna was defending him. "You should finish him off. So his death isn't agonizing." The troll's face dropped as he realized what Legna was implying.

"Spare me, please!" Chud pleaded. He looked rather pathetic with no arms or legs, but it wasn't gruesome for trolls don't bleed. They are but hollow mixtures of evil and dirt.

"You cannot be saved," Legna said briskly. "You are ripped to pieces as it is, and soon your energy will be sapped from your very body. Both ways, you die, and quite honestly, I'm growing impatient *and* indifferent toward which way it happens. Now either you are killed right now, or you die a slow and painful death three hours from now, thinking about all the mistakes you have made in your lifetime. Now which is it?" Legna demanded. Chud cowered at Legna's commanding presence.

He lowered his head and said, "I shall die now."

"Good," Legna responded, and Aspör lit Chud on fire. He burned faster than Stag, with his limbs taken care of, but Legna did feel a small sense of pity when she realized that neither of the trolls would have ever had a chance even if they had weapons.

A bright light where Aspör was standing distracted Legna. When it disappeared, Aspör was still there, but he had grown. He was four feet taller than Legna and his silver hide had changed to a sparkling blue. For the first time, Aspör was able to fully spread his wings, as they had been too small before.

"Grab the spirit jewels and get on my back," a voice said.

Legna was startled as the only living thing she could see was Aspör. "Who are you?" Legna asked the voice.

"It is I, Aspör. Hurry, we must get back to the others."

Legna did not ask any questions. Instead, she scrambled to pick up the small spirit jewels, and climbed onto Aspör's back quickly. She put the jewels continuity issue into the bag she was carrying, and the instant, she got ahold of one of the spikes on his back, Aspör took off.

And they were flying.

# THE MESSENGER

They soared high above the trees, the mix of green, gold, and silver leaves making for a dazzling display. Aspör's tail whipped back and forth in long sweeps, and he would let out an occasional roar to show his excitement. They were going incredibly fast, and soon all the forest below became a blur.

"Hold on!" Aspör shouted. He suddenly dropped his nose and they became a vertical line, heading straight for the trees.

They soon neared the ground, and just when it seemed as if they would crash into the ground, Aspör heaved his body so they were moving forward again, and he lightly landed on the ground.

They had landed a short distance away from their camp, so Legna got off of Aspör and they treaded back to their companions.

"There you are!" yelled Traven. "Do you think you can just run off with that dragon of yours whenever you want?" His eyes widened as he inspected Aspör. "What happened to it?"

"Excuse me!" Aspör said. "I am not just 'that dragon'! And I am most certainly not an 'it'!"

"It can talk?" Traven exclaimed.

"Again with the 'it'!" Aspör responded, frustrated. "I just told you not to call me that!"

Traven sighed, not wanting to argue with a talking dragon. "Where did you go?"

"Well," Legna began, "we went out for a short walk in the woods and had a small problem with a couple trolls. But it's taken care of now."

"Trolls? Where have you been, Legna?" Bátor asked, who had just sauntered over from a conversation with the nymphs.

"We only went for a walk in the woods, but we ran into some trolls."

"One of them thought I was a fire-breathing dog. The end result wasn't exactly pretty. At least, it wasn't for the trolls," Aspör said.

"And what happened to you? Last time I saw you, you were about as high as my knee! And you could only make an assortment of grunts," Bátor said.

"I'm not exactly sure what happened to him. He killed those two trolls, there was a bright light, and then he was like this. It was the strangest thing," Legna said.

"I see," Bátor said. "Look, Legna, as long as you're in my care, and as long as you're the hero of this quest, you can't go romping around like this! This isn't a game! These monsters really can hurt you! If you had died, what would we have done? Korrtar would have won without even trying! Traven and I? We are here to protect you. You may think you can handle yourself, but you have much to learn. Take it from a man who is over three hundred years old. If we lost you . . . I promised your father . . ."

All eyes were on Bátor. "You know my father?" Legna asked.

Bátor sighed. "Yes, Legna, he was a good friend of mine. Did he ever tell you what happened to his legs? *I* was the one who was there when that Rangun almost killed him. He made me promise to be a father to you if something happened to him. And Traven"—Bátor motioned to Traven—"I was there when your father passed. Or disappeared, is the better word, I suppose. The Rangun just looked at him, there was a flash of light, and he was gone.

"It was also the night I was trapped in that blasted apple."—
Bátor looked at Legna—"that night could not have gone worse if
Korrtar herself had been there. And I promised I would keep you
safe no matter what. And I don't intend to break that promise."

"Oh...I don't know what to say."

"Just say you won't put yourself in danger like that again.
Anyway, Wisteria needs to speak to you before we part ways.
Something terrible has happened. But I'll let her explain."

Legna walked to Wisteria slowly, wondering what the nymph
would tell her. She stood there for a solid two minutes, waiting
for Wisteria to stop talking to Lotus. When Wisteria finally
turned to Legna, a sullen look was on her face.

"What's wrong?" Legna asked.

"A messenger came while you were gone; a messenger from the
Elf king." She paused, exhaling slowly. "He told us that evil has
come unto the world of Giza, across the abyss. It has been there
for many years, as long as our race has been. The evil is as old as
Korrtar herself, but Aryanis has allowed it, choosing a small race
of Gizaans to be his imperfect people. But now, the evil is so great
that Aryanis has to travel across the abyss separating Zerúa and
Giza and provide an escape from evil. While he is there, part of
him shall also reign here. But still, our creator must pay the price
the people of Giza have earned."

Legna panicked for a small moment. Who would kill their
king? Would they be without rule from then on? Then she
remembered that Wisteria had said that part of Aryanis was left
to rule Zerúa. Aryanis had three forms, a spirit form, a kingly
form, and a fatherly form. "When will he be back?" Legna asked.

"It will not be for many weeks, for his journey shall be harsh.
I will not hold back the truth, Legna. Aryanis will die at Giza."

Legna was overcome with grief. "But you just said that he will
return in some weeks!" she pleaded.

"Ah, there is where he will show Giza that he really is the
most powerful and wonderful being in both our worlds. After

three days of their time, Aryanis will rise from his torturing in Mëkator and prove his love for those hopeless people."

"So he's sacrificing himself for them, just so they won't have evil?" Legna asked.

"No, evil will still be there, but its effect of an eternity in Mëkator can be avoided by believing in Aryanis."

"Oh," Legna said. She couldn't believe Aryanis would give his own self for this imperfect people. But she trusted Aryanis with all her heart and knew that everything he did was for a good, solid reason.

"We must leave now that you have heard this vital news. Please, be swift of mind and slow to speak." Legna nodded at this, and Wisteria smiled. "Legna, I really do know you will succeed in your task. Never give up hope."

Legna smiled. Wisteria really was a kind woman, and Legna wished that they could prolong their relationship. But Windör was so close that Legna could see its dark, twisting trees and ominous mountains. And the weak state she was put in from the Light of Truth was a large setback.

"Good-bye Wisteria. And good-bye, Princess Lotus," Legna said.

"I really wish I had gotten to be well acquainted with you, Legna. You are a woman of valor, and if you ever need anything, I welcome you with open arms into my father's court."

"Thank you, Your Highness, I appreciate that," Legna said, nodding her head in respect.

"Please, call me Lotus. I was never fond of the formal way of things."

Legna smiled and turned to Anais. "I will miss you Anais," she said.

"Legna, you are probably the most spirited young woman I have ever met."

"Thank you, that means a lot." Lastly, she looked to Judd. "If you become the champion of anything else, please tell me."

Judd smiled, saying, "Keep in touch, Legna. I want to hear about the next Demon King you kill, and I want every detail." Legna hugged him, and his grin widened.

Traven and Bátor said their good-byes and picked up their things. Each got on a brown horse, leaving Legna with the perfectly white one. They waved one last time and then kicked their heels into the horses' sides and galloped off. Aspör lifted off the ground, flying gracefully through the air.

As the nymphs watched them gallop off, Anais studied Judd. "You really liked that girl, didn't you?" Anais asked.

"Yes," Judd answered, "I did."

They reached the Mountains of Windör at noon.

The dark trees in this forest cast twisted shadows over their faces, and it was eerily quiet. All the happiness and warmth in Engjëll was contrasted by the cold, uninviting darkness of Windör. There were no birds chirping, no bees buzzing. At dusk, no crickets could be heard. Each tree was mangled uniquely, and almost all of them were a deep black. No, nothing pleasant was in Windör. It was as if when Aryanis created Zerúa, he had put everything good and beautiful in his people's lands and everything bad into Mëkator. Then, all of the leftover, mediocre components were thrown onto Windör.

"No wonder no one ever explored this place," Traven said. "Even the trees look evil." The wind curled through the forest, sounding like a million dying whispers.

A mile later, they found a wide river flowing from a waterfall, which was spilling over the edge of a nearby cliff. The water was a dead white, fluorescent in the dingy light coming through the trees.

They stopped, dead tired from the day. They built a fire and sat around it, ready to sleep. Legna lay up against Aspör's warm belly.

"Aspör," Legna said. "Will you tell me about dragons?"

"What about dragons? I don't know much myself. I don't remember what my life was like before you."

"You don't know the history of dragons? Or where they come from? Nothing?"

"I do know; we don't like to be interrogated."

"I'm sorry. I'm just curious." Legna stopped asking about dragons, but she was still curious. She made a vow to find someone who knew about them.

⁓

They rode for three days, only stopping to eat and sleep for a few hours. Bátor made a crude bow with the black limbs of the trees and used hemp for the bowstring. It was only powerful enough to kill a rabbit, but rabbits were really the only living thing in Windör. Or so they thought.

Little did they know that three small pairs of eyes were watching them from the bushes, following them, each licking their lips in anticipation of the feast laid out before them. They didn't know that the creatures cast their voices with the sound of the wind, so no one could hear them. The creatures also knew a way to kill something silently, with no weapon, so the victim wouldn't have time to scream. Like the creatures' voices, no one would hear them. They wouldn't know what it was until it was too late.

"Please," the first creature whispered, "can we eat them now?"

"Yes, yes, I'm so hungry," the second whispered.

The third was silent for a minute, letting the questions hang in the air. Then, in a horrible, bloodthirsty voice, it spat out, "So be it."

# ARYANIS'S KEEP

Zemër felt his way along the walls of the Keep, groping for the switch that would light the torches. Finally, he found it and jerked it up, lighting up the magnificent cave.

The walls were made of pure ivory and the floors, of jade. Torches of blue fire were spread across the walls. Beautiful carvings of the creation of Zerúa stood around a throne made of gold. Here Aryanis sat, staring at Zemër with love and wisdom. He had a grey beard and grey eyes but agelessness was portrayed in his face, so he did not look old. He wore robes of gold and silver. He shimmered because he was only an illusion. While whatever he said were Aryanis's own words, Aryanis was back at his palace, on the Holy Island, in the middle of the Eben Sea. Each group of his people had their own Keep, where they presented their concerns and questions to him.

"My Lord," Zemër said, kneeling on the ground.

"Yes, my child?" Aryanis said softly. Zemër sensed that Aryanis already knew what had happened. He did, after all, know everything.

"My King, something horrible has happened to my son. I believe it was Korrtar. She transformed him, My Lord, and I am heartbroken that he would turn against us as he did."

"How did you hear of this, Zemër?"

"The mural I was given had his picture there, screaming, and there was Korrtar herself, laughing at my boy's pain." Zemër was crying at this point, mourning his son's soul.

Aryanis watched him, letting him weep. Then, he said, "Little king, I know your grief. I feel it every day when my creation dies. From a single flower being stepped on, to an Engjëllen passing away, I know grief. Just today, I had to send part of myself, my creation, my *son*, down to the world of Giza, across the abyss, to pay for their sins. I know he will die there. It is certain and it is necessary. Zemëroj's death will play a part, I assure you. It is but a tiny existence in the grand scheme of things. Your heroes will need to use him as a way to weaken Korrtar. His demon form shall perish in the hero's triumph, but they shall triumph nonetheless."

The King cast his gaze down, still unhappy. "How, My Lord? How will my son weaken Korrtar?"

"Your son will do nothing. The real Zemëroj is dead. But when Korrtar made her new pet, she poured most of her strength into him. When her Demon dies, she will be too weak to fight your heroes."

"Tell me, my Lord. Will the heroes succeed? Will they kill Korrtar?"

"They will not kill Korrtar, only weaken her. But they will disgrace her enough that she will have to leave Zerúa as she had to leave Ederra when she challenged me."

The king nodded. "I have one last question, My Lord. Who shall be the heir to the Engjëllen throne?"

"Choose who you see fit, and then consult me, and we shall decide."

The King nodded and bowed and then turned to leave. But Aryanis stopped him, saying, "Do not grieve too much about your son, my child. You will see him again." Then the lights went out and Zemër returned outdoors. He walked back to his castle and entered the massive garden his wife had planted years ago. Plants of every kind, from every part of Zerúa were planted there, and it all turned out to be a kaleidoscopic masterpiece. He turned just in time to see a young boy, about the age of fifteen, with his bow pointed toward a far off elk.

Just when he was about to fire the arrow, the King screamed, "No!" He leaped and bounded, covering yards with each step. He had startled the boy enough to delay the shot, and in seconds he had wrestled the bow from the boy's hands.

"My King!" The boy sputtered. "What is wrong?"

"Don't you know that every time you kill one of those," he said, pointing to the elk, "You bring grief and pain to Aryanis?"

The boy stared at him in horror. "I had no idea! I am so sorry, My King!"

"From now on, I only want you to shoot what you absolutely need. Does your family have enough meat right now?"

"Well, yes, they do, My King."

"Then leave that poor beast alone. From now on, I want the majority of our meals to be made up of plants. Do you hear me, boy? No excesses of meat."

"Yes, sir, I understand."

"Good. Now, go tell the rest of the village that your king orders them not to kill any animal unless they have no meat at all."

The boy nodded and the king handed him his bow. Then, the boy ran away to the village below.

"If the Elves can survive on no meat, we can stand reducing the amount of meat we eat, at least," the King mumbled.

Putting the small matter out of his mind, he entered the castle, arriving in the sitting room. A fireplace made of gold sat unused in the hot weather of summer. Sitting down on the soft, red upholstery that covered his chairs, Zemër thought about what Aryanis told him. Korrtar would not die but would only be banished. She would be banished by shame, and she would be less powerful.

It was strange, Zemër mused, how completely different death worked for holy and evil. When Engjëllens died, they went high up, to the world of Ederra. The place that Korrtar had fallen from. In this way, they didn't actually die. They just traveled to a different place, to lead even more extravagant lives. They didn't have to worry about eating or sleeping. Really, the only thing they had to worry about in Engjëll was drinking the water, but they ate rich foods for pleasure.

Korrtar and her Demons, on the other hand, were knocked to a place so awful there was an abyss separating Zerúa from it. A place that was not quite as evil as Mëkator but close.

The only thing that was the same about the lives of Demons and Engjëllens was the way they died. They could acquire no sicknesses, nor starve. The Engjëllens required water, but no sleep, although they performed better with it. The deprivation might have been uncomfortable, but it was livable.

No, the only way either died was through combat. They were immortal in some senses, but not even they could be stabbed through the heart and live to tell the story. Not even Korrtar could. There was only one truly invincible being. And that was Aryanis.

*It was truly fascinating,* Zemër thought. Truly fascinating indeed.

Now, he had large problems on his hands. Two young heroes had been sent to stop something deadly. Zemër knew that his kingdom needed the water, and they always kept large amounts in the castle cellar. But he didn't know if Korrtar had infected those also. If so, they would have to migrate to Naïfon and ask for refuge.

There was no more time to waste. He had to check the water.

He navigated the large castle, weaving through a maze of torch-lit corridors and extravagant rooms until he reached the heavy, wooden door to the cellar. He hesitated before flinging it open and walking down the eerie steps. The room he entered was filled with barrels of all sizes, each holding a supply of water.

He slowly pried off the top of one barrel, eyes closed, dreading the results. His eyes opened long after the top had come off, and his heart dropped.

Green. Every last drop was green.

He quickly opened four other barrels and the results were the same. A grotesque, moldy smell filled the air until Zemër couldn't breathe. He put the top of his robe over his nose and ran back up the stairs, slamming the door behind him. He cursed the day Korrtar fell, and then he cursed Korrtar herself. He stomped to the diplomat's quarters and opened the door.

"My King, what is wrong?" his head diplomat asked. The man was dark skinned, with a black, bushy beard covering half his face. He had serious brown eyes and curly black hair. He was slightly big-boned, but somehow it made him look even more verbally adept. He wore a simple, striped tunic and the typical brown cotton trousers. The King had always offered him finer clothes, but the man refused, saying he was more comfortable in the clothes he grew up in.

"The water is what is wrong. There's no more. None!" he fumed.

The diplomats stared at him in stunned silence. "None, my lord?"

"None. I need you to gather six of your best diplomats and ride to Naïfon. Ask if their king could find it in himself to welcome the Engjëllens. I need it done as fast as possible. I will send guards with you, in case there is danger on the way."

"Yes, my king," The man answered. He hurried off, walking deeper into the quarters to find men for the mission.

Zemër pointed to a woman. She was younger, with long red hair and light blue eyes. She enjoyed the finer ways of a diplomat and showed that in the way she dressed. A sage green robe hung down to her toes and she wore a small necklace of gold. "You will come with me now, and I will tell my people of our dilemma."

The diplomat bowed her head. "Yes, my liege."

They made their way through the castle, not looking sideways at the familiar tapestries covering the walls, and only nodding to people who passed them. They finally arrived at the front, where they walked into the sunshine, which seemed very inappropriate considering the events of the day.

They walked through the village to the town square. Everyone waved, but none of the villagers suspected anything unusual because the King usually made it his duty to walk through the village and speak personally with many of the villagers daily.

The regular bangs and clangs of hardworking craftsman could be heard, and the chatter of old friends talking. The potter and his apprentice were carving a beautiful design of dragons onto a large pot. The silversmith was making a small teapot. The produce vendors were cleaning their vegetables. Everything seemed much too normal.

There was a large stage in the middle of the square, where many plays and public announcements had been made. All good announcements, like marriages and births and the victory of a battle. Nothing like this. He and his diplomat walked slowly up the stairs, and suddenly all eyes were on him.

"Excuse me, all of you. I am sorry to…interrupt, but I have something to tell all of you." More villagers had gathered. Everyone had heard. The King was making an announcement, and they had to hear it.

"It seems that we have run out of good water." The crowd stirred. Everyone began to mumble to each other. The King knew that now the entire village was there, not a face missing but his diplomats and the two heroes.

The mumbling got louder, and his diplomat silenced them.

"I have sent some of my diplomats to negotiate with Naïfon, so that we may flee there until our heroes return. My expectation is that the answer is yes, so I am going to send all of you with them."

A voice sounded in the back. It was Läken, the father of one of the heroes. "What about you, my King? You are coming with us, right?"

The King's eyes welled up with tears. "No, friend. I will stay here and wait for your daughter and her friend." The entire crowd gasped.

"No!" Another person, a woman, yelled. "You will die, my King!"

"This is a chance I must take for the heroes. I have spoken to Aryanis, and he told me the heroes will succeed. I want to be here when they return." He could hear sobbing now, from many women. "Do not fear for me. I am not afraid to make the journey to Ederra." Now he could hear the children crying.

"Please," his diplomat cried. "Do not cry, women. You must be strong for your children." That landed a blow. Much of the weeping subsided, and only the wails of the children remained. The King knew he had picked the right diplomat to come. "Nothing is faster than the female mind," Zemër always said.

"Even though I understand any one of you would be perfect for the job," Zemër said, "I will choose only a few of my best soldiers to stay and help me defend this village." At this many shouts went up. They were shouts of one hundred fearless men who would give their lives for the King.

Zemër carefully chose ten strong warriors to stay with him, including Neör, his warlord, and Garren, the son of the late Malin. They all joined him on the stage. The sound of hooves caught his attention. There were the seven diplomats chosen to ride to Naïfon. He yelled to them and leapt off the stage, pushing through the crowd to them.

"We are ready, my King," the head diplomat said.

The King nodded and replied, "Good. Listen, I don't have enough time to wait for you to come back, so I am sending the village with you. I don't expect that Naïfon will refuse, especially if I send the entire population with you. Wait another few hours for the people to pack their things, and then you will be off."

"I understand, my King."

Zemër turned back to the crowd and yelled, "I will give you five hours to pack only the necessities for the trip. Nothing more, do you hear? Those of you who own horses may ride them. If not, you will walk." The King once again pushed through the crowd to a different location, where Läken stood.

"Läken, I want you to stay and wait for your daughter with me. You are in no condition to walk to Naïfon."

"Agreed, my King. Thank you for your kindness."

"Anything for an old friend, Läken. Besides, you are probably my mightiest warrior, despite your injuries."

Läken smiled and said, "That may have been true ten years ago, sir, but I think I've lost the spring in my step for that sort of thing."

"You never know 'til you try, right? Maybe that cane could come in handy. We could be a team! You whack the Orcs, to stun them, you know, and then I'll lop their heads off! We'll kill millions!"

Läken chuckled. "That might just be the solution, sir. I'll keep it in mind."

"All right then. Now, you better go speak with your wife. You and I both know that she'll want to stay, too."

Läken nodded, smiling, and limped away. The villagers had already begun to prepare. Five hours later, they had gathered again in the square. Zemër was sure his tears were visible in the waning light, but he didn't care. So was everyone else's. He told the village about Zemëroj. He felt like he owed it to them. Then, they sang one song to Aryanis before they slowly filtered out of the village.

Then, the King was left alone, with eleven other strong men. And each of them wept like a child.

# WINDÖR

There was a sound. That was what first caught Legna's attention. Normally, it wouldn't have bothered her. The world was full of sounds. But in the days she had spent in Windör, she knew sounds were a rare treat in the dismal forest.

For three days, Legna had felt like something was watching them. And she knew that if she didn't confirm her suspicions, she would go mad. Not that she doubted she already was going mad but not knowing would drive her too far.

They rode into a clearing, and Legna saw a small white light, which disappeared quickly.

"We're not alone . . ." Bàtor whispered. He pulled gently on his horse's reigns.

The forest was incredibly dark, and it took a few moments for them to realize they had reached a dead end. They looked at their surroundings, and it looked like the ruins of a town. Weather-worn gravestones littered the ground to their right, and to their left stood three houses, all made of stone. In front of them, a temple of some sort stood. Strange, goblin-like creatures carved out of stone protruded from each building. They had wings and horns, and long, curled tongues. Their evil eyes had a strange, inward glow to them.

"We should leave. Now." Legna took her bow from its place on her back and notched an arrow and then backed her horse away, catching a glimpse of something grey flying close to her. She looked around her. One of the stone carvings was gone. The sudden realization that they were being stalked made Legna feel sick.

They turned around, so that Traven's back was to the temple. He felt breath down his neck. Even worse, he knew no one was behind him. And there was no wind. He slowly turned, face-to-face with the grinning face of a flying stone carving.

He pulled out his sword and swatted at it, sending it crashing into a large gravestone that may have resembled a lamb. It shattered, and green mist hovered above its remains.

"Go! Now!" Traven yelled. They galloped back toward the forest, only to be cut off by three more carvings. Legna's horse reared, kicking one in the face and breaking it. Four more swarmed above them, their wings making small creaking noises. Legna shot two down with her bow; the contact making small explosions that killed the monsters around it. One clung to Bàtor, biting into his shoulder. He yelled in pain and shoved one of his daggers into it, plucking it off like a kebab and flinging it into a wall.

"What are these things?" Legna shouted above the sound of their psychotic laughing. There were hundreds now, filling up the skies and covering the trees with a dismal grey. Legna's white stallion fought ferociously, valuing its life above all else. Traven was covered in the creatures. He had at first taken to Bàtor's method of daggers but found that the creatures were overwhelming him quickly. Now, he just wriggled hopelessly under the beasts, undoubtedly being eaten.

"Gargoyles!" Bátor yelled, desperately ripping them from his body and smashing them on the ground.

Three gargoyles slammed into Legna, knocking her from her horse. She tumbled helplessly onto the ground, and the necklace that her mother had given her tumbled from inside her shirt. The gargoyles stopped, ironically still as stones, watching the necklace. She realized what was happening and ripped the necklace from her neck. She wasn't sure how to use it. Her mother hadn't told her.

"Aryanis help me," she whispered, holding it up and slowly standing. Her necklace tapped a gargoyle frozen in mid-flight, and it dropped, writhing, to the ground. It let out a horrible scream before bursting into green flames.

What followed in the next few moments was the exact sound of death.

Blood-curdling screeches filled the air as the gargoyles disintegrated. Green flames enveloped the forest around them, not burning the trees, but rather melting away the filth from the pitch-black bark, leaving creamy, eggshell-colored wood. A bright white light blinded Legna momentarily and then faded away. Then, she heard singing. It was a beautiful, symphonic melody, sounding at many different octaves, creating a mysterious song. There were no words, only notes, and it seemed as if whoever was singing was throwing their voice to sound as if many people were singing.

The trees above her grew sparkling, silver leaves. Suddenly, she could see the sun again. The singing continued, ringing throughout the forest now, echoing against the trees. It seemed to have no source, until, amidst the trees, Legna saw movement. She hesitated and then called out, "We know you are there."

An elderly woman, only about three feet tall, like a nymph, stepped out from the trees. She wore a twinkling white dress and a tiara that glittered like stars. She was very beautiful, despite her grey hair and wrinkles. Her mouth was open in song, and suddenly, she closed it, ending the haunting melody.

"You have freed my beautiful forest and I," the woman said. The power in her voice surprised Legna.

"Who are you?" Traven asked. Legna looked back at him and winced. The gargoyles had eaten off skin from his elbows, forehead, and knees, and the wounds were seeping blood.

"I am Trayona. Most call me Ona, though. Not that anyone has spoken to me in a good four thousand years, of course. Those horrible creatures overwhelmed me and trapped me in the very trees, containing me."

Legna gasped sharply. Lady Trayona was a name she had heard from many legends, and had been taught to respect. Trayona had been the keeper of ancient relics and guardian of Windör until she mysteriously disappeared. Afterwards, the nymphs evacuated Windör and never returned. "What happened to Windör that made it so ..." Legna didn't get to finish before Ona interrupted.

"Abysmal? I'll tell you what happened. Windör used to be a sacred place, where the nymphs lived. This was before Korrtar's fall, of course."

Ona stopped with a look of disgust on her face. "Good heavens, boy! We can't spend time talking! You look like death itself. Come, hold onto my robe, and we shall arrive at the Elvish village, Mär-Linna. There, they will tend to your wounds."

The heroes hesitated. Legna thought about what might stall Ona, for she wasn't sure she trusted the old woman. A rush of wind and a loud roar answered her questions. Aspör dropped down beside them, knocking down three crumbling gravestones.

"What is it? Why have we stopped?" He stopped and looked at Ona. "Mistress Trayona!" He fell flat on the ground in a bow. "You're Excellency! We are graced to be in your presence!"

"Do I know you, master dragon?" Ona asked.

"You do not know me, but when I lived in my homeland as a very young hatchling, my parents would sing of your grace, your forest, everything about you! It's such an honor to meet you! You are very well-known in our folklore!"

"I'm flattered, master dragon. We must talk about me more when we get to Mär-Linna. I will have your name and then we will be off."

"My name? Aspör, Mistress."

"Please, call me Ona."

"Ona," Aspör repeated.

"Good. Now, are we leaving or not? I very much want to see the Elves again, so I'm leaving with or without you."

"We'll come. Thank you, Ona." Legna approached the woman and laid a hand on her robe. Traven and Bátor followed her example, each grabbing ahold of the glistening material. Aspör trodded tentatively up the Ona and then gathered up a piece of her dress in his mouth.

Once each had a firm grip on her, Ona resumed her strange singing and the trees around them blurred, going out of focus until they were entirely gone. In their place, the mouth of a cave appeared, covered in ivy. Ona turned them around to face a beautiful city, looking like it was enveloped in white flames from the sun's rays.

"Welcome to Mär-Lïnna, heroes."

# ALONE IN DARKNESS

Zemër and his men kept watches, rotating throughout the night. The town was quiet and eerie without all of the Engjëllens bringing it to life. During his watch, Zemër noticed only slight sounds, like a squirrel chattering to its friends, or a rabbit scampering under a bush. The town seemed darker and more sinister without the women and children, even with the colorful buildings surrounding the men.

There was little excitement for a time, and what felt like days passed by without any noise. Lacking any servants to help him with his daily life, Zemër took on the responsibilities of the everyday man. He cooked his own meals, scrubbed his own clothes, and refused any offers of help from the other men.

He knew he looked foolish, doing his own work. He burnt his first few meals, and he did not know how to wash his clothes the way the chambermaids did. But, he had never bothered to learn the ways of the home. He had far more important things to do than cook and clean, such as discuss war plans and carry out diplomatic missions.

He was sleeping when Vildir, his head counsel, shook him violently and said, "The alarm has been risen, my lord. The Orcs have come to slaughter us in our sleep."

Zemër glanced around at the other men. Each was rushing back and forth, preparing for an unfair battle of twelve to two hundred.

"Well," Zemër grunted, "it's a good thing none of us are sleeping, now, is it?" Vildir began to help Zemër up, but Zemër pulled away and said, "Go, Vildir, tend to other matters. I can very well stand up without help."

Vildir stood from his crouched position and nodded. "Yes, my lord, of course." He trotted away to get fitted for armor.

Zemër heaved himself to his feet and made his way to Läken, head of weaponry and father of the hero they were waiting for.

"Is it true?" Zemër asked.

Läken nodded grimly. "They think they are catching us by surprise. They have well over two hundred Orcs out there, sir."

Zemër leaned closer to Läken. "Then we will just have to kill two hundred Orcs."

"Yes, sir. But with my … disabled state, I am unable to defend myself as well as I might like." Läken glanced down at his own legs, limp and useless.

Zemër looked back and forth and then snatched a bow from a table nearby, along with a full quiver. He pointed to the second story balcony of the inn. "Position yourself on that balcony, and try to take out as many as you can. In turn, we will barricade the inn and defend you as best as we can."

Läken nodded, took the weapon from Zemër, and then started toward the inn. Zemër trudged to the bakery, which was, at the moment, filled with the men's armor. There stood Garren, guardian of the ancient weapons and provider of baked goods. Zemër smirked as he thought how strange the two careers were together.

"Master Garren! Where is my armor?" Zemër called to the extremely young baker.

The boy looked at him wearily and then said, "Just a minute, sir." Garren ran back to the kitchen and returned with Zemër's armor of deep black. The helm, breastplate, and shield were lined with bright diamonds. The style of armor, called Dragonslayer armor, was only to be used by the royal family. It was gifted the name Dragonslayer because the armor looked to be made from the hide of a dragon. The first set of Dragonslayer armor had belonged to Melise, the Powerful, who had been queen millennia before Zemër was born.

"Thank you, Garren." Zemër extricated himself from the crowd of men in the tiny bakery and strode back out into the night air. He pulled his hauberk over his head and then attached his greaves and breastplate. He strapped on his bracers and gauntlets, and, finally, pulled on his helm, which had a design of a large, serpentine creature on it.

He drew his sword, a falchion, and swung it through the air, testing its weight like so many other times. Like his armor, the sword's blade was dark black steel. The cross guard was bright white, and a diamond was implanted into the hilt. The white design of a dragon graced the thin blade.

"If war is what you want," Zemër whispered to himself, "war is what you will get."

He heard a voice behind him. "They are advancing, sir." It was Vanir, now dressed in elegant, gold armor, with a red hauberk and a golden helm with eagle wings on either side.

"Prepare to retaliate. We are not children to be toyed with. I expect every Orc dead by the end of the day."

"Yes, sir."

Zemër marched to the edge of the village, and gazed out at the Orcish army. Normally, an army that size would be pitiful, but considering the Engjëllens only had an army of twelve, the Orcs had the advantage.

"And once again, we are at war." Neör said. Zemër flinched, as he had not noticed Neör's presence. Neör sighed. "As it should be."

"Yes," Zemër responded. "But only with the Orcs. War should not start between the true inhabitants of Zerúa." He turned to face Neör. "Let us never start war with our brothers, the Elves, or the Naïfonians, or even the nymphs."

"What if there is cause for it? What is they rise against us, angry that we are favored higher than them?"

Zemër paused, looking out at the Orcs, feeling a strange peace. "Would you kill your son, Neör?"

"Of course not, my Lord!"

"Would you deign murdering your sister, or your uncle acceptable? Or crossing blades with your father? Would you kill your wife because she did not appreciate the way you spoke to her before you left for the day, and she decided to tell you her feelings?"

"Well…no! Never!"

"Then why should you think any differently about our fellow citizens?"

"I am sorry, my lord, I was only thinking of your safety."

"I know, but sometimes we Engjëllens can become bloodthirsty. Almost like we *need* to kill. We have to remember that we are merely servants of our High King, and to kill is a dangerous path that all too often leads to evil."

Neör looked away and then muttered, "So we will fight?"

Zemër smiled. "Yes, we will fight."

# MÄR-LÏNNA

Legna stared at the sparkling city in front of her. Each building was made of some sort of marble, that shimmered and shined in the sunlight. Intricate, beautiful designs covered pillars and walls. Even the market stands were gorgeous. The silversmith, produce vendor, and jeweler stands stood in a circle atop a raised stage of wood. Chests of their goods stood around the stands, overflowing with incredible merchandise unavailable anywhere else.

Ona pointed to a grand building in the distance. "That is the palace, where Queen Bella lives and reigns.

"Incredible," Bátor breathed. The palace was, indeed, amazing. It stood well over two hundred feet in the air and like all the other buildings, was made of white marble. But this building was iridescent, displaying a rainbow of fantastical colors that danced across the other buildings. Legna saw what looked like little black dots on each block of marble. The pointed roofs of each tower were red and seemed to sparkle like a crystal, and Legna wondered if they were truly made of rubies.

"It's amazing," Aspör said. "I don't believe we made it this far…"

Ona tapped her foot impatiently. "Are we going to just stand here gawking, or are we going to go see the city?"

Legna nodded, and Ona led the way into Mär-Lïnna, down a path of silver bricks. A grand, silver gate with patterns resembling eagle wings on it stood in their path. From above, a younger elf with black hair and brown eyes called down, "Who goes there? State your business!"

"It is Trayona and some friends. We are just passing through. Our reasons are our own."

The elf's eyebrows drew together and then shot up in surprise. "Trayona? As in Lady Trayona, the Keeper of Windör?"

"The very same," Ona said, with a hint of amusement.

The elf seemed to jump. "Oh! Please, wait one moment while I open the gate!"

He disappeared from his place on the tower, and moments later, the gate slowly began to open. They stepped back, so as not to be smacked by the approaching gate and watched as the City of Marble appeared.

They hesitantly stepped past the guards, dressed in white and red mail and white helms, with crimson ebony blades strapped to their waists. They nodded to Ona and then watched the Engjëllens and their more fearsome compatriots closely. A thump sounded behind them. The gate was closed.

The young elf that had opened the gate for them dashed down the steps in the guard tower and rushed toward them.

"My Lady! I am Feor, Queen Bella's nephew. You have returned!"

"Yes, Master Elf, these heroes have brought me back to Zerúa."

"How?"

Legna held up her necklace, which she still had in her hand. "With this."

Feor's mouth moved, forming silent words. "That…where did you get that?"

"My mother gave it to me…as a gift. It belonged to an ancestor of mine."

"That is an ancient Nymph relic, meant for dispelling darkness." He looked around, seeming skittish and excitable.

"Put that away and follow me. We must speak with my aunt immediately." He began walking toward the palace and motioned for them to follow him. They began the trek through the City of Marble, amazing sights surrounding them. Acrobats were performing in the streets, twisting their bodies in incredible ways an Engjëllen could not accomplish in a million years. An elf next to her lit a piece of wood, tossed it in the air, and caught it in her mouth, swallowing it whole. She watched as an elf spoke to a deer, a squirrel, and a bear cub, and seemed to be making them do his chores for him.

She heard a shout of "Ready...Now!" close to her and looked over to see ten Elves shoot arrows, each hitting the middle of the bull's-eye simultaneously.

As she observed the Elves around her, she noticed they dressed much differently than Engjëllens. Their clothes were flowing and colorful as opposed to the simple, sensible way the Engjëllens dressed. Each female deigned appropriate to wear a tiara on their heads, and each man wore a circlet. Instead of wearing fur boots, these Elves went barefoot, only some wearing flimsy sandals. The Elves were naturally gorgeous, not one the same. Some had sharp, cat-like features, and others had round, curved features. Each had a perfect complexion, save for some battle scars, and many had oddly colored eyes such as yellow or red, and some had irises that were striped like tiger skin.

Legna continued to marvel at the town as they walked to the castle, and in turn, the Elves marveled at her and her companions, although she suspected half of the attention was directed toward Ona, and the other half at Aspör.

As they approached the castle, Legna realized that the black dots she had seen on the stones of the castle before were actually runes in the Elven language.

"Feor?" Legna asked the young elf. "What do these mean?"

Feor stopped suddenly and a spark of excitement lit up his eyes. "No one knows why, but ever since the Elves settled here in the Isles and built this castle, every time an elf is born, their name and date of birth is magically inscribed on a stone on the castle. Then, when they pass, their date and reason for death are inscribed under their date of birth, along with a short recount of what they are remembered for."

"Incredible," Aspör remarked. Then, he read aloud, "*King Eisley, born on the twenty-fifth day of the third month of the four-hundredth century. Died in the Battle for Hollin on the fourth day of the twelfth month in the nine-hundredth century. He helped us through many hard times and raised up a fine successor. He will be remembered for his role as king, veteran, father, husband, grandfather, and friend to many. May he rest in peace.* This all just appeared here?"

"Yes. And it truly does tell of what kind of person they were, where they died, and how they died. On more than one occasion, we have found out that people were spies for the Demons through these stones. Read this one." Feor gestured toward another stone higher up.

This time, Legna read, "*Tyrann, born on the nineteenth day of the fourth month of the eleven-hundredth century. Died by way of assassination on the thirtieth day of the ninth month of the thirteen-hundredth century. She was a spy and a traitor to us all, who was married to a Demon. Long may she burn in Mëkator.* Wow. Harsh. Who writes these?"

Feor lowered his voice. "That's just the thing! Nobody knows, and nobody has lived long enough to have been doing it for all this time! It really is incredible and mysterious. Some say we built on top of a crypt, where the dead from a past race were buried. Others say Aryanis himself blessed the stone. But we never seem to run out of stones for the newborns all over the Isle. And no one that was there when the castle was built is alive anymore. It's a marvel! We call them the Talking Stones, although they never truly talk, now that I think about it." They stood in silence for a minute, reveling in the mystery of the thing.

Bátor was the first to break the stupor. "Shall we proceed?" he asked Feor.

"Oh! Of course, I do apologize; I can get quite distracted from time to time. My aunt tells me I have the attention of a squirrel at sometimes."

Feor pulled open the heavy, iron doors, revealing the corridors of Queen Bella's castle. Windows lined the walls, open and allowing sunlight to stream gloriously through, lighting up the hallways. Deep red banners with the Elven symbol, an eagle feeding a dove, hung between each window. A large, sparkling chandelier hung from the ceiling, throwing iridescent sparkles around the room. A winding, marble staircase at the far end of the room led to a balcony only slightly visible to the companions below. Ancient tapestries hung where banners were not, depicting coronations and the wealth of kings and queens past.

With some trouble, Aspör managed to fit through the doors and slowly crawl through the grand hall.

"We are taking this corridor," Feor said as he pointed to their left, down a large hallway that looked big enough to fit two dragons side by side.

A silence accompanied their trek down the corridor, giving Legna time to think. They had made it this far, yes. But they were only at the top of the Elvish Isle. Going at their pace, on their horses, it would take at least another couple of weeks to get out of the Elvish Isle and into the forbidden land, Korrtar's land. After this, they would have to discard of their horses, going by foot to be stealthier. If it were only her and Traven, they could fly on Aspör to Mëkator, which would only take one or two days. But with Bátor, they had no choice to continue as they were. Aspör just could not carry three people on his back.

Or she could…no, she did not want to think about that. She could not just leave her friends in the villages. She knew that Traven would just chase after her, throwing himself blindly into danger for her. She could not bring herself to do that. Traven was the closest thing to a brother she ever had. She was comfortable telling him things that she would never tell anyone else: not Garren, Aspör, or even her father.

A pang of heartache hit Legna as she thought about Garren. She felt guilty when she realized she hadn't thought of him in weeks, what with all the excitement and danger.

The further from home she got, the more she forgot what her old life was like. Sleeping in the woods, fighting monsters, and traveling to faraway places were slowly replacing her old life. She felt older, more mature. She had a new view on life. Not everything was easy, and now she knew that. It frightened her how quickly she had changed. She had as many scars now as an old war hound. Her bow and sword were a part of her, and she never went anywhere without them. She even slept with them.

She was becoming everything she was told about in legends.

Legna's thoughts and self-reflections were abruptly stopped by soft whack to the head, caused by an overhead wooden plank. "Genius," she muttered to herself.

"Don't worry, Legna," Feor said next to her. "The queen herself has done that a dozen times if not more. That beam is absolutely inappropriately placed if you ask me. We are almost to the throne room. Hurry, everyone!" Feor scurried ahead, motioning for them to follow. Being an elf, Feor's legs were longer and faster, and he was tall, even for an Elf, so the Engjëllens had to jog to keep up, and poor Ona had to sprint.

A grand door stood in their way, a red door carved from pure ruby and laced together with silver. Feor knocked on the door, and it slowly opened. The throne room opened before their eyes, and Legna breathed in sharply. They stood in a huge room with marble floors, walls, and ceiling. Columns around them were made of ruby and silver, like the door. In front of them sat Queen Bella. She was beautiful with spindly fingers and long, white hair. Her eyes were blood-red, and her skin was white as snow. She had a stern but gentle look on her face as if she would like you if you behaved. She wore a long, red dress that seemed to be made of cardinal feathers. She donned a similar headdress with silver beads streaming down the sides of her face. Her eyes were slanted, as were her ears. She wore no shoes—strange for royalty—but only transparent ankle socks that were laced with silver chips. Her feet sparkled as she shifted to see who had entered her hall.

She sat on a throne made of silver and red satin, in between two smaller thrones. Above her hung a tapestry of the royal Elvish family tree. It started at the high ceiling, at least three hundred feet in the air, starting with the first royal family of the elves, King Denmand, and Queen Zethara. The tree ended in the middle of the tapestry with Queen Bella and her deceased husband, King Ingund, and their nephew, Feor. Legna already knew that Queen Bella took an oath of maidenship when she was a young girl, so she never had children. Feor was the rightful heir to the throne, but somehow, Legna could not see the man leading a country.

Legna thought that Queen Bella was about as beautiful as one could get. And then, she spoke. Her voice sounded as if all of the loveliest songbirds had a child and then put it in Bella's throat in place of vocal chords. "What do you seek in my hall, Engjëllens? You are far away from home."

Legna gulped down her nervousness. "We are on a quest to save our people, Your Highness. We seek passage through the Isles to Mëkator and also your blessing. Will you grant us what we seek?"

Bella raised an eyebrow, amused. "Passage through my Isles *and* my blessing? What is this quest, which you need to go to Mëkator? What business does Zemër have sending two teenagers and..." The Queen stopped. "Oh my," she said in a smaller voice. "Bátor? Is that truly you?"

Bátor knelt. "It is, my queen."

"You...You were dead. Trapped in an apple. How? How are you back?"

Bátor pointed at Legna. "That hero released me"—he lowered his voice—"I think she is it. The chosen one."

Legna looked, startled, at Bátor. His expression was grim, no sign of jest in it.

Queen Bella did not seem to be surprised. She gestured to Ona. "And who might you be, my lady?"

Ona lifted her chin. "I am Trayona, keeper of Windör. I brought these young heroes here to Mär-Linna, and I intend to see they are treated well. Bátor is right. She is it."

Queen Bella's mouth upturned in a slight smile. "I always knew it would be a woman. All of the songs and prophecies spoke of a man. But I knew it would be a woman." Bella turned to Aspör. "What is this monster doing in my palace?"

Aspör spoke then. "I am Aspör, Your Majesty. Legna is my good friend. I follow her."

Bella looked at Legna. "You have a pet dragon?"

"More or less. Dragons aren't monsters, Your Majesty. They're just large and…scaly…Your Highness, we really do need to—"

Bella interrupted. "Yes, yes. I grant you full pass to everywhere on the Elvish Isles. Also, I gift to you the empty house in my city, which you can use for your leisure. It has enough room for all of you, over ten bedrooms. It is next to the blacksmith's forge."

"Thank you, Your Highness." Legna was stunned at the generosity of the queen.

Bella nodded. "You are quite welcome. Furthermore, I make an offer to Bátor. I offer to let Feor take your place in this quest. I gift to you my nephew, Feor, as your faithful servant. He is young and quite a warrior, and he has a few unique…talents."

Legna was about to ask what talents Feor had, but just then, Bátor drew in a sharp breath. "Truly, my queen?" He asked.

"Truly. You may stay in Mär-Linna until their return."

"I don't know if I can just leave these children alone…" Bátor said.

"Bátor, you have been trapped in an apple for sixteen years. You need rest. And Mär-Linna is beautiful. We could teach you so many things. Come now, you have done your part in this quest. You have mentored these heroes. They need to do this on their own."

Bátor looked at Legna. She knew he was thinking about the promise he made to her father.

"It's okay," Legna said. "I'll be fine."

Bátor nodded. "I know." He smiled. Then, he looked back at Bella. "I accept your offer, Queen Bella. I will stay, and Feor may take my place."

Queen Bella nodded. "Feor, Legna is your leader until this quest is over. I am giving you this responsibility, Feor, to test your humility and bravery."

"Yes, Your Majesty. Thank you for the honor."

Bella smiled; a beautiful event that should have been witnessed at least once in a person's lifetime. Legna could tell Bella was quite fond of Feor.

"Lastly, I give you my blessing"—Bella tossed Legna a silver ring with the Elvish crest—"that will grant you access to anywhere on the Isle. It also has special powers that…enhance your performance, I suppose. Keep it safe."

Legna slipped on the ring and felt refreshed. "What does the ring do?"

"Let's just say when you have it on you'll be able to endure a little more pain than usual. Every race has them. They are given to ambassadors to give them full freedom, like they are a member of the race themselves. Each ring does something different. The Elvish ring increases your pain tolerance and damage resistance. Wear it, and you'll be a match for Korrtar herself."

"Thank you for all you have done, my queen." Legna suddenly had an idea of what she wanted to do before she left. "Are there any scholars here? Or librarians? One that would know a lot about the ins and outs of Zerúans?"

"Well…There is the man Absom. He lives in the meadow down by the creek. He is the oldest of us and spends his time learning new things and stuffing knowledge into his brain. But he is quite a hermit and will only talk to certain people. You can try to ask him your questions, but there is no guarantee he will answer them, or even respond, for that matter."

"I'll try. Thank you again."

"Go now, with my blessing! May you succeed and bring peace to Zerúa."

They turned to leave, but Legna caught sight of Traven's wounds again. "Your Highness, do you have a healer here? My friend is badly wounded."

"When you walk out the door of the castle, turn left. Pass the bakery and masonry and then it is on the right. You will see it."

"Thank you."

They left the castle and followed Bella's directions to the healer's shop. They dropped Traven off there and then set out to the house they were gifted. When they finally arrived, Legna's eyes widened with wonder. The house was six stories tall made completely from cherry wood. It was fully furnished inside, along with herbs and food to cook. A fire was roaring in the corner, ready for them.

"Why don't you all rest?" Legna asked. "I have something I want to do."

Her companions agreed, so she set off to find Absom.

# ABSOM

As Legna approached the hermit's house, she looked around her. The house stood in an outcropping of trees in the middle of a meadow. A small stream flowed next to it, and salmon swam near the surface. The house was round in shape, built into a small hill, which made up the roof. A green door blared in the front, with a gold doorknob. The white paint on the stone walls had begun to chip.

She apprehensively approached the door, glancing in the window, seeing nothing but a pulled blind. She knocked lightly on the door. At first, there was only silence. Then a loud voice boomed, "Who dares disturb my studies? Come in! Show your face!"

Legna, startled, jumped backwards and almost lost her balance. She twisted just in time to catch herself mid-fall and regain her balance. She laid her hand on the golden knob and twisted. The door swung open, as if caught by a strong gust of wind. Legna stepped inside.

"Hello? Absom? I have come with questions, seeking your knowledge." Legna waited for an answer, but none came. The floor she stood on was wooden, swept clean. Little round tables were everywhere, covered with strange relics that made no sense. One held a little gold cube that looked to be made up of more little cubes. She picked it up and twisted the top, and only the top row moved with her hand. She put that down and walked away, hoping she hadn't broken it. A table nearby held a large sphere of sapphire, surrounded by white puffy things that looked like clouds. Legna assumed it was only a sculpture, but when she touched a cloud, it evaporated on contact. She gasped softly and moved on.

"I really need to leave the Isles soon, but I was hoping to receive some answers before I leave! Please!" Legna cried as she wove her way through the tables.

A voice, to her left, said, "Get out! I have no time for questions! Leave!"

"Please! I'm Legna, daughter of Läken and Zopporah. I've been sent to Mëkator to kill Korrtar."

The same voice sounded to her right. "Läken? Daughter of Läken, you say? Come, I may consider your questions."

She turned a corner to the right. "Where are you?" She asked.

Only humming answered, in front of her. She followed the sound until she came to a large library. The library had bookshelves that stood ten feet tall and were completely filled with books. Here, a very old elf stood leafing through a book that read *Grooming Your Unicorn*. Legna decided she would ask about that later.

Legna assumed the old man was Absom. He had wiry grey hair that stuck out in all directions. His ears were still pointed, but so many wrinkles covered him; the lobes sagged. He had twinkling grey eyes with an eccentric look and a large nose. He wore brown trousers and a green overcoat that looked like it hadn't been washed in decades. He was barefoot, with ragged toenails and fingernails on each appendage.

"Are you Absom?" Legna asked.

The man looked up, seemingly surprised she was there. "Stupid question, girl. What other old man were you expecting to find in this house?"

"Um … none, I guess. Sorry I asked."

"Are you Legna?"

Legna was tempted to respond sarcastically, mimicking Absom's own words. But, instead she only sighed and replied, "Yes, I am." Then she muttered, "How many other girls were calling for you?"

Absom smirked. "You've got spirit, girl. I like that. Sit and I might answer your questions."

Legna glanced at the leather chairs next to the dozens of bookcases in the room. She ambled over and sat down. She waited for the old man to sit down, but instead, he continued to read his book, learning how to groom the unicorn he probably never owned. Once he finished, he shut the book with a bang and strode over to the chairs. He settled down and rested his chin in his hand.

"So, what did you need?" Absom asked.

Legna hesitated and then blurted out, "What do you know about dragons?"

"Dragons? Beautiful creatures. Can sometimes be hostile toward smaller races. Why?"

"My dragon doesn't remember much of his days among other dragons. I wanted to find out about them."

"*Your* dragon?" Absom exclaimed.

"Yes, sir. My mother found him on our doorstep as a hatchling and took him in. I am his master."

"Taming a dragon. Imagine it. All right, I'll tell you about dragons. Everything I know. Ask away."

"Where did they come from?" Legna asked.

"Dragons are the ancestors of Naïfonians. They are their Ederran state, I suppose you could say if you would like to compare to Engjëllens. They live in their own country, far to the east of Zerúa, a place they named Pâne. That is where Naïfonians supposedly go when death rears its ugly head. They go to Pâne, and become a dragon."

"Like Engjëllens become Ederrans," Legna said.

"Right. Now, it is very unusual for a dragon to have any contact with Zerúans. The dragons consider themselves higher than us, which for the most part is true. But, it is possible to journey to their land, and they to ours, unlike Ederra. Sometimes, when a dragon is chosen by Aryanis to be a destroyer of evil, it is sent to Zerúa to fulfill its destiny because there is no evil in Pâne. That must have been your dragon. He was sent down to help you with your quest."

"So Aspör is a chosen one too. Birds of a feather flock together, I suppose," Legna said.

Absom cleared his throat. "Excuse me?"

"I was chosen by Aryanis also. And by the baker in my village, who is dead now."

"The baker chose you? To do what, taste his new recipes?"

"No! He gave me this bow." Legna stroked the bow on her back. "It's magical."

"A baker with magical weapons . . . I really should visit Engjëll more often. Anyway, what other questions do you have?"

"Why does my dragon change colors when he kills monsters?" Legna asked.

Absom's eyebrows went up. "Now *there's* an interesting story. You understand that each race in Zerúa has different talents, to balance each other out. You Engjëllens are war savvy, while we Elves are one with nature, full of grace. Nymphs are gifted with magic, and Naïfonians, our lizard folk, are talented with mechanics and blacksmithing."

Legna nodded. "An old nymph taught me that, yes."

Absom continued, "Well, the first queen of the dragons wanted something for her race too. So Aryanis let her decide. Well, she thought and thought and thought but couldn't think of a gift unique enough for her race. So, finally, she asked Aryanis to give her people a rainbow of talents. So he did. And from then on, each time a dragon kills a certain amount of monsters, it will turn a more beautiful color and get bigger and bigger until it can get no more beautiful and no bigger. By then, it will be colossal, and iridescent, the ultimate dragon, the Energia, as they call it. That is why it is such an honor to be chosen to go to Zerúa to fight because that will give you a chance to achieve that ultimate goal."

"Why is that the ultimate goal?" Legna asked.

"You see, my dear, the rule of the dragons is not passed down through bloodline. When a monarch of Pâne passes or steps down, the next leader is chosen on account of respect and strength. When you are this Energia, this mammoth of a dragon, you are highly regarded and respected. Reaching this ultimate goal increases your chances of receiving the position dramatically. And each dragon yearns to make his land better. *That* is why it is the ultimate goal."

"With great power comes great responsibility," Legna remarked.

"Yes. And great sacrifice. When a dragon reaches their Energia state, they are unable to have children from then on. This is a great woe to most dragons as they treasure their hatchlings, and live to see them grow up big and strong."

"A great sacrifice," Legna agreed. "What do they do in their spare time? What are their focuses, their goals in life? Other than Energia, of course."

"What do dragons do in their spare time? They love to fly, of course. They base a lot of their respect on how well a dragon can fly. But, they also love to read about the ancient histories of their people. I don't blame them. They are quite intriguing indeed. I wish I had a copy of the book *The History of Pâne* just to read. I would give much to learn of dragon heroes. But alas, I am old and becoming weaker. People wonder why I stay in my home and read, but it's all I can do, really. I get too tired to swing a sword properly, and my hands shake too much to aim a bow. I'm almost three thousand years old. I've seen a lot and done a lot. But I never traveled to Pâne."

Absom looked at Legna, and his eyes lit up. "Would you go to Pâne for me? And find that book? I'm not asking you to go right now, but someday? When you are idle in your questing, would you think of old Absom and find it for me? It would mean a whole lot."

Legna looked at the wise old man. "If I ever have the time, I would be honored to go, Absom."

Absom clapped his hands in joy. "Oh, thank you, thank you! It's been a long time since I conversed with a hero, and now I remember why I love it! Oh, thank you! Now, are there any other questions?"

Legna thought for a moment and then thought of a final question. "Yes, just one." She gently took the necklace her mother gave her from her neck. "What is this?"

Absom's face darkened. "Where did you get that?" he asked.

"My mother gave it to me, to protect me. My companions and I ran into a horde of gargoyles and...they seemed afraid of it. They burned on contact and then they exploded, and the entire group was gone. They vanished."

Absom gingerly took it from Legna's hands turning it over and stroking it with his fingers. He traced the heart shape, stopping at the diamond in the middle. "This hasn't been seen in centuries," he finally said.

"What is it?" Legna asked.

"What is it?" Absom asked. "It's many things. An ancient relic, for one. It's also a weapon, and a lovely accessory if I do say so myself."

"Why was it made?" Legna was becoming a little bit impatient, feeling antsy.

"It was made by one of the first nymphs, Adarr. He was the strongest of the nymphs, very gifted in magic. When Korrtar fell, some nymphs turned to follow her. Those nymphs turned to gargoyles. Adarr created that necklace to repel gargoyles. Unfortunately, he used it too much, and it stopped working. So, calling it useless, Adarr threw it away and ordered all nymphs to evacuate Windör. Only Trayona stayed because she still had hope they could defeat the gargoyles. But, without the necklace, the gargoyles became too much. They trapped Trayona in a tree and left her like that for centuries, living in their despicable hives in Windör."

"Why did the necklace stop working?" Legna asked.

"Like I said, he used it too much. The magic began to wear out. You have to let magic rest for a while before using it again."

"So why is it working now?"

"Think, girl! It's had almost four thousand years to charge! That magic will not be wearing out for a very, very long time."

Legna nodded her understanding and then stood. "I really need to leave. But, before I go..." Legna gestured to the book, still in Absom's lap. "Do you even own a unicorn?"

Absom laughed. "Do I own a unicorn? Ha! Come with me!" He sprung from his seat faster than Legna thought possible and then he scampered between two bookshelves and down a hallway Legna had not noticed before. She hurried to catch up, and they twisted and turned through the corridors. Just when Legna began to wonder if the house went on forever, they reached a dead end. The wall was completely empty, except for a round indent, conspicuous on the bare wall. Absom reached into his pocket and pulled out a golden medallion. He pushed it into the indent and the wall disappeared, replaced by a stable door. The smell of hay filled Legna's nostrils.

Absom pushed open the door. "*This* is my unicorn, Vella." And so it was. A tall, white horse stood in a huge stall, snorting and eating golden hay. Her mane and tail were both white, but with the setting sun lighting the hair, they looked pink. She had big, blue eyes like sapphires and a light gray star on her nose. Most prominent of all was the sharp, iridescent horn that protruded from her forehead.

"Wait...vella is Elvish for rainbow."

"Yes, it is."

"So you named her Rainbow the unicorn? That's kind of cliché, isn't it?"

"It's so cliché; it's not cliché."

"I…have no response to that."

"As it should be."

Legna studied Vella. "I must admit," she said, "she is very well groomed."

Absom winked. "I take my books to heart."

"How did you get a unicorn?" Legna asked.

Absom smiled. "A story for another time. Come now, you need to rest and continue on your journey. You have a long way to go yet."

Legna nodded and stroked Vella. "Another time, Vella." Then she and Absom made their way back to the library and back to Mär-Linna.

# BATTLE FOR ENGJËLL

"My King," Garren said behind Zemër. "The Orcs are at the gate. Their general is requesting to speak with you."

Zemër let go a pent-up breath. "Take me to them." He followed Garren through the empty town to the front gates. There, the small battalion of Orcs waited. In front, a large Orc stood, with more armor than the others. He was missing an eye but made no attempt to cover it up. He held a wooden club that was covered with deadly green spikes in one hand and a black mace in the other. He grunted when he saw Zemër and saluted to him. Zemër glared back in return.

"What do you want, Demon? If you are looking to take over this village, it's not going to happen." Zemër fixed the Orc with a stare that would have stopped a charging bear.

"*Nejsem chtějí bojovat. Já jen chci s tebou mluvit, a pokračovat v našem smlouvu,*" the general said in the Orcish tongue.

"Speak Engjëllen, you beast. I refuse to speak in your repulsive language."

"Very well, king. I speak in your tongue. We are not here to fight. Only want to talk. Resume treaty. Ask forgiveness."

"I shall give no forgiveness. That treaty was idiotic in the first place. No. I will not be at peace with you again. Not now or ever."

Then, he yelled behind him, "Gather the men! Line for battle! We fight now!"

The Orc smiled grimly. "It is not war we want, little king, but if war is what you want, you will get it."

Zemër sneered. "Send your worst. It's nothing compared to the mighty warriors of Engjëll." Zemër stepped so close to the general; he could smell the Orc's repulsive breath. He grabbed him by the collar and lifted him slightly off the ground. "If you think you'll win this war, you are gravely mistaken." His voice was barely a whisper now. "If you understood the might of men deeply scarred, you would be frightened. You *should* be frightened." Then, Zemër threw him backwards, causing him to land painfully on his bottom.

Zemër marched away, stewing. The nerve of those Orcs, proposing a treaty after they attack an innocent girl and an old man was preposterous. They would receive what was coming to them. They all would.

He joined his ten men, Läken having stayed back, and took his place at the front. He looked the general straight in the eye and then drew his sword and raised it skyward. "For our families!" He yelled to his men.

"For our families!" the men repeated.

"For our High King!"

"For our High King!"

"For Legna," he said quieter, to himself.

Garren standing close to him, heard this and yelled, "For Legna! And Malin!"

"For Legna and Malin!" the other men agreed.

Zemër hesitated, hoping the suspense would unnerve the Orcs and then he screamed, "Charge!" His men barreled forward, and the general's smug look changed to fear as the Engjëllens struck the Orcs.

His sword like a blur, Zemër killed five Orcs with one stroke, spinning in a wide circle, cutting through weapons like butter.

An Orc struck Zemër's helmet with the butt of his sword, but it didn't make a dent. Zemër screamed at the Orc, making him flinch and then he sliced the Orc's helm open and decapitated him. The sound of steel striking steel rung everywhere. When he was able to still his sword, he was able to glance at Neör performing a backflip and simultaneously cutting an Orc in half and then bringing his sword down just in time to block a thrust from another Orc as he landed. His marksman, Yuler, stood a ways back, knocking ten arrows at a time and hitting dozens of Orcs a minute.

*I'm so lucky to work with these men,* Zemër thought. This thought was cut short by an Orc with a spear, jabbing at him clumsily. He caught the end of the spear with his sword and flipped it into the air, catching it in one hand and stabbing the Orc in the stomach with it. He turned and smacked an Orc in the neck with his spear and then stabbed the Orc in the throat with his sword. He discarded the stolen spear and picked up a shield from a fallen Orc. He raised it just in time to receive an arm-numbing jolt from a mace. He looked up to see the fat face of the general glaring down at him.

"You've killed too many of my men, little king. Now you die to pay for them."

"I'd rather not," Zemër responded. He swung at the Orc, but it was blocked by the club. The mace slyly swung around to pierce his mail on the side, but Zemër rolled backwards and caught the mace with the tip of his sword. They stood, locked in a silent strain, until the Orc swung his club at Zemër's head to finish him. Zemër quickly bashed the hit with his shield and stabbed the Orc in the leg when he staggered. The Orc howled in pain and Zemër thrust his sword through the Orc's mail and into his chest. The Orc dropped to the ground with a thud, and Zemër watched as the Orcs slowly retreated. They fell back, slowly but surely, noticing that their general was dead. They fell into chaos, making it easy for the Engjëllens to pick off the rest of them.

Yuler killed the last three Orcs with arrows right into the eye-slits of their helms.

The Orcs had gone. None were left alive.

"Is that it?" Neör asked.

"That's it for now, friend," Zemër replied. He gazed into the distance. Puffs of dirt still rose from the battlefield, shrouding the horizon in a hazy fog. "How many casualties?" he asked.

"None are dead, my king. Only a few minor wounds, and...one that may be a problem."

"What do you mean?" Zemër asked, suddenly worried.

"Come. I'll show you." Zemër followed Neör back into the village. Lying there, on a bench, was Garren, Malin's son. He had an arrow sticking out of his arm, with blood trickling from his mail.

"It seems that the Orcs had an archer, too, but Yuler killed him before he could kill anyone else. But he did manage to inflict some pretty bad damage on this young fellow." Neör patted Garren and Garren smiled at the king.

"You can't go through battle without a few scars," Garren said; his voice hoarse. He winced as he shifted his position to look at the king. "But my scar may be a bit more ailing than others."

"Now, don't you worry a thing, boy. You're going to make it just fine. I was smart enough to keep our medic around, so you don't need to worry. He'll fix you up quicker than you can say 'ouch.' Just hold on." Zemër signaled for Neör to go fetch the medic, and Neör obliged.

"Thank you, King." Garren closed his eyes and then became still. Zemër panicked, thinking the boy's life had suddenly ended, but then he saw the rise and fall of his chest, and the panic left as quickly as it had come.

That night, they traveled to the Kaparan Meadow, like always, and built a bonfire. They sat around and ate dried meat, warming themselves near the flames. Garren sat with them; his arm in a splint.

"Where do you think they are now, King?" Garren asked.

"Who?" Zemër responded.

"Legna and Traven. Where do you think they are?"

"Well, they're probably in Windör by now, exploring the unexplored. Or they have just arrived with the Elves."

Garren nodded, seemingly satisfied. Then, Yuler, also rather young being only twenty-four, called out, "Tell us a story, your majesty."

"A story?" Zemër thought, then he said, "All right, I'll tell you a tale." He settled down onto his log, then began:

"Once, there lived an Engjëllen named Hypont who wanted knowledge greatly. He begged and begged Aryanis to give him his request. Finally, Aryanis told him he would grant Hypont's request if he could figure out what a person's most precious jewel was. Hypont went back to his home and thought and thought and thought until an old man mysteriously showed up at his doorstep. Desperate, he asked the old man the riddle, and the old man responded, 'The spirit, of course.' Hypont returned to Aryanis and gave him this answer. Aryanis smiled and said, 'So be it.' He snapped his fingers, and Hypont's very spirit came out of his chest and into his hands, in the shape of a small, blue jewel. Hypont, of course, received knowledge, more than most minds could fathom.

"Aryanis explained to Hypont that he had just discovered a significant fact about Zerúans: that their spirits were jewels of the highest value. This is when Aryanis created our water and dubbed spirit jewels the way to cleanse it. At first, spirit jewels were inside Zerúans instead of monsters, but when they ran out of jewels to clean the water with, they began to think murderous thoughts. That was when Aryanis taught us a valuable lesson on greed and deceit. He knew that it was not correct to have the Zerúans's source of water inside the people themselves, but he wanted them to know how horrible civil war was. Out of our own greed, we formed ranks and marched against each other. Just as the general of one army was about to clash swords with the other, Aryanis came in between them, stopping the weapons. He asked the people if this was really what they wanted, fighting their brothers. The Zerúans looked around and realized that war was the worst possible solution to the problem. So, Hypont, with his new knowledge, came up with the idea that Aryanis already knew. So they wouldn't have to kill each other to live, instead, their spirit jewels should be transferred to monsters, so they could get them in an honorable way. So, Aryanis transferred the jewels into monsters, and from that day on, we have been relying on heroes to keep our water clean and our world alive."

Everything was silent. Only the crackling of the flames was to be heard.

"Do you think Korrtar will ever die, King?" Garren asked.

"I have been told," Zemër began, "that the people of Giza will make a prophecy about the death of Korrtar."

"You heard a prophecy of a prophecy?" Neör asked.

"Indeed. The prophecy will say that Korrtar will raise up one last Demon, but on Giza this time, and he will rule Giza for years until, finally, the Zerúans will fight a final battle with the Demons, and Aryanis will slay Korrtar."

"So Legna and Traven will not succeed?" Yuler asked.

"No, they will succeed. Their quest is to extract Korrtar from our world. They will battle her, and they will win the battle, but Korrtar will only be weakened. I believe she will be banished from her home in Mëkator and sent to live among the Gizaans; invisible, but still able to plant lies and tempt them."

"Then what happens?" Retin, an old warrior with a scruffy grey beard and deep black eyes asked.

"Then we wait for what our High King tells us to do. He'll know what is best."

Changing the subject, Läken called out, "My lord, tells us of how you met your wife!"

Zemër smiled. This was a story he loved to tell, even if she was gone. "Her name was Opal," he began mistily. "I always noticed her in the market because she would always accidentally bump into me and then flash her silly smile and keep going, daydreaming the whole way. She was a flower girl in the market, just because she loved making people smile. I remember one day, I finally got up the courage to talk to her. She was holding a lily, smelling it, her eyes closed in delight. I watched her until she opened her eyes and noticed me there. She smiled, bright and warm. She had a waterfall of blonde hair that tumbled down her shoulders. Her eyes were purple and had a striking glow to them. She was short, but slender, and she had a simple way of dressing that made her look as regal as any queen.

"'Hello,' she said. 'Do you want a flower? The roses are especially beautiful this time of year.' So, naturally, I picked up a rose and smelled it. But, apparently, there happened to be a bee on this rose. As soon as I lifted the flower to my face, the bee stuck its stinger right into the end of my nose! My nose was red as a cherry. She giggled, caught the bee in her hand, pet its head, and then let it go again. The bee buzzed happily, and I was jealous. But then, Opal looked back at me and told me to meet her back at the flower stand that night. I did and that was the night that she first kissed me"—his eyes began to tear up—"four months later, I proposed to her, in Kaparan Meadow, during the Celebration, in front of everybody. I remember that when she accepted, everyone cheered, and the sound was deafening, but neither of us cared. I only cared that I finally had her.

"Our wedding was beautiful, held in the forest. She was wearing a dark green dress, and a crown made of silver apple leaves. My father married us. Then, a year later, she gave birth to Zemëroj. And then, when Zemëroj was twelve—"

"My King, you don't have to explain," Laken interrupted gently.

Zemër waved him off and then continued. "When Zemëroj was twelve, Opal was walking in the woods. A Lahti intercepted her, and...he murdered my defenseless wife." He took a deep breath. Everyone was quiet, watching the king. A few men had tears in their eyes.

"The funeral was simple, but there were flowers everywhere, just like she liked it. The Elves were able to weave a coffin out of roses, and we buried her under a garden. I don't know why, but I didn't cry for a while. I guess I was too bitter to cry. I became harsher with my servants and son. Eventually, a good friend of mine told me that everyone was worried about me. They mentioned that the path to darkness is through resentment and anger. So, finally, I allowed myself to cry. After that, I was able to let it go. I will never love another, though. Never." With that, he stopped talking, got up from his place, and walked back to Engjëll, leaving the men in stunned silence. Only Neör and Läken had ever heard the story of Opal's death, and Zemër was sure they weren't expecting to hear it again tonight. The other men didn't know the cause of the queen's death. Zemër avoided talking about it. Not everyone needed to know. But he figured if he would be fighting beside these men, they should know about his life.

He did not lie. He did let go the pain caused by his wife's death. But he still cared for her. And he did not want to spare a Demon's life any more than before he let go.

He continued to walk mindlessly back to his empty town. He reached the market square and lit a small fire. He gazed at the night sky and could pick out constellations. An archer shooting an arrow across the sky. A milkmaid petting her favorite cow. An Elf fighting an Orc. A Naïfonian, his hammer raised, ready to strike steel to make a new sword.

And his favorite, though he never understood it, an old Elf riding a unicorn.

# ABSOM'S GIFT

Legna returned to the mansion and fell into the first bed she encountered. She didn't realize how long she had gone without good sleep until now.

*She dreamt she was in Mëkator, sneaking among ranks of Demons. She was all alone, and she was wearing no armor, only a simple white blouse and a deerskin skirt. Her sword and bow were still on her back. She dove behind a rock as an Akull passed by, looking just as Bátor had described it. He had a fuzzy head, with a nose and ears that resembled a rabid monkey's. His bottom half was half the body of a dragon, with glinting, white scales. Ice hung from everywhere on his body. He had fangs like a tiger and pupil-less eyes. He looked directly at Legna, smirked, and spoke. "I knew it would work," he seemed to call to someone behind him. His voice sounded kind of like icicles smashing, and as he spoke, little snowflakes curled from his mouth.*

*A Lahti strode over to him. Legna's eyes widened. She had never seen a Lahti before. He hardly had any features on its face, only a ball of fire with black, twisted horns curling up from his head. A gaping mouth that reminded Legna of the furnaces in her father's forge was slathered across the Demon's face, along with two matching eyes. His hands were made of red-hot coals and he had no legs. He seemed to just float across the air.*

*"What did you say?" the Lahti asked the Akull.*

*The Akull pointed at Legna. "I said I told you it would work."
The Demon yelped as the Lahti's heat began to melt the icicles on the
Akull's scaly hindquarters. "Not so close! You're going to hurt someone
with those incessant flames!"*

*"That's rather the point," the Lahti snickered. He jerked toward
the Akull, making him flinch. Legna began to get the vibe that the Ice
Demons and Fire Demons weren't too fond of each other.*

*"Stop that! I contacted the girl, just like Her Highness directed."*

*"Congratulations. Why tell me?"*

*"Because we had a bet, Blazing Butt. Pay up."*

*The Lahti grumbled as he pulled out five large amethysts
from unnoticeable pockets and threw them to the Akull. The Akull
frantically blew on the amethysts with his blizzard breath, freezing
them. Satisfied, the Akull dropped them into his mouth and swallowed
them. Legna curled her lip in disgust.*

*The Akull waved his hand, dismissing the Lahti. The Lahti
growled at the Akull and then stalked away. "Come on out, you
despicable girl. I know where you are. This is only a dream, so I can't
hurt you... for now."*

*Legna hesitated and then stepped out from behind the boulder.
"What do you want with me?" she asked, spitting out the words.*

*"Believe me, I don't like talking with you any more than you like
talking with me, but my queen ordered it of me. She wants to give you
an offer."*

*"Tell her she can take her offer and stuff it up—"*

*The Akull interrupted her. "Just hear me out, you creature. Korrtar
is giving you a way out of the quest you were forced into. She can save
your pitiful race and your friends."*

*Legna smirked. "Yeah? What's the catch?"*

*"You join her. You are already a powerful enemy. You would be
even more powerful as an ally."*

*"You can tell Korrtar she can ask all she wants. I still won't relent.
Get out of my dream."*

*The Akull shrugged and then said, "You'll be sorry. You all will."*

*"Yeah, right. And the next rabbit I see will fly. Get out of here."*

*The Demon dissipated, along with the scenery of Mëkator. Instead, she was sitting in the middle of Kaparan Meadow, blowing the fuzz off of a dandelion. She looked up and Garren stood above her, smiling.*

*He was just as wonderful as ever, with his brown hair and brown eyes.*

Wait, *Legna thought,* Garren does not have brown eyes.

*She looked at him suspiciously. "What are you?" she asked.*

*"It's me, Garren," he said. "Are you okay?"*

*Legna took a deep breath. It was just a dream, after all. "Yeah. Sure."*

*"Walk with me?" He offered her his hand, and she took it and pulled herself up.*

*They walked deeper into the meadow, and Legna began to feel uncomfortable.*

*"You don't have to keep doing this," Garren said.*

*"Excuse me?"*

*"This quest. Come back home. Abandon the mission. We can just migrate somewhere else. You and I can be together, no worries, no trouble. Submit to Korrtar. Let her have our land. We can just go elsewhere. Wouldn't that be easier?"*

*"Korrtar killed your father and now you want to cooperate with her?"*

*"Listen, Legna when those Orcs stabbed my father, I was angry. I—"*

*"Wait," Legna's eyebrows furrowed. "What did you just say?"*

*"I said I was angry."*

*"No, before that."*

*"I said that when those Orcs stabbed my father, I was angry."*

*Legna grinned in triumph. "Your father was shot. By an arrow. Not stabbed."*

*"So? What are little technicalities? I wasn't there when it happened."*

*"Oh, little technicalities can mean a lot. Such as, my Garren's eyes are blue, not brown." Legna began to study the imposter more*

*carefully. "Your skin tone isn't that dark. Your feet are too big. Your half smile goes the other way. Hey, I saw you change it!" Legna looked at the imposter with narrowed eyes. "Who are you? Tell the truth. Dreams don't just come to me."*

*Garren smirked and then his body morphed until Legna was staring at the face of a middle-aged woman, with blonde hair and cold eyes. "You're a smart girl."*

*"Korrtar?" Legna guessed, not surprised.*

*"Yes. So you discovered my little ruse. And still, you stand strong to your quest and your people. Impressive."*

*"I'm not so fooled by honeyed words,* Your Majesty. *I see right through your lies."*

*"Well, you will soon see that I would make a much better ally than an enemy."*

*"I wouldn't work for you if my life depended on it."*

*"Oh, but it does, dear." Korrtar got closer to her face, so their noses were almost touching. "I will break you," she whispered. "And you will serve me."*

*"I doubt it." Legna pulled her sword from her sheath.*

Suddenly, she was awake. She realized that she had drawn her sword in her sleep. She yawned and put the sword back in its place. She would duel Korrtar another time. She got out of her bed and had the feeling that someone had been in the room while she was sleeping. She looked around, and found everything as it was.

Peaceful paintings of nature covered the green walls. Little wooden sculptures of animals sat on the corners of a desk and on the windowsill. A bureau sat, with a pail of warm water and a silver brush. In the corner stood a wardrobe. It had been empty before, but Legna had the feeling that something had changed overnight. She opened the wardrobe and found a set of Elvish armor tailored to be her size and changed so a female could fit into it. The armor was completely silver, the mail sparkling like platinum. It was light but still tough. There was no matching helm, but Legna did not mind. She ran her fingers along it and marveled at the quality. She locked her door and dressed in the armor, then admired it in the mirror. It fit her perfectly.

She left the room, and wandered around the house until she found Feor, Bátor, and Traven sitting in the kitchen sipping tea.

"Well," Traven said. "Good morning, princess. We thought you'd never wake up."

"What time is it?" Legna asked.

"About ten o' clock. Slept well?" Feor asked.

"Not exactly." Legna explained her dreams to them.

Traven's expression hardened. "Korrtar used Garren to convince you?"

Legna blushed a little bit. "Yes. She didn't do a very good job of it, though."

Bátor rubbed his chin. "It's not natural for Demons to be able to contact anyone through dreams. That's very unusual even for Korrtar to do that. She usually doesn't speak to heroes directly. She must think you're a pretty big threat."

"Am I supposed to be flattered?" Legna asked.

"The more scared she is of you, the better. She won't think clearly that way," Feor said. The Elf was now wearing steel plate armor, with a huge broadsword almost as tall as Legna strapped to his back. She could tell that Feor meant business. It looked rather strange for an Elf dressed for battle to be sitting and drinking tea from a porcelain cup with flowers on it.

Legna pushed that thought far from her mind to avoid laughing. She nodded her agreement and then asked the question that had been at the back of mind since the previous day. "So, Feor…What special talents do you have, exactly?"

Feor smiled mischievously. "You ever heard the expression 'born in the shadows'?"

"Sure, I guess," Legna said.

"Well I can…emphasize that point. You want me to be invisible? Done. As long as there are shadows around, only the sharpest of eyes will see me. It cannot be fully explained until you witness it, but I can sneak into pretty much anywhere unnoticed."

"That will be helpful once we get into Mëkator," Traven said.

"I guess that's why my aunt wanted me to come. So I could prove my worth to the city and the other races by using my talent. I'm not exactly highly regarded around here. I'm more of a dark horse ... no pun intended."

Legna laughed. "Well you're welcome with us"—she turned to Bátor—"so you're really not coming along? You're going to stay here?"

Bátor nodded. "Yes, it's time to rest for a while. Maybe I'll try to learn, I don't know, pottery or something."

"Well, we'll miss you," Traven said.

"More than you know," Legna added. She changed the subject. "I visited the Elf, Absom yesterday. He explained about dragons. Now I understand why Aspör does what he does, where he comes from. He also told me about my necklace." She explained to them most of the information she acquired from Absom, leaving Vella the unicorn out of it. Her companions did not need to know everything.

Suddenly, the door to the outside slammed open. Legna stood from her chair in surprise, drawing her sword. A muddy shape tumbled into the door. It unfolded itself and Legna realized that it was really an Engjëllen, half-starved and obviously dying of thirst.

"What on earth?" Feor said. He drew his broadsword, and Legna was amazed that he was able to hold it up. "Explain this!" He said to the Engjëllen.

Legna ran to the man, who she recognized as one of the messengers from the Engjëllen court. "Please! water." The man gasped. Traven dashed outside to well while Legna held the man's head in her lap. Traven returned with a bucket full of water and began to pour it into a cup, but the man stopped him and motioned toward the bucket. Legna took it from Traven and handed it to the man. The man grabbed the bucket and gulped it down greedily, right from the bucket. Water ran down his cheeks, making clean trails down the dirt on his face. It drenched his shirt, but it was quite obvious that he did not care.

Once he had finally drunk his fill, he gasped for air and looked wearily at them.

"You are Legna?" he wheezed.

"Yes. Why? What are you doing here?"

"Sent … by king … Zemëroj … missing for days."

"Zemëroj still hasn't returned? I thought he had gone back to Engjëll!"

"So did I. He was gone in the morning. He couldn't have followed us all the way here," Bátor said.

A look of fear dawned in the man's eyes. He was finally beginning to catch his breath. "Where could he be, then?" he asked.

Legna shook her head. "I don't know, but first, what's your name?"

"Hayde. My name's Hayde. Please, may I eat something? I've gone a week with no food, no sleep, and hardly any water. I'm starting to doubt when people say we can survive without food or sleep. That was the closest to dying I've ever felt."

"It's the water deprivation," Feor said. He grabbed three biscuits off of the table and handed them to Hayde. "Here you go."

Hayde gobbled down the biscuits and slowly stood from his place on the floor. He stumbled, but Legna caught him.

"I never want to ride another horse again. Ever," he said.

"It's okay, you're done now," Legna coaxed. "You can rest here. I'm sure Queen Bella would be willing to send a messenger back in your place"—Legna looked at Feor—"she would be willing, correct?"

Feor shrugged. "If she's in a good mood, and you look pitiful enough, which you do, I think she would be willing to send someone to Engjëll."

Hayde nodded gratefully. "Thank you. I think I'll just … just …" He yawned and then dropped in Legna's arms, already asleep.

Legna began to struggle under his weight.

Traven hopped up. "I'll take him to a room." He took Hayde from Legna and stumbled along to a bed to drop Hayde into.

Legna felt a pain in her head. Suddenly, visions of Demons and death entered her mind. She dropped to one knee, clutching her forehead.

"Legna?" Bátor said.

She didn't respond. She watched as, in her mind, her battle with Korrtar played out. She didn't see much of the fight, only one clash of their swords. Korrtar brought down her scythe onto Legna's sword. The large black sword broke.

There was a catch in the vision, a pause that only lasted for a millisecond, but it was prominent enough for Legna to notice. After this, Legna watched in horror as she was stabbed by Korrtar, completely helpless without her sword.

The vision left her suddenly, and the headache subsided, but she could not erase the memories.

"Are you all right? What happened?" Feor asked. He helped Legna up.

Legna regained her composure and then said, "I had a vision."

"A vision?" Traven asked. He had returned from his escapade to find a bed for Hayde, and was now sitting in the chair next to Bátor.

"About our quest," Legna said. She described the vision to them.

Bátor shook his head in disbelief. "That can't be true! That sword is unbreakable! And you—you're supposed to be it! The one to finally complete what was started. To make all evil fall down."

Legna thought of where she had heard the last line of Bátor's statement. Suddenly, she remembered. "That song I heard in the market square the day this all started. That was about me?"

"That song is about the one who will slay Korrtar. According to what you just experienced, it doesn't look like you will be doing much slaying."

Silence followed.

"Well, this has been an eventful morning, but I do believe it's time for a quest to continue," Feor cut in. "We should leave."

Bátor narrowed his eyes, for a second, but they quickly softened again. "Go. But don't expect victory, or you will lose sorely." Bátor got up from his chair and strode out of the room.

"Well, isn't he optimistic," Feor said.

Legna waved the comment away. "He's just not a morning person. I think everything has him really worn out. He'll be fine." Legna sipped tea from a cup that was set on the table for her. "It is time to go, though. I'm afraid we've delayed too long."

Her friends nodded. They stood in unison and looked at Legna. Legna hesitated, not sure what to say. Then, she realized that they were waiting for her to lead them out. So she took a deep breath and walked to the door, placing her hand on the knob.

She pulled open the door and stepped into the sunshine. The city looked just as it did the day before. Except for one thing.

Near a fountain, in the middle of a circle of homes stood an old Elf, leading a white horse.

"Absom?" Legna called. The elf looked up with a start and then beckoned to her. She looked back at Feor. He shrugged. Legna turned and headed toward Absom.

"What are you doing out here?" Legna asked Absom as she approached. "I thought you didn't like to come out of your house."

"I will for special occasions, such as this," Absom responded. Legna looked at the white horse and realized that it was Vella, Absom's unicorn. She stroked the horse's neck. Her hair was as soft as silk.

"Is that a unicorn?" Traven asked, incredulously.

"Is that an Engjëllen?" Absom said, mocking Traven. "Of course it's a unicorn, boy. It doesn't take a genius such as myself to figure that out."

"Is he always like this?" Traven asked Legna.

Legna shrugged. "Most of the time."

"That's why people love me!" Absom exclaimed.

"More like why people avoid him," Feor muttered under his breath.

"I heard that! When I was your age, you were forced to eat four toads for disrespecting your elder!"

"What's so bad about eating toads?" Feor asked. Legna was unsure if he was joking or not.

"You'll get warts in your stomach. Now, don't get me ranting! I have a task I intend to complete!" He gave Feor a stare filled with daggers and then turned an affectionate gaze onto Legna. He handed her Vella's reigns.

"I am giving you Vella. She can't talk, like a dragon, but she will get you where you need to go."

"You're giving me your unicorn?" Legna asked.

"Sure. I never ride her. She needs exercise, which I cannot give her. She would love an adventure like this."

Legna gazed at Vella. She looked faster than her current horse. "All right, I'll take her. Thank you. Now, how do you ride a unicorn?"

Absom winked. "Why don't you find out?"

# LEARNING TO RIDE
## A UNICORN

Legna sat uneasily on Vella in front of Absom's house. The unicorn's girth was thinner than a horse's, so it took a lot more balance to stay on.

"Just pat her neck, and she'll go," Absom said. Legna did as instructed, and Vella trotted forward, eager to have exercise. Her gait was gentle, but fast. It had a nice rhythm that was easy to follow. Legna trotted around the house, enjoying herself. Then, she pushed her heels into Vella's sides and the unicorn began to canter. It was refreshing for both rider and horse to feel the wind in their hair.

Unable to resist the urge, Legna urged Vella on a little faster into a gallop. They sped up the slope behind Absom's house and out of sight, into the small woods that lie beyond. Legna became one with the unicorn, flowing and moving with Vella as if they were the same creature. Vella's horn glinted in the sunshine, throwing pearly sparkles around them, though Legna could hardly see, their speed was so great. Legna let out a cry of excitement and then urged Vella on faster. She whinnied in response and sped on happily, tossing her mane. Legna looked behind them and realized they had ridden off far into the forest, so she pulled lightly on Vella's reigns and turned them around.

Absom and her friends were small figures, but they were getting closer at a surprising speed. As they were just about to trample Feor, Vella skidded to a stop.

"So, how was it?" Absom asked.

Legna did not respond at first, too breathless to speak. Then, she said, "It was incredible."

"You went out of sight. How fast were you going?" Traven asked.

"I don't know, but it was faster than any other horse I've ridden. Absolutely exhilarating!" She patted Vella's neck, and Vella whinnied softly in response.

"Well, now you have a unicorn, an unbreakable sword, and a magical bow. Are we ready to set off again?" Traven asked.

Legna smiled, hopped off of Vella, and then seized his hand. "Whenever you're ready."

Traven started; his eyes becoming uncomfortable. Legna knew that was exactly what she had said to Garren so many weeks ago. But her old love life seemed unimportant now. She just felt so distant to her old life that she was ready to start new with everything.

"Well then, let's go!" Feor said. They made a strange procession through the city, the Elves watching them and marveling at Vella. They stopped at the huge cave granted to Aspör the night before.

"Come on, we're going!" Legna called in to him. He tumbled out, bickering with the caretaker assigned to his quarters. Legna noticed that Aspör was wearing armor similar to her own, sparkling and silver, and big enough for the dragon to be comfortable.

"No! Stop! I need no more food! I must leave now!" Aspör shouted.

The caretaker, an elderly Elf woman with silvery grey hair, shoved a spoonful of something brown at him. "Eat it! You need to grow up big, and strong! Eat!"

Aspör shut his mouth tightly and shook his head. "No! Get that vile food away from me, woman! I want no more of your infernal mush! It tastes like the mud off of an Orc's boot after tromping through the bogs in Mëkator!"

The Elf adopted a look of pure horror. "I cooked this especially for you! I don't care if you don't like it, you'll eat it and get your vitamins!"

"Did someone forget to tell me that my mother died and left you to take care of me? I hope the funeral was nice!" Aspör said sarcastically.

"Hey!" Legna shouted. "I have had a stressful morning already! We've got a long way to go and a lot more serious matters to worry about than who is whose mother! So just calm down!"

They both stared at her defiantly and then bowed their heads sheepishly. Glad to have some silence, Legna left the caretaker, thanking her for her hard work, and led the way to the stables, where their horses not only slept but were groomed, fed, and exercised. Legna told the Elves they could keep her white horse, then took the other two horses and headed toward the gate. They arrived and saw Ona, waiting for them.

"I suppose you are setting off now?" she asked.

"Yes, ma'am," Traven said. "Are you staying here?"

"Possibly. Or I will go back to my people and show them the way back to Windör."

"I hope you will be safe, Ona," Feor said.

"I would worry more about yourselves. Listen, once you cross the border of Mëkator, you cannot come back unless you win. Unless you defeat her. That's how her twisted magic works. Until you complete the quest you were sent to do, you are technically her prisoner. Be wary of danger. Even a team like you can't survive everything." Ona swept a stray hair from her face. "It only gets harder from here."

Then, Ona said words that helped Legna through many trials. "The only way to be a real hero is to sacrifice everything. But, that which you think you could never give up are the easiest to let go of, when facing life or death situations. It's those things, those *people*, which you take for granted that will be ripped away. Only then, when you survive, will you be a true hero."

Legna looked at Traven. Her best friend. Had she taken him for granted? Had she taken her mother, her father, or even Garren for granted? What would she be forced to give up? In front of her, the gates groaned open. The world looked so wide open, so frightening. So big. And Legna felt so vulnerable.

She tightened her grip on Vella's reigns and walked forward, her armor jingling softly. There was no celebration, no farewell from the elves. Only weary glances and skeptical stares accompanied their exit. Feor kept his head down, and almost seemed somewhat transparent, melting into the background. Legna wondered if that was his special talent. They turned once they crossed the gate. Queen Bella stood there, a hand raised in farewell, a grave expression gracing her ageless face. Legna responded in a likewise way, raising her hand and then turning slowly as the gate slammed shut behind them, depositing them once again into the wilderness.

# A KING'S ADVICE

Zemër licked his dry lips and took a tiny sip of what little water they had left. Neör had gone and retrieved the spirit jewels produced from the many Orcs slain on the battlefield and then melted the jewels down and thrown them into the water. Only three people knew how to really cleanse water: Zopporah, Läken's wife, an Elf named Katria, and a Nymph named Wisteria, not including Aryanis. Aryanis personally cleansed the Naïfonian's water.

The spirit jewels had not done much, but Korrtar's poison was held off long enough to scoop some drinkable water into a few canisters.

Zemër looked down at his hands and noticed how dry they looked. Skin crumbled when he touched anything. Soon, they would all turn to ash, and there was nothing they could do to fight it. Korrtar would win.

Their only hope rested in the hands of a small teenage girl—a girl who hardly looked strong enough to lift a sword. Zemër put his head in his hands. Where was their small race going? Were they meant to just slowly die off like this? His thoughts were ripped in two by a shout of surprise.

"There's someone coming, my lord! They are crawling to the front gate!" Yuler shouted.

"This is the last thing I need," Zemër mumbled. "Friend or foe?" He called.

"Friend, I believe. He looks like a Naïfonian! But he has no tail!"

A puzzled look came onto Zemër's face. "No tail? Greet him, but bring your weapons. Drawn."

Yuler nodded and ran off; the rest of the men following him. Zemër stood and drew his sword, stalking after them. If this was another trick from the Orcs…They arrived at the gate. A Naïfonian it was indeed, lying on the ground, gasping for water. With green scales and a reptilian face, the Naïfonian would be ferocious if he was not squirming on the ground, half dead.

"Water," Zemër barked to his men. Yorin, an old fellow with bulbous muscles, scurried off to scavenge what little water they had left. Zemër studied the man at his feet. Long, razor sharp claws protruded from his fingers and bare feet. Glistening white fangs graced his mouth, and a forked tongue rested in between. Green eyes speckled with red glistened under a brow of blue scales, revealing a spirit that worked hard but enjoyed mischief.

Yorin returned with a small canteen of water. He gave the lizard-man a drink of water.

"What is your name?" Zemër asked.

"Skeedro," the man hissed. "That's my name. Skeedro." Zemër smiled. The Naïfonians were known for their strange names.

"What are you doing here, Skeedro? It is not often that your kind deems it worthy to visit our fair city."

"Yes," Skeedro said, panting. "I come seeking solace for my people. Korrtar…she's taking our water…we are dying by the dozens! You must help us, I…where is everyone?"

Zemër stared at him in shock. "We sent our people to Naïfon to seek refuge from Korrtar. I thought she hadn't attacked your people yet. Did you send heroes?"

"We sent none of our warriors. We assumed that we could find solace in Engjëll, and you could send someone. I brought this as a gift from our most skilled blacksmith." He pulled a huge battle axe from his back and handed it to Zemër. "Its name is Maldak, demon slayer. Take it, although I see no reason now for me to linger. I might as well go back and die in honor with the rest of my people."

"Dying by the mercy of Korrtar is no honor, friend. Stay and fight with us. We have Orcs swarming, ready to attack. Won't you stay? We need more men."

"Yes, I can see this," Skeedro said as he glanced around at the meager amount of men the king currently commanded. "I will stay and fight."

Zemër smiled and gripped the handle of the axe. "Welcome to the family, friend." He used his free hand to pound Skeedro on the back and then he took the heavy axe and helped the man up.

"Läken," Zemër barked. "Take this man and get him cleaned up. Give him new clothes and armor. Läken nodded and hurried Skeedro off. Zemër studied Maldak. It had a blade on each side of the metal rod, each rounded and dark grey. Intricate designs were imprinted into the blunt of the blade, and the very top of the rod was carved into a man with a gaping mouth, open in a scream. It was an unnerving weapon, and it gave even Zemër the chills.

Zemër had no need for the weapon, but he did not want it to go to waste. He glanced over his shoulder and caught sight of Garren—tall, muscular and young, in need of a proper weapon. All he had was a simple, iron blade forged in a hurry by Läken.

"Garren, come here," Zemër said quietly. Garren approached him uncertainly.

"Is something wrong, my king?" He asked.

"No…I only noticed that I already have a weapon, and you are left with that pitiful needle you call a sword." Zemër tossed Garren Maldak, and he caught it with expert reflexes. "Take this, as a gift."

Garren stood, speechless. "But this was a gift from the Naïfonians. It would be a dishonor to them if you were to give it to me. I'm just a baker."

"No, you're a warrior. And you deserve a warrior's weapon."

"But..."

"Listen. All of the warriors you have looked up to are getting old. Just because we are immortal doesn't mean that we can't get tired sometimes. We need a younger generation to take over, and you are part of that generation. You have to stop discrediting yourself. You are one of us, not a child anymore."

"I..." Garren stared at the axe and then something changed in his expression. "Thank you, king." He unsheathed his sword and looked at it. "I guess this is farewell to you. I'll take it to Läken to use as scrap metal."

"There's a good lad. Something troubling you, Garren? You seem upset."

"Yes, it's just...It's nothing. I'm fine."

"Tell me." Zemër sat down on a log close to the fire and patted the place next to him.

Garren sat down next to him and his head dropped into his hands. "I miss her," he said; his voice muffled.

"Who?" Then Zemër realized. "Ah, you're in love."

Garren brought his head out of his hands and looked at Zemër. "To put it bluntly, yes. I just feel like she's too good for me now."

"Why?" Zemër asked.

"She's a hero. She's on an important quest, and I'm stuck here. I'm not outstanding or special. I'm just me."

"Typical love story. Trust me; I've been through it. So, who is this girl?" Zemër thought he already knew. What other female hero Garren's age was there other than Läken's daughter, Legna?

"It hardly matters. She's off saving the world with another man. Tragic, isn't it? I even offered to come along, and she refused to let me. I just feel like I'm desperately failing with her. All I want is for her to be ready to start a family. But she's reckless."

"It's always hard to know that the one who you think is supposed to love you is doing something that makes you feel small. But trust me, you'll get your chance. Once this is all over with, you'll prove yourself. You already have."

Garren looked at him. "How?"

"Well, you are a fierce warrior. You even have your own battle wound! You are very attractive to young women, you have a charming personality. What's not to love?"

"We just have such a different view on life. I want simplicity, not too much excitement, but all she wants is adventure."

"She's special, I'll give you that. That adventurous spirit is normal in Engjëllens and quite encouraged. It will calm down in a few years, once she sees what adventure is truly like."

"I never get to spend time with her now."

"That's not your fault. You can't follow her to Mëkator now; she's probably already in the Elvish Isles. There's nothing you can do but wait. Take a king's advice. I told you the story about my wife. It took me a long time to get up the courage to talk to her. I thought it was no good. But then, I realized that she was as scared to talk to me as I was of talking to her. The best love is one that takes work."

"This just feels like too much work."

"If it feels like too much work, you must not really love her! If everything was easy, there wouldn't be any heroes or warriors. You have to be a man and tell her straight up when she comes back how you feel! And if she doesn't feel the same way, which I don't find possible, there are plenty of other beautiful girls in Engjëll! You'll find someone."

"But there's no one like her," Garren murmured; his eyes drifting out to the horizon. The day was fading slowly, and amber light spilled delicately from the puffy clouds.

"Every girl is unique. But some are similar. Everything will be all right, I promise."

"Every girl is unique but it seems like every girl is ready to marry except the one I'm in love with." Horns sounded, interrupting him.

"Here we go again," Zemër muttered. "We will continue this discussion later. What do you see, Yuler?" Zemër asked his sentry.

"Three Ranguns, my lord! And six trolls!" Yuler yelled.

"Can we have no rest? Prepare for battle! Show them absolutely no mercy!" Zemër bellowed. He slapped Garren on the shoulder and stood from his log. "Let's go fight to take your mind off this girl."

Garren nodded slightly and stood along with the king. "Let's go."

# A GAME OF DARKNESS

"Here we go again," Traven said and looked over at Feor. "Which way is south?" Feor pointed to their right without the direction of a compass or a map. Legna was impressed at the Elf's sense of direction, along with a many other things. He was a little bit odd but still had all the strength of an Elf.

They rode south, toward a thin forest filled with small hills and valleys. No one spoke, only thoughts passed through them. Aspör flew above them, sometimes disappearing into the clouds.

"Well," Legna said, when they had come into a cozy-looking clearing. "This has been quite the productive day. I believe we covered about twenty miles. We can stop here." Traven dropped down from his horse gracefully and Feor stretched his arms.

"I can keep going for a while yet," Feor said. "We don't need to stop."

"Maybe it's different with Elves, but Engjëllens perform better when we aren't exhausted. We camp here," Traven said. Feor shrugged and dismounted his horse also.

"Hey," Feor said to Legna as she slid off of Vella. "You want to fight?"

"Excuse me?" Legna asked, surprised.

"Do you want to spar? To train?"

"Oh. Sure." They were in a clearing surrounded by a ring of trees. Feor made Legna and Traven stand back to back in the middle of the ring, weapons drawn. Then, he disappeared into the forest.

Legna jumped as she heard Feor's voice somewhere in the forest. "Where am I?" Legna surveyed the tree line but could see nothing but shadows.

"Feor?" Traven called. He shifted nervously and held his sword a little higher. Legna fingered the arrows in her quiver.

Suddenly, she felt a cold blade on her neck. "I win," a voice whispered. She turned to see no one there, only empty space. The blade on her neck was gone, and so was Feor.

"Look for movement, not for shape. The leaf that you think is falling from the trees may be me. Or a moth fluttering its wings. Watch for me," Feor's voice came again, seemingly from all angles.

Legna scanned the forest again, with a new perspective. She looked for movement, as Feor had said, and she was successful. She saw movement, there in a tree. But as soon as she caught it, it was gone. She found him many more times, but could never manage to pinpoint where he was exactly. After a long time, much longer than the first round, Legna glanced at Traven to see a large blade on his neck and a dark figure standing behind him. Legna took her chance and lunged at Feor viciously. Feor brought his sword up just in time to catch Legna's violent blow and they both set to work, slashing, stabbing, and rolling to avoid each other.

Eventually, Traven joined the fight and Legna had to concentrate on fighting both of them at once, without killing either one. Soon, they seemed to gang up on her, and she held her ground, twirling in a whirlwind of fury and ferocity. At one point, Legna twisted Feor's sword right from his hands and tried to strike him down, but Feor pulled two long knives from his sleeves just in time to block her blow. She could sense Traven coming up behind her, so she whirled quickly to come almost nose to nose with him, barely missing his neck.

"Hey!" Traven exclaimed. "Be careful! This isn't an actual battle, you know!"

"Sorry!" Legna responded apologetically. "I didn't mean to!" She accompanied this with three swift blows to his sword, resulting in his disarming and defeat. She turned and smiled at Feor. "One down."

"One to go," Feor responded and slashed at her with his knives. She knocked them aside and rolled between Feor's legs. As soon as she unfolded, she turned to press the point of her sword to his back, but he had already turned, knives ready. He brought them down upon her in a flash of metal and she barely brought her sword up in time to meet block his slash. Feor smiled, adrenaline rushing through his tan face. He faked to the right and then dove to where his sword lay, picking it up and performing a full front flip at the same time.

"All right, show off," Legna mumbled. "You want to get fancy?" She copied him, swiftly performing three front flips until they were facing each other again. From here, their fight turned into a performance of acrobatics. They rolled, flipped, and tumbled, all the while avoiding each other's blades and attempting to catch the other off guard. Traven sat by and watched in amazement, occasionally letting out a yell of warning.

At one point, when neither felt they could continue, Legna finally caught Feor off balance on his landing, ripped the sword from his hand with a swift kick to the hilt, and spun around to rest her blade on his neck.

Feor smiled. "All right, you win!" He strode over to where his sword lay and sheathed it. "You're pretty good. Where did you learn all that?"

Legna sheathed her sword with a huff. "My father has been teaching me since I was able to hold a sword."

"He taught you well. A lot of Elves couldn't have fought with that level of skill…and style, for that matter."

"You weren't so bad yourself. Who taught you?" Legna asked. She wiped the sweat that had begun to bead up on her forehead.

"My uncle. He was a very skilled acrobat and warrior and obviously our king. He passed away when I was twenty. It was a very hard time."

"I'm sorry," Traven said.

"It's all right. He's in a better place now."

"How old are you, exactly, Feor? The king passed away before we were born," Legna said. She was wrapping a small gash she had received on her arm from her skirmish with Feor.

"Almost one hundred, exactly."

Legna raised her eyebrows in surprise. "You look as young as us."

"Elves can choose whether we want to age or not. People like Absom, who are very old and want everyone to remember it, choose to age. I, on the other hand, prefer to look twenty for the rest of my life. Maybe, when I get older, I will want to look like an elder Elf, but for right now, I prefer to keep young muscles and a young face."

"Elves can do a lot of things we can't do," Traven said softly.

"Excuse me? Like what?" Feor asked, cocking his head.

"Well, you can choose not to age. You are natural acrobats, you can talk to animals. I saw someone swallow a ball of fire, for goodness sake. Is there anything you can't do?"

"Eat meat," Feor said. "That's what we can't do that you can. We don't envy you for it, either. The animals are our friends; our family, even. Eating them would be like cannibalism."

Legna felt a little bit queasy. She had been eating meat her whole life. Was she a cannibal?

Feor must have seen the sickened look on her face because he laughed and said, "Don't worry; it's only the Elves that are that close to animals. You are allowed to eat meat. I won't blame you for it. Just do not ask me to eat it."

Just then, Aspör swooped down from the sky; the night sky dark against his bright blue wings, his steel mail sparkling in the moonlight. He was carrying a deer in his jaws, and when he had landed he gently placed it in front of Legna.

"Figured you could use some meat," Aspör said. "I didn't know what kind Feor liked, so I just chose venison. Everyone likes venison."

They stared at him in silence and then each burst into laughter. Aspör stood, pawing at the ground as the three laughed. Eventually, he had had enough of the confusion. "What is so funny?" he demanded.

And they laughed again.

# EDIAK, THE DEFILER

L egna pulled off her overcoat, sweating and laid it on Vella's hindquarters. The unicorn whinnied and shook her mane, obviously hot. As they neared the southern Elvish villages, the air had become more humid and the plants more tropical. Legna's body was made to live in the cooler, milder climate of her northern home. They had passed a few villages in the days they had been traveling but had not stopped in any as they were aware of their lack of time. A few sentries had spotted them and watched inquisitively as Feor melted into the background and left Traven and Legna in plain sight. It was quite obvious by now that Feor was not a people person.

As for her relationship with Feor, they had rapidly become good friends, sparring every night and talking together whenever they could. Feor had a deep intelligence that Legna did not expect. At one point, she had finally vented her feelings about Traven and Garren and her old life.

"So who would you choose now?" Feor had asked. Legna had just told him about her confused emotions toward Traven, and Garren, who was waiting at home for her.

"I don't know!" She had said. "Just a few weeks ago, I would have easily chosen Garren. But now...I just don't know. Traven has saved my life a few times; we have been more than a sufficient team, sticking together. He would follow me right into one of Korrtar's traps if I asked him. But so would Garren. They are both wonderful, but…it's just too confusing."

"Yes, I remember when I was as young as you…I was shy. My aunt was worried about me. I spent so much time reading by myself or sitting in the shadows of trees that one day, I kind of just became part of the shadows. But now, I see how vital that was. If not for my attitude at that age, I would never have lived through many predicaments that I got myself into. Once I got a little older, I became more outspoken, but I preferred to be alone. And alone I have been for one hundred years." He looked at Legna with his careful, probing gaze and the conversation ended there.

Their conversations always left Legna with something to think about, a quality that she did not see in most people.

Her friendship with Traven had become more and more tenuous as she began to see his more attractive qualities. The quest had made him more muscular, and he had a tired, knowing look in his eyes that captivated her. After that conversation, though, she had decided to harden herself to those feelings. She was doing something important, and her emotions could not get in the way of it.

She looked around her now and felt uncomfortable in the strange landscape. They had not had any trouble from Demons or Orcs since Mär-Linna, and she was becoming suspicious. Suspicious that something far more terrible than they had faced before was in store.

They were on the east coast of the Elvish Isle, and she could hear the waves of the Eben Sea. Far away, the rushing sounds were soft yet prominent in the silence surrounding them. Sand covered the ground, white as a summer cloud. Little tufts of dry, brown grass puffed up out of the sand. The majestic oaks and elms had slowly melted away to huge palm trees, with leaves that shaded them like umbrellas. Rocks littered the sand in all places, charcoal black and smoky grey.

Unused to the vulnerable openness of the beaches, Legna felt exposed. They rotated watches at night, but there was still no cover, nothing to guard their backs from approaching predators. *Nothing to hide the predators either*, Legna thought. That was encouraging.

Legna detected a flapping noise behind her, but thought nothing of it, considering Aspör was up in the sky, following them. A sudden burst of air behind them signified the landing of a dragon. Legna turned, but the dragon she saw was not Aspör. This dragon was larger, a dim green color like sewage, with many pink scars lining his legs and stomach. It roared and spat blue fire to the side, lighting a palm tree on fire.

Legna rolled to the side just in time to avoid a fireball aimed at her. She felt the fire sear her right arm, and she looked down, cringing. A long, red mark was on her forearm, and it burned badly. She drew her sword weakly, but the dragon knocked it from her wounded arm with his front foot. He growled loudly with a sound like crackling thunder. The waves roared in unison. Rain began to fall. Legna fell over wearily as the dragon swung his head, hitting her squarely in the back.

"Legna!" Traven cried. He dove at the dragon and stabbed its eye. The dragon roared again and shook him off, but he seemed very focused on Legna. Feor ran right up the dragon's tail and onto his head, attempting to find a kink in the mottled green armor. He was easily thrown off, and the dragon enclosed his claws on Legna's body. She weakly fought his squeezing talons, but to no avail. He carried her off into the dark sky and consciousness left her.

When she woke, she was lying on the ground on her side with her arms and legs tied. Her bow was gone as was her sword and her armor was stripped from her. She lay in her original white shirt and brown trousers. Her necklace was also missing from its place on her neck. From her view on the ground, she could see a bonfire and about thirty Orcs gathered around the dragon that had attacked her and her friends. She listened, careful not to move so as not to alert them to her consciousness.

"Lord Ediak!" A voice squeaked. It sounded like an Orc runt. "Is she really it? The hero who denied the Queen? I knew you would be the one to get her! And so easily, too! You truly are magnificent, truly incredi—" The voice stopped short as Legna watched the dragon, Ediak, curl his tail around the runt-Orc's neck and lifted him from the ground.

"Flattery will get you nowhere, you little slug. I will not forget that you were among those who let the Nymphs go." He tightened his grip, and the runt stopped struggling and went slack.

*Is this really what they do? Murder each other?* Legna thought. She kept quiet and continued to listen.

"Dinner, my servants," Ediak chuckled. The Orcs flocked hungrily around the dead runt and Legna closed her eyes as the limp body was tied to a spit and set above the fire.

"Can the girl be next?" An Orc asked.

"No!" Ediak exclaimed. "After the Queen gets her hands on that nymph, then you can eat her."

The Orcs groaned in disappointment. They wanted to eat her! Legna took a close look at Ediak and realized that something was very familiar about him. She could not place what.

Ediak rose from his position curled up on the ground and stalked toward Legna. She tried to keep herself calm, but could not stop from shivering slightly.

"She's awake!" He called to his horde of Orcs. "Let the fun begin." He scooped her up in his tail, much like he had the runt, and held her by the waist. Then he set her in a sitting position and kept a hold on her head, forcing her to look directly at him.

"So you are the one my Queen has been searching for so frantically? You don't look like much." He turned her head to the side to examine her. "Leave us!" He ordered his Orcs. They ambled away from the fire without an argument, into the darkness. Legna sat and watched as another fire went up far into the distance. She was alone with the dragon.

Ediak let go of her head and plodded along in front of her, back and forth. It was a long time before he said, "You have given my queen a lot of trouble. Did you know that?"

Legna stared at him in anger before managing to say, "I know it, and I'm proud."

Ediak smiled coldly at Legna. "You won't be so smug when she gets her hands on you." He brought his huge head closer to her. "First, she rips off each of your fingers. If you don't squeal, she goes for the toes, too. Then the arms. Usually, you break by then. But you seem especially strong of will, so I will continue. After that, she burns off your legs, nice and slow-like. And she keeps you alive long enough after that so she can catch your friends and family and murder them painfully while you are forced to watch and know that *you* are the cause of their suffering. How proud do you feel now, worm?" His voice had risen to a shout. "So proud you will kill those closest to you? Talk to me about pride if you still have the will to live after that."

Legna closed her eyes as his hot breath curled around her. She was afraid of this beast, more than anything else she had encountered. But she fought her desire to faint and continued the conversation, "At one point, I would have believed you. I would have given up in fear of my friends' deaths. But now I realize that if I did, to save them, I would be dead to them already. No, they know where I stand. And they stand with me. If I gave myself to you, they would die anyway, and it would be by my hand. I would rather die through torture and end up in Ederra than join you and burn in Mëkator. So go ahead and take me to Korrtar. I am not afraid of her."

Ediak nodded his head thoughtfully. "These words seem like wise, noble words to the weak-minded. But I am not so easily fooled. I know where life lies and where death creeps. Where danger wreaks havoc and where peace lies. You are foolish; to believe your friends care enough about you to want to die like that."

"We will see who is foolish when you are burning in the fires of your own existence," Legna said softly. "Your mind is troubled, isn't it? There is something, some*one* you are trying to avenge. Who?"

Ediak's eyes widened, and for a second, they changed. They became pleading, open, and scared. Then, the moment passed and they hardened again. He slammed his front foot on the ground, making it into a fist. "Don't try your mind games on me, Glowston! You are mine now, and soon you will be hers. And I will laugh when you die."

"Such pain," Legna continued. "Why are you in Zerúa anyway? Shouldn't you be in Pâne, with your people?"

"Well…" The look in his eyes came again, and this time, it stayed. "I guess it doesn't matter, if you're going to die anyway. I used to live in Pâne, with my kinsmen. I learned one day from my mother and father of an egg in the nest that was to become my brother. I was excited, nervous, apprehensive, everything a future older brother could feel. He hatched, I bonded with him, and it was clockwork. Then…that king of yours came. He came and took my brother away. My family didn't protest. No one did. They *celebrated*. They celebrated that he was gone." Ediak looked at Legna as a person for the first time. Suddenly, his eyes hardened again and acquired their cold glare. "But now I have a home with Korrtar. And she has promised me revenge."

Legna looked at him even more closely than before. She knew he looked familiar, but she could not place why. Then it hit her like an arrow. *He looks like…* her thoughts were interrupted by a movement, which she caught barely in the corner of her eye. Her thoughts instantly jumped to Feor. She dared not look in his direction in fear of giving him away, so she continued talking.

"Your brother was chosen to be a hero," Legna said. "You don't need to have revenge on us. I believe he is still alive."

"I know he is still alive, maggot!" Ediak snarled. "I've come to take him back. Back to Pâne."

"They won't accept you back in Pâne. Look at the destruction you have already caused." She wiggled her foot slightly and found that the dagger she had stuffed in her boot before they had left Engjëll was still there.

Ediak sneered at her. "I'm proud of the destruction. I am truly an original. I do my work well."

"You certainly are something different." Legna said. She watched as the background behind Ediak slightly shifted and changed. She caught a glimpse of red hair. Traven. Ediak had his back to them. She shivered in spite of herself, nervous for what might happen.

"Are you cold, Glowston?" Ediak asked; his voice changing to a kinder tone, relatable and less evil. Legna wondered why these changes were happening.

"A little bit." An idea came to her. "I probably wouldn't be if I had my armor on." She didn't expect it to work, but to her surprise, Ediak nodded.

"Then I won't have to hear you complain through the night. Very well, but just for right now." The change in his voice happened again. It switched back to the dragon that almost killed her, that described her torture. Instead of the dragon that wanted his little brother back. "Turn so I can cut your bonds, worm."

She did as she was told, and he cut the bonds on her hands and ankles. She flexed her wrists and winced at the chaffing the ropes had given her. Her arm was feeling better, and as she examined it, she realized that Ediak must have treated it. *Who am I dealing with?* she asked herself. He seemed like he wanted to kill her, but he had healed her wound and cut her bonds.

Ediak retrieved her armor from a pile close to the fire, where Legna spotted her sword and bow. He threw the armor toward her, and she slipped into it. She discreetly pulled the knife from her boot and pressed it against her palm, hiding it from view.

Ediak turned to face her and looked her over. She caught another movement. It was Feor. She had become good at seeing him even when he was invisible, from the shifting of the shadows. Ediak turned away again, and she focused her gaze on Feor. He briefly became visible and pointed toward Ediak, and then toward his own eye. He disappeared again, lost to the shadows.

Legna thought she knew what Feor meant, but she was not sure if she could execute it. *Oh well,* she thought. *I'm going to die soon anyway.* As soon as Ediak turned his head in her direction she flipped the knife into the air, caught it, and threw it at the dragon. It planted itself firmly in Ediak's eye. The dragon stumbled backwards and Traven leapt from the bushes, landing on Ediak's back and savagely severing the dragon's leg with his sword. Feor attacked also; his broadsword looking as if floating by itself before Feor fully let go of his invisibility and performed a backflip, landing on Ediak's thrashing tail and slashing upward, stilling the wriggling tail. It fell to the ground in a sickening heap and Ediak bellowed in pain.

Legna dashed to the pile of weapons that Ediak had seemingly collected. She scavenged for her bow and found it just in time to loose an arrow into Ediak's leg, creating an explosion that singed the ligament and rendered it helpless.

Ediak threw Feor and Traven off his back, each landing motionless far away from the fight.

A looming, black mass of muscle sped down from the sky, slamming into Ediak and tumbling around. A cloud of teeth and claws eventually reformed into the disheartening image of Ediak on top of the squirming figure, Aspör. Ediak growled maliciously in Aspör's face but stopped suddenly, his lips curling in an uncertain expression and his eyes growing confused.

Ediak shook his head slightly, as if just coming out of a deep sleep. "Brother?" He muttered. "My brother?"

Aspör took the opportunity to flip over and pin Ediak to the ground; his claws digging shallowly into Ediak's soft chest.

"I am no kin of yours. How dare you call me that after what you have done to defile our race? After you have betrayed us and disgraced our kind." He pressed his claws deeper in, blood running down Ediak's belly. "You make me sick. Why do you call me this insult? Brother?" He spat; the spit boiling in an unappetizing muck from the flames hidden at the back of his throat.

Ediak's eyes bugged in pain as Aspör pushed harder on his chest. "Please!" He gasped. "Let me explain! Don't kill me! You are my brother! I came looking for you!"

Aspör's lip curled in disgust. Then, after looking down at the bigger dragon, something softened in Aspör's eyes. "Ediak? Big brother?" His claws loosened. Ediak's look changed to one of malice, so quickly it startled Legna. She had heard of beings with multiple personalities, those who switched back and forth between two people hiding in them, screaming to be let out. She began to wonder if this was what Ediak struggled with.

Ediak threw Aspör off of him and lunged at Legna, bounding as fast as he could with his useless leg. His eyes gleamed greedily. Legna pulled one arrow from her quiver and calmly fired it into his stomach as he leapt at her and…nothing happened. The arrow stuck but created no explosion, as it had countless times before. The dragon continued his terrifying sprint toward her.

"Aspör!" Traven screamed. He was tumbling like a drunken man back to the fight. The violent trip he had been given had obviously resulted in a head injury.

Feor was in no better condition. He stumbled from the other direction; his leg bleeding profusely. "Aspör! Go! Save her! What are you doing?" he shouted. He lifted his sword and limped toward Ediak, eventually kneeling on the ground and throwing the sword with expert precision into Ediak's good front leg. Still the dragon did not stop in his blind rage.

Aspör stood in shock, watching Ediak lumber toward Legna. Legna looked over, helplessly begging for aid with her eyes. She projected her feelings of fear to Aspör, although she knew he could not feel them. She stared forward wordlessly, waiting for the huge dragon to come kill her. Her weapon was useless, her friends were half dead, and her dragon had left her alone. She closed her eyes, accepting her fate. The thundering of feet got closer, reverberating in her ears and shaking her very soul.

She waited for him to take her, for her mission to be over, but he never came. Instead, the footfall stopped. The snarls stopped. She heard nothing but dead silence. She opened her eyes, figuring she was dead, but she still stood in the same place, staring at the bonfire.

A sickening noise drew her attention to the left and she watched as Aspör tore his evil brother to pieces, with a look of sorrow and eyes of stone. He stomped on where Legna's arrow had planted itself and the arrow exploded, incinerating the near-dead Ediak and reducing him to nothing but a pile of ashes. The flames billowed around Aspör, but none touched him. They gave him reasonable space to calmly walk from the debris toward Legna.

Legna stood, still in shock. The dragon licked her face and nudged her with his nose.

"You are my family. Not him," he said quietly to her.

She smiled. "You will always be part of my family, Aspör. I love you." Aspör grunted and nuzzled Legna again. She placed her hand on his nose and glanced around her.

The flames around Ediak's carcass had quickly extinguished themselves and the dragon that had been so massive before was there, an empty skeleton. The bones were black, and Legna was unsure if the color was from the flames or just the dragon's equally black heart. Either way, Ediak, the betrayer, was dead.

Legna noticed Vella, her poor horse, cantering bravely near the Orcish camp farther in the distance. She ran her deadly horn through them and kicked them back, but they had seen the explosion, and they wanted to know what was going on.

"This isn't over yet!" Traven called to them, pulling himself to his feet once again and stumbling to Legna, landing with his arms around her neck, his face just inches from hers. She stared into his green eyes, unblinking. "None of this is," he said. And he hugged her, picking her up and spinning her around in happiness. "But I'm just happy you're alive." Feor approached and clapped a hand on Traven's shoulder.

"Well that was fun! I'm beginning to like you guys! Now let's go almost get killed again, shall we?" He motioned to the Orc camp, where Vella was desperately outnumbered. Feor grinned at both of them and started to his sword, still stuck in Ediak's carcass. Legna grabbed his arm and pulled him back, wary of the wound on his leg.

"Not so fast, Feor. You're injured," she said, quickly ripping off a section of her sleeve and handing it to Feor. "Wrap that up and stay here until it stops bleeding."

"But that could take an hour! I want to fight! I've fought with much worse wounds."

"I won't lose you over this. You are to stay here. And considering your aunt said you are under my command…I *order you* to stay here."

Traven smiled apologetically. "You really should stay here, Feor. Leg wounds are serious."

Feor gave Traven a sarcastic look. "Thanks for standing up for your fellow man, Trav. I know how hard it is to resist the female charms."

Legna turned to Traven. "I want you to stay too."

"What?" Traven sputtered. "Why me?" As if in response, he clutched his head and swayed uneasily.

"Because you can't walk straight. Aspör and I can handle this. If things get out of hand, Feor, I give you permission to come help. But only if it's absolutely necessary."

"All right, Your Highness," Feor mumbled.

Traven rolled his eyes at Feor's sarcasm and gave her another hug. "Stay safe. I can't lose you again."

"I will." She peered into his eyes again. "I was born for this." She knocked an arrow and smiled mischievously at them. She and Aspör set off to the camp. She released the arrow, creating an explosion that, to her satisfaction, caused many Orcish screams. She dashed past Ediak's pile of weapons once more and plucked her sword out, swinging it happily and slinging her bow across her back. Aspör took off into the sky.

Legna rolled headfirst into the encampment, thrusting her sword right into an Orc's stomach. He screeched with a horrifying crescendo then toppled to the ground. All weapons were focused on her, but her adrenaline was pumping and showed no signs of stopping. She watched as Vella galloped gratefully away, into the darkness, seemingly in the direction of Mär-Linna.

She stabbed an Orc maliciously in the chest giving her sword a painful twist before extricating it from his body. He toppled forward in a mass and Legna leapt to the side, narrowly missing being buried by the Orc's bulk. As she sidestepped, she pulled her sword smoothly from the Orc and thrust it behind her into an Orc she had been able to sense coming for several seconds. The blade planted itself firmly into the monster's forehead. The Orc fell backward, taking her sword with him.

She nodded in acceptance to her small setback and pulled her bow from her back, along with an arrow. She drew the bowstring, shot the leader of a row of Orcs, and they each combusted in a neat line. She turned face-to-face with an ugly Orc, dark green with black tusks. He snorted heavily; his acrid breath making no effect on Legna's battle rage. She calmly raised her bow, aimed, and fired a sparkling arrow right through his eye. She dove away as he erupted into flames, destroying four other Orcs with him, each who tried to put out the flames but failed.

She caught a glimpse of something in the sky and got an idea. She aimed her bow at it, confusing the Orcs and making most of them turn to see what she was trying to kill next. As they were distracted, she tilted her bow down and shot four of them easily, each in different spots, and the crowd of Orcs burst into bright flames.

Aspör sped down from the sky and ripped the remaining Orcs from the ground, dropping them from high in the air into the slowly dying flames. Legna looked around her and the battle rage faded. All the Orcs were dead and she still wanted to kill something. A large bird flew overhead and without a thought she took aim and then stopped herself. Malin had told her to kill nothing but evil with it, so she pushed down the bloodlust and replaced her bow to its place on her back.

She shook herself, trying to get rid of her feelings of fault and continued back through the wreckage, pulling her sword gracefully from where she left it in the body of an Orc without pause. She strode back to where her companions were sitting and raised her eyebrow at Feor.

"I wouldn't have lost my sword, hotshot. But you did okay," Feor said in a subtly approving manner. Legna smiled, knowing this was the closest to praise the Elf would give. She planned to take it and run with it.

"How's your leg?" Legna asked, kneeling down to examine the wound.

"It stopped bleeding," Feor said, wincing as Traven helped Legna unwrap the bandages.

"But it still hurts, am I right? You fractured the bone, Feor," Traven said as he inspected the leg.

"That's ridiculous," Feor said. "I'm just fine." He tried to stand, but instantly fell again. "All right. I'm not fine. You win. Can you do anything about it?"

"It's going to set us back a few days. I can splint it with some wood but it will take at least four days to be able to even limp on it again," Traven said. Legna and Feor looked at him, wondering where he learned this from.

Traven smiled. "The Elvish healer liked to talk a lot," he explained. Legna stared at him for a moment longer and then let the matter drop. She looked back at Feor and thought about the best thing to do. Then, she remembered the vials the king had given them. She rummaged in her pack for a few minutes and brought out the vial, the glass glinting in the moonlight.

"Here, Feor. It will stop the pain." She let one drop out of the vial onto his wound, and it instantly lost some of its redness. "You still shouldn't walk, but it won't take as long to heal."

She thought about what they should do with their injured companion. They simply could not stop for a few days' time. They were late as it was and another setback could cost them the entire mission. She felt a sense of hopelessness close in on her as she realized the height of the mountain she was about to climb.

*What am I doing here?* she thought to herself. She stared intently at Feor's wound, wondering how she would ever get herself out of this. Suddenly, a thought came to her. It was so simple and easy that she wondered why she did not think of it at first.

"Aspör?" she called to the dragon. "Would you be able to carry Feor for a while?"

"I could carry all three of you! That puny Elf is nothing to me!" Aspör said proudly.

"You better watch who you call puny, you overgrown gecko," Feor growled.

"Puny. You are all puny compared to me."

"You're puny compared to Ediak," Traven pointed out.

"You have a point there, Trav. Only tough 'til your big brother comes and shows you up," Feor said.

"That *defiler* was not my brother!" Aspör roared.

"Well then why did you almost let him kill Legna? If you have such disdain for him, why did you not kill him when you could?" Traven shouted. "We almost lost her! All because of you!"

"It's fine Traven, I'm fine now. Really, don't blame Aspör," Legna said, taking Traven's hands in hers and turning his face toward her. "Wouldn't you hesitate to kill your own brother?"

Traven stared into her eyes for a minute and then turned away, shaking his head. "I have no brother. I have no father. My mother is hardly there at all." He turned back to her. "The only one I have is you. So no, I wouldn't hesitate. Because quite honestly, you're everything to me."

Legna stood perfectly still as Traven calmly helped Feor to his feet and onto Aspör's back, who took off with the Elf without comment or complaint, glad to leave the tension brewing between the two Engjëllens.

Legna stayed where she was while Traven went through the pile of weapons Ediak had collected and, seeing as he did not seem to want to talk, she set off to try to find Vella. But, it was hopeless. The unicorn had returned to her master in Mär-Linna. And Legna had never felt so alone.

# MËKATOR

It was three long days of constant walking before they finally reached their destination. Feor's leg had healed, with a little more treatment from the king's medicine, so he stopped riding Aspör and took his place walking with Traven and Legna. They had turned their horses back toward Mär-Lïnna as soon as they saw Mëkator's border. The creatures did not deserve such horrors.

Legna inhaled sharply as she approached the border between the Elvish Isles and Mëkator. The tropical, sunny look of the land abruptly died away and became black, dead, and cold. The ground changed from sand to black stone, plants ceased to exist. Even the sky darkened where the border lay, looking like a sword had cut straight through the clouds and turned half of them grey. A shadow lay across the land in front of them, one of oppression and pain and sick happiness.

This was their destination. That did not make it any more desirable to finally be there. They stood still, staring down at the blatant border. Legna placed one foot cautiously onto the black, sooty earth of Mëkator. She stayed this way, one foot on the Isles, the last connection to her home, and one foot on this new, strange land before her, where her destiny awaited. She took a deep breath, thought once more of home, and let go of her past life completely. And suddenly, her feet were carrying her completely across the border into the open, into the belly of the beast. Her friends loyally followed.

She saw something in the distance. It was tall, and red, and in their path. As she neared, she felt her heart slowly sink. It was a huge gate, well-guarded and impenetrable. A dozen Demons of all sorts patrolled the outside. She crept closer and rolled behind a large rock, contemplating her next move. Traven pressed close to her and whispered "Look," pointing toward the gate.

She watched, and her eye caught movement that she had trained herself to see. Feor was on the move. She smiled as she watched the liquid figure slip in between two Demons and stab both in the back without a sound. As the two Demons fell, he slipped away, to the rock Legna and Traven crouched behind.

"Why didn't you—" Legna began.

"Just watch," Feor murmured, interrupting her. She focused her attention back on the gate. The Demons were checking the bodies in a confused frenzy, some searching the area while others stood, nervously glancing from side to side.

Feor vanished before Legna's eyes, and she watched the transparent Elf pick up a stone and throw it an impressive five hundred yards away. The Demons heard the thump and saw the little cloud of dust rise and immediately stormed after the assassin facade.

"Quickly! Go!" Traven hissed. They dashed to the gate. Feor reached first, and began pushing on it with all his strength. Legna and Traven joined him and the gate began to pry open. The Demons were still occupied, having dashed into the Elvish Isles to pursue their attacker. They pushed for two minutes, and finally, with a final desperate attempt, Legna threw her entire body weight against the door. The gate creaked vehemently and swung open, revealing the city they had waited for so long to reach. This was the final stretch of their journey.

Legna exhaled a tired sigh and whispered, "Finally."

There seemed to be no one around. The city was huge and deathly quiet. Unnatural trees with black bark and purple leaves curled like wisteria against buildings and in town squares. They cast eerie shadows in the waning light of dusk. The buildings were seamless, not a crack or crevice in sight. As opposed to the brick or wooden foundations of Engjëllen structures, these buildings seemed to be made entirely out of black stone. The city stretched on, alleys curving off to the side occasionally. The three companions stole through the city carefully, staying with the shadows, but they found there was no need.

The city was abandoned. Completely deserted. No one was there, and the solitude began to settle like a rock in Legna's chest. It felt wrong. Something was about to happen.

Legna could see Korrtar's palace from the time they arrived, but as they quickly slinked through the city, the feeling of dread toward the upcoming battle hit her like an arrow. She reached out to Aryanis, something she had not done in a while, and she still felt the comforting presence there.

"Please help me, my king. Help me do what I was sent to do," she whispered. She felt a reassurance from somewhere beyond herself. She smiled. Suddenly, she felt a sharp pain in her wrist and the presence withdrew quickly from her reach. The pain faded, but the hope she received endured, and she pressed on with a newfound vigor.

They trudged through the city with no sign of any other life. By the time they reached the castle gates, Legna was desperately confused.

Traven glanced around. "Where is everyone?" he asked. "Did someone beat us to it?"

Feor shook his head. "No. Look." He pointed to the castle. It was impressive, even larger than Bella's home. Grey and purple, the castle gave a sense of cold beauty that Legna had only seen once before: At the bottom of Greenwater Lake, on a warm summer day.

She followed Feor's eyes to a balcony at the top. There, leaning out against the railing and feeling the breeze on her face, stood a woman. She was of average height, with icy blonde hair and very pale skin. Her smile seemed translucent. She gave the appearance of someone who was once powerful, but had suffered a terrible ailment and was now weak and frail. Legna felt an ounce of pity for her.

And then she realized who she was looking at.

Korrtar—betrayer, seductress, megalomaniac, and her worst enemy—was only a few hundred feet above her.

# THE DEATH PENALTY

Zemër stood, wounded, and overwhelmed, and watched the chaos around him. What had started as a simple force, a few Demons and a few trolls, had quickly progressed to an army of thousands. Even his elite force of Engjëllen warriors could not defeat them. They only had twelve men, thirteen counting Skeedro, who had regenerated in a few hours and joined the battle. He carried a staff and a knife, slamming Orcs in the nose, then slitting their throats.

Now half of the king's force was wounded, and the other half was begging for retreat. He saw something he had not recognized in Engjëllen faces in many years: Pure fear. Two had died. His marksman, Yuler, and Ganzan, an older warrior. Yuler was right next to Zemër when he was firing a volley and an Orc stabbed him in the back. Zemër fought as he cried in grief and received a draining leg wound because of his mourning.

One by one, his Engjëllens were struck down. Finally, as Zemër stood and calculated their pathetic chances against this army, he called for retreat.

"Retreat! Fall back! Fall back to the forge!" he shouted to his remaining men. He limped away with them, but was suddenly choked by an iron grip.

"Going somewhere?" A brutal voice whispered in his ear. He knew this voice. This voice, hardened by years, was recognizable. This was a voice he had last heard sixteen years ago, a voice that had all but faded from his mind.

"Gidön…" Zemër choked out. The crowd of Orcs, now silent, hissed at the sound of the name.

The one who had grabbed him spun him around and Zemër took a close look to pick out any similar features. There were none. This Demon, this creature was not his former friend. Only a shadow of him. He was huge, and bulking with ridiculous muscles. He had blackish blue shining skin and a squashed up nose that made him resemble a bald gorilla. He had no shirt, but white tattoos covered his chest, pictures of gore and war, of death and grief. They seemed to weigh him down and gave him a weary look in his black eyes that did not fit his bulky body. The Demon turned Zemër to face him, keeping his hand enclosed around his neck. His voice quivered, and his eyes momentarily seemed to cry for help as he said, "What…That name…My king…" The Demon shook his head and his eyes hardened. "That name is forbidden. The mere mention of it"—he leaned close and tears began to show in his eyes—"is punishable…by *death*."

The Orcs began chanting in bloodlust. "Death, death, death, *death, death, death!*" The volume increased, until Zemër's ears boomed with the sound of death for hours afterward, the word imprinted into his being.

The Demon stared at him with a murderous gleam in his eye. Then, he tossed the king aside. The Orcs caught him and shackled his wrists tightly, pushing him around roughly.

"Leave the rest," the Demon said to his colonel. "We can come back for them." He smiled smugly at Zemër. "We have a special prize to enjoy." The Demon boomed with maniacal laughter, and the Orcs joined him. The Demon turned and strode away; his back straight and confident, but his gait slow and limping. The Orcs seized Zemër firmly by the arms and led him after the Demon out the gates of Engjëll into the outside world, open and wild.

For the first time in his life, Zemër felt completely vulnerable and genuinely afraid.

∽

They marched for hours before dusk, when the Orcs stopped and shoved Zemër roughly to the ground for the night. They lit a fire and pulled some mead from their packs, drinking bottles upon bottles and throwing the alcohol into the fire to watch it leap up in agitation. The Demon sat alone, drinking no mead and not speaking to the others. He sat brooding and relentlessly staring at Zemër, a contemplating look troubling his hideous face.

An Orc staggered up to him and put a drunken hand on his shoulder.

"We gonna execute him tonigh'?" the Orc asked loudly. Suddenly, all interest was focused on this conversation.

The Demon considered this, glanced at Zemër, then glanced back at the Orc. He balled his fist, and without moving the rest of his body, punched the Orc, sending him flying into the shadows.

The Demon stood, spreading his arms to the crowd of soldiers. "Shall we execute him tonight?" The Demon said mockingly, a deadly tone in his voice. The Orcs were deathly silent, as if a fly buzzing might set the Demon off on a rampage.

"Shall we?" he asked again, screaming. He stared at Zemër, and Zemër was overwhelmingly disturbed to see this sick creature smiling while his eyes cried desperately for help.

The Demon stared, and the pleading in his eyes was slowly clouded over by a darkness—a disease full of blood lust. He snatched an axe from one of warriors and strode toward Zemër.

He raised the axe. "All hail *the King!*" He roared ferociously, tauntingly. He swung, right for Zemër's neck.

And as Zemër watched the Demon's eyes, disregarding the weapon swinging at him with full force, he saw something. He saw an apology, written right there in the Demon's eyes. It was this moment that Zemër was sure, that he knew the Demon really was Gidön. He closed his eyes and waited in darkness for the axe to end his long life.

It was time.

# ALL FALLS DOWN

As Legna stared up at Korrtar, the woman closed her eyes. Legna could tell that Korrtar knew they were there, but the woman did nothing. She turned her face to the sky and, almost on command, the heavens opened, and it began to pour; the drops of rain running down her face. She savored every drop. Then, so suddenly it made Legna jump, Korrtar snapped her head down to stare in their direction. A grotesque smile snaked onto her lips, as she stared directly into Legna's eyes.

Korrtar mouthed two words to Legna as she stood in the rain. "We're ready."

With a look of complete glee, she whirled around and entered the castle. Legna was stunned and confused.

"How are we supposed to respond to that?" Feor whispered incredulously. "Should we march in after her and just announce the place is ours?"

"I- I don't think it's that simple," Traven said. He looked at Legna. "What do we do now?" he asked.

Legna thought. She knew what she had to do, but she was so frightened of what was to come that it was hard to face. She turned to Traven and Feor. She looked deeply into Traven's deep green eyes, light brown wisps hewn here and there into his irises. She reached her hand toward him, letting her hands land as her heart chose. One hand cupped his cheek, caressing it tenderly. The other gripped his shoulder, for support and warmth from his very alive body.

"Traven…" Her face so close to his; she could hear his ragged breath and could see the tears threatening to overflow from his eyes. He knew what she was about to say, the pain on his face displayed it, intense and cutting, like a double edged sword.

She tried again. "Traven, I—"

He stopped her words with his lips, kissing her gently. It surprised her, the intensity of it, but she leaned into it. When he stopped, she was left wondering what the kiss meant.

Then he whispered three words that revealed its purpose: "I love you."

She was speechless, unable to think, unable to organize her own feelings. Did she love him? She was not sure. She thought of Garren, trying not to compare the two men, two completely different people, but she could not stop herself.

Garren—quiet and thoughtful, a simple baker, someone who could give her a family, security. Traven—outspoken and her best friend, a warrior, with a thirst for adventure, just like her. Both of them loved her, she knew this. Deep down inside, her heart knew which one she loved, but it just was not letting her know.

But as she gazed into his eyes, the danger of the moment forgotten, she knew what she wanted.

The words came easily as if they had been water pent up behind a dam for many years. The floodgates of her mind opened and it came rushing out.

"I love you too, Traven," she whispered back and kissed him again, placing her hand gently on his cheek. As she pulled back, she dreaded her next words.

"I have to go alone," she said carefully. "All alone. This was my quest to begin with, and I want you both to be safe. If Korrtar wins…Get back to Engjëll and tell them to evacuate. All will be lost then…" She trailed off as she thought of the weight of the moment. Here she was, with her odd little family by her side. For the first time, she had no backup plan. This was it. The final moment had arrived. It was either succeed or die, and Legna was fairly certain of her preferred outcome.

Traven's look of grief was imminent. He caressed her cheek; his hand moving down to her neck and then slowly stroking down her arm to intertwine his fingers with hers. He was too dejected to speak, so Feor spoke up.

"Legna, we're your friends, and we aren't about to let you go in there and die for your own pride."

"This isn't pride, Feor. This is something I have to do. And I feel like I must do it alone."

Traven finally found his voice and said, "At least let us come in with you, please. Don't leave us here to watch you die."

Legna sighed. They did not have time for this. So, she compromised. "If I'm in there for ten minutes, follow me and see what you can do."

Traven looked at her with a defeated look and Feor narrowed his eyes indignantly, but both nodded halfheartedly in agreement. She nodded back, in reassurance. Then, she stood and strode with dignity away from her companions and into the castle, hearing a *thud* behind her as Aspör landed among them.

"She's leaving without us," she heard Aspör whisper, broken. Murmurs of comfort came from Traven and Feor, and she continued on. Through the gate at the beginning of the path, straight into the doors she went, just like an old friend might.

The hall was huge, much like Queen Bella's castle. Fibrous strands of amethyst with internal light, no doubt magical, were strung delicately across the black stone walls. Disturbing satin banners hung from the walls, each with a picture of murder stitched into it. A man smiling gruesomely with blood on his hands hung on the east wall while his victim, a woman screaming in agony with a knife through her heart, hung on the west wall.

Legna averted her eyes from these scenes and focused on the carpet. A rich, blood red graced the floors. As she stepped on it, she was surprised to find it wet and sticky. She bent down and wiped her hand across it, and her fingers returned to her with crimson liquid dripping down to her arm.

The carpet was drenched in blood. Legna tasted bile in her mouth and swallowed hard to avoid vomiting. She had not expected Korrtar to be so unstable of mind, but she realized that she had just walked into the castle of a madwoman.

Pushing back her fear, she trudged along the carpet in silent dread. What else would Korrtar conjure up? There was a grand staircase in front of her made of black marble. She began to ascend it, taking each step with caution.

The worst part, Legna concluded to herself, was the lack of choice in the castle. There was only one path. No hallways trailed from the foyer, like most castles. There was only one way, one hall, no doors or windows. One way in. One way out. It made Legna feel claustrophobic, the lack of discernment greatly disturbing. She was like a sheep to the shepherd.

"Or a lamb to the slaughter," she whispered to herself. Her whisper echoed, so great the silence around her, and it continued to bounce from the walls until she was listening to thousands of whispers. She was sure that she heard other voices than her own repeating the words.

Something began to itch at her, to close around her mind, and she began to feel increasingly paranoid. She clutched her sword hilt, and soon, the anxiety became too much for her. She drew the sword and continued up the steps, which seemed to continue on forever. Then, the staircase abruptly stopped, and Legna continued down a narrow hallway lit only by the twinkling amethysts on the walls. Creaks of the castle began to invade her sense of sound, moans and groans of the fortress's inner workings.

The hallway opened up to a wide terrace, and Legna was shocked to see the sky full of stars. It was night. How was this possible? Why had Traven and Feor not come after her by now?

"I guess I really am facing Korrtar alone," Legna murmured to herself. She suddenly felt very small as she looked at the balcony around her. It was completely empty, made of more black marble. She could not see whatever was below it, just deep, ominous darkness. It was a dead end.

Legna turned to leave back through the hallway, to check that she did not miss any doors or tributary hallways, but to her surprise the hallway was gone.

In its place, three thrones sat. A large, cold stone throne reclined in the middle, made of amethyst and dark granite. To its right was a complex throne carved from cedar wood to look as if a dragon was holding the seat up. The last throne was made of a glorious white mineral, shining in the dark like a fallen star.

Her mind was being played with, she realized. Now she stood, uncertain of how to proceed. As she stared desolately at the thrones, two figures began to appear in the first two thrones. They were just shadows at first with their heads hanging loosely as if dead. Soon, they began to solidify and take form in her eyes. In the wooden throne sat a demon, with a crown. He had wrinkled black skin that fell in flakes from his bald head every so often. He wore a sparkling set of armor and an axe clung heavily to his back.

In the stone throne, Korrtar lightly reclined, raising her head to watch Legna with seeming amusement. The demon joined her; his black eyes twinkling coldly.

"Finally," Korrtar whispered; her voice soothing and raspy, both high and low, melodious and a cacophony, completely indescribable. She chuckled, raising her arms to some unknown deity her depraved mind had conjured up.

"Finally!" she shouted; her giddy laugh unnerving Legna. Korrtar surged forward in her seat and stood, her black dress flowing behind her like an executioner's cape. The woman strode forward with gusto, right next to Legna. Korrtar grabbed Legna's chin in her hand and inspected her face.

"You're quite beautiful. Almost as beautiful as me," Korrtar said.

"Just not as conceited," Legna said with venom, pushing Korrtar's hand from her jaw.

Korrtar smiled a smile void of humor. "You remind me of myself in many ways. You defy tradition; you're witty, quite brave. You make me proud."

Legna kept a straight face. "The only difference is our sense of honor."

Korrtar's eyes took on a sad look. "Ah, yes. You're committed to your *king*. You see, my dear, honor is an opinion. Your definition of honor and my definition of honor could be two very different things."

"They obviously are," Legna shot back. "And what is your definition of honor? Betray those who love us for more power? I guess somehow, in your mind, you see that as honor. You gave them a chance to serve you and make what you believe to be the right thing for the world a reality. You make me sick."

"I gave them a chance at a better future!" Korrtar exclaimed gloriously. "I had ideas, wonderful ideas for this world. And they threw them aside." Anger began to creep into Korrtar's voice, and she shook her head in an attempt to clear her mind. "But no matter. Today is *your* day!"

Korrtar turned to face the thrones, where the demon sat in stoic silence. She gestured to the throne on the end.

"I've been preparing for your arrival," Korrtar said intimately. "This throne is yours. I can give you more than you have ever dreamed of."

"I've had one too many nightmares to agree to that," Legna whispered steadily.

Korrtar seemed unperturbed by this news. "All right. Suit yourself," she said; her voice no longer warm and inviting. "Care to meet my newest pet? I mean...prince."

The Demon stood, rising to full height and bared pitch black fangs. As he drew his battle-axe, Legna tightened her grip on her sword.

Korrtar disappeared, into thin air, without sound or indication of returning. "Isn't he beautiful?" Her voice sounded from all around, ringing coldly in Legna's ears. "Well...he was, anyway. Legna, meet your old friend." Just like that, the voice of Korrtar dissipated, leaving only Legna and the Demon.

Old friend? What did she mean? Legna hardly had time to think before the Demon's axe came crashing down, barely missing her head as she rolled out of the way.

Suddenly, she understood something. She was not fighting Korrtar. She was fighting this Prince.

She stood from the roll, now to the left of the Demon. He roared in protest and swung his axe at nothing, a form of intimidation that Legna recognized from her own people. *Especially one person*, she thought. She could not for the life of her remember which man it was. Again, her thoughts were smacked aside by her survival instinct as the Demon came charging at her. She rolled again, swinging her sword blindly and landing a lucky hit on the back of the Demon's calf. The gash wounded him, but it was hardly enough to prove fatal.

A voice sounded above them. Korrtar had returned to watch. "My dear girl, have you guessed who this is? Once loved, now despised, but still a prince. Give me your best guess."

Legna felt sick. "Father?" She murmured, flattering the queen with her cooperation.

"Hmm. Why don't we find out?"

The Demon before her morphed into an exact likeness of her father; everything of his figure was present but his crippled leg and cane. Korrtar had healed him.

Her father charged. The axe had become his familiar sword, a disturbing sense of betrayal emanating from the weapon. The very sword that had shown her the movements of sparring was now trying to kill her.

Their swords clashed loudly, and her father smiled in false kindness at her. "It's good to practice. Remember your training," the Demon said mockingly.

"My training was to kill without mercy, *father.*" She swung her sword deftly at his neck and the Demon ducked, stabbing at her legs. She hopped back and slimly avoided the blade. "There is no way my father committed to you, Korrtar. I have faith in that." "My child, you have faith in the pettiest of things. It will be your downfall," Korrtar's voice boomed. Finally, Legna spotted her in an unnoticeable balcony seemingly floating in the middle of the stars. "But, in this case, your faith shows you the way. My prince is not your father." The Demon morphed back into the faceless black figure he had been before.

"Guess again, my beauty."

It could not be Garren. Legna was sure of that. But, sure enough, as soon as her thought materialized, she saw her old love swinging a Naïfonian axe at her. She shrieked and dropped to the ground as the axe barely missed her neck. Garren swung around and brought the blunt of the axe blade crashing down onto her back.

Legna cried out in pain as she felt a rib crack and quickly rolled out of Garren's way. They stood in a deadlock, facing each other in a war of the eyes and a battle of the mind. She knew of only one way to figure out whether this was Garren or not. She surged forward and, obviously startling the Demon, kissed him. The lips she felt were cold and dead, refusing to kiss back. This was not Garren. She stabbed him through the stomach while their lips were still locked and let him fall away, the disguise melting from the Demon's physique like mud from glass on a rainy day.

Legna glanced up at Korrtar. The woman clutched her stomach as if she had taken the blow also. She looked paler, and for a moment she looked weaker. She quickly regained her composure, and said, "You are good at games of the mind, girl. For that is all this is. Only a game of the mind." Her voice became a whisper. "Guess once more."

*Aryanis, my king, don't let it be my companions. Please, I couldn't kill them,* Legna thought feverishly.

"Ah, I believe you've just dug yourself a hole you can't get out of," Korrtar rasped. The Demon's body began to peel apart into three different parts, skin closing over the wounds caused in a grotesque fashion. Each section threw itself to the ground, and in a series of spasms and convulsions formed themselves into Bátor, Feor, and Traven.

"Kill me now," Legna whispered to herself.

Korrtar waved her off. "All in good time, my dear."

Legna laughed in spite of herself. She was going to die today, and there was nothing she could do but continue to fight every person she had ever loved.

"Which one could it be, which one could it be?" Korrtar said in a melodic tone.

All three stormed her at once, surrounding her in a deadly triangle. She rolled between Traven's legs, kicking out his legs and crying out as her instincts forced her to stab him in the back. Tears ran down her face as she watched him fall, dead in an instant.

"No," she whispered. "This is wrong." Feor swung his broadsword at her, and she jumped out of the way quickly, hearing the sword hiss through the empty air where she had just been. She stabbed at him, but he deflected every blow she tried to land. She pushed him back into the shadows near the thrones, a plan forming quickly in her mind. As Feor was enveloped in the deepest, darkest shadow, Legna faked a roll under his legs and then jumped as high as she could, raising her sword and bringing it down hard on Feor's skull. He collapsed to the ground, unconscious, and Legna drove the sword through his stomach, hating herself for doing so.

Then, she realized she had not killed Feor. He had not blended with the shadows. The real Feor would have done so. The guilt faded, although the trauma could not be erased.

Bátor ran at her maniacally, screaming, "Expect the unexpected, my dear!" She shrieked as she was trapped against a wall and she felt the cold point of his sword digging into her neck. She pushed on his arm, but he kept it firmly in its deadly position. She moved her hand down his arm to his wrist, grabbed hold of it, and, before Bátor could do anything, twisted his wrist, breaking it. He yelled in pain and dropped his sword, falling to the ground, clutching his arm. Without thinking, she drew her bow, pulled back and took aim for his head. The arrow slid from the string and planted itself into his forehead. His eyes lulled back in his head as the arrow exploded, burning his skin away, revealing just a skeleton.

The Demon reformed, skin spreading across the bones and organs growing in high speed before they too were closed over by skin.

A thought came to her. Where *had* Zemëroj gone that day if he had not returned to Engjëll?

Korrtar gasped up in her balcony. "You've figured it out! Good job! A little late, but I'm impressed you guessed it."

"Zemëroj? Our prince…he's your prince now."

"That's right."

The Demon's skin peeled and flaked away until it left the chiseled physique of Zemëroj.

"You betrayed us," she said to him; her voice hard and cold.

"I took the better path. Look at all I have!"

"You're second in command to the most insane woman in Zerúa, and you're destroying everything you once loved. You're right, sounds like a great way to spend the rest of your life."

Zemëroj smirked. "You're just as foolish as you were before I left."

"And you're just as dishonorable."

Anger boiled in his eyes, and he assailed her, this time knocking Legna to the ground with the flat of his axe. He stood triumphantly over her and raised his axe to finish her, all too easily, but she quickly rolled backwards, her feet kicking Zemëroj's legs out from under him and bringing him down. She realized she would get nowhere with melee, so she plucked her bow from its position on her back and laid an arrow on the quiver. As Legna turned, she saw he was already up and running at her. She had no time to respond before he had tackled her, knocking her back into the throne Korrtar had made for her.

"You will submit," Zemëroj said heavily, pinning her down on the throne. "I always win in war."

Legna, her bow still prepared to fire, drew the string slightly back and shot the arrow deeply into the Zemëroj's stomach.

"You see," Legna whispered, "the problem with war is there are too many rules."

He fell back onto his rear end, onto the ground, clutching the wound. "You cheated," he said incredulously.

"Precisely," Legna said. "I wish I didn't have to do this. But you made your choice." She stood, and with a victorious smile, stomped heavily on the arrow in his stomach; the shaft exploding into flames around them. In the final seconds before the fire engulfed her, she saw Traven sprint through a doorway she had not seen before, screaming her name, reaching out to her. And then everything went black.

# RESTORED LIGHT

Traven knelt over Legna's limp body. How could he have let this happen? This girl, this angel in his life, had meant everything to him, yet he let her sacrifice herself. Tears threatened to spill over.

"Korrtar!" he screamed into the empty air. The sound of his voice bounced around the empty space. The night sky nothing more than an illusion on a ceiling. The voices covered him, consoled him, convinced him. Pulling Legna's head into his lap, he began to weep bitterly, realizing how costly his quest had always been. He recounted to himself the events before he had followed Legna into the castle.

When Legna had left into the castle, Feor and Traven had been suddenly surrounded by an army of Demons. The commander of the army, whom he heard referred to as Errk, was fearsome in every aspect. With black, soulless eyes, long horns protruding from his temples and leathery, ripped wings poking from his back, Traven almost thought he was looking at Korrtar.

The Demons cornered them, Errk stepping forward and jabbing his spear at Traven.

"Come in peace, and your death will not be quite so painful as I planned," Errk growled.

"You, my friend, are a true diplomat," Feor said. "But unfortunately for you, so are we. How about you leave and we don't slaughter every last one of you?"

"Feor," Traven said softly, warning him.

Errk was not amused. He shrugged indifferently, turned and breezily said, "Kill them." Suddenly, Aspör, who had flown to look for hidden armies in the city, swooped down and took out an entire brigade of Demons with his massive tail. Errk stared, stunned, and Traven took the opportunity. He pulled the bow from his back, notched an arrow, and shot Errk in the neck. Errk paused, stricken fear crossing his eyes, and fell to the ground, vomiting blood and pointing dastardly at Traven and Feor.

"Kill them!" Errk hissed and then slumped forward, dead. Traven and Feor leapt over the rock they were hidden behind and took off through the city. Feor was behind Traven, giving Traven a lead as they both knew who the better fighter was.

The company of Demons behind them began to gain unnatural speed, overtaking Feor quickly and seizing him by the arms. He kicked and bit, fought as hard as he could, but they carried him away, into the city. The army continued to pursue Traven until Aspör landed heavily in front of him and allowed Traven to climb onto his back. They flew away, and Aspör sped toward the courtyard of Korrtar's castle. Traven jumped desperately when they were twenty feet above the ground. The landing rattled his bones, and he considered that he might have broken a few toes, but he stumbled into the castle nonetheless. He was so frantic to get to her, to see her face, that all pain left him. Fires had erupted all over the castle, but Traven just jumped over them or swerved around them. He sprinted up a very long staircase and down a narrow hallway, until he burst through the doorway and watched as Legna combusted her opponent, along with herself.

*She still looks so perfect,* Traven thought. His eyes ran longingly over her face, wanting his old friend back. Her lips, which he thought were the most perfect shade of pink, curved gracefully, so painfully alive on her cold, paling face it put a terrible weight on his chest. Her eyes, still open, still warm, were a beautiful brown. He could still see the heavy sorrow that had seemed to accumulate in her throughout their journey.

He loved her the whole time, from when they were children to this moment.

"At least I could tell you I love you once," he whispered to her. "I love you." He kissed her forehead wistfully and looked hopelessly to the sky.

"I remember everything," he said to her, to relieve the tension he felt. "I've been sure to. Every moment I've kept in my mind. Do you remember your fifth birthday? I do. It was the first time you hugged me." He proceeded to recount many of the moments they had together, until his words broke with grief and he could only silently allow the tears to roll down his cheeks.

"You're gone," he whispered, barely audibly. "You are everything, to me and now you're gone."

His eyes lifted once more to the skies. "Save me, my king," he breathed. "Take me away from this place." To his surprise, a bright light appeared above him, enveloping the star filled sky and turning synthetic night to day.

A man, handsome and gentle, with undefinable features, materialized right before Traven's eyes. Shocked, Traven could only gape at the man. His face looked familiar, but Traven had never seen him before.

"Who are you?" Traven asked half-heartedly, not wanting any more adventure.

"I'm your king, Traven. It's me. It's Aryanis," the man said softly.

Traven glanced at Aryanis, his mind not processing or caring about the words he heard. Suddenly, he remembered who he was speaking to. He gently lifted Legna's head from his lap and knelt down respectfully.

"My King," he murmured in awe.

"Rise up. Something troubles you." Aryanis's eyes flickered down to Legna and then back to Traven.

"Yes," Traven said. "To put it lightly, my King, something is troubling me. My friend has died."

Aryanis laughed a rumbling laugh that made Traven feel joyful in spite of his anger.

"You assume too much, my son. Your girl is not dead. Only sleeping."

"Sleeping?" Traven breathed in disbelief. He knelt by her side again and felt her pulse. Yes, she was alive. She was alive! Legna was not dead after all! "How long will she sleep?"

"Oh, a few days at the most."

Traven remembered something that Wisteria had told them so long ago, when they were still in Engjëll. "My King," he said, looking up at the deity. "You're supposed to be dead. You left Zerúa to die for the Gizaans."

"Ah, yes. The sin filled people. They did kill me, yes. But I'm about to come back to life."

"What do you mean?" Traven was puzzled. No one, not even in Zerúa, came back to life.

"See, I knew I would die, and I would be trapped in Mëkator where all lost souls go. I've been in these dungeons for a fairly long time, but now I'm ready to return. I spent thirty years in Giza, and I'm ready to go back for one last visit with the people I love."

Traven's eyes displayed doubt. "But it was only a few weeks ago that you left! How could you have spent thirty years there?"

Aryanis shrugged, "Time runs differently there. It goes faster. It has something to do with a continuum, but I doubt you would understand." Aryanis smiled kindly. "Now, I won't return in my fullness for a long time, but for now let's get you back to Engjëll."

Everything blurred, and Traven fainted.

When Traven woke, he was lying in his own bed, sunlight streaming through the large window close to him. His dirty, torn clothes were gone and replaced by cotton night clothes. His sword and bow leaned against the wall across the room.

He lifted his hand from under the covers and stared at it in amazement. Was he dreaming? Or was he really home?

He sat up abruptly. "Legna!" he cried. He tore from the bed; his head pounding. He rent the clothes from his body and quickly dressed in whatever he could find and then he sprinted out of his room, through their atrium and to the front door. He flung open the door and halted. The town was empty.

# AWAKENING

Legna's eyes snapped open from her deep sleep. It had been a tiring sleep; a sleep that made her want to curl up again because in that sleep, she had fought with herself to stay alive. She had wrestled with her will and told herself that she would stay alive no matter what.

Here she was now, unless it was a dream, in her room. How did she get here? As she turned her head sleepily, she saw her father intently gazing at her with concern.

"Look who's finally awake! Now I know you've never been much of a morning person, but really, you've been out for days now!"

Legna smiled. She was home. "Where is Mother?"

Läken cast his eyes down. "She isn't in Engjëll. She went with the rest of the village to Naïfon."

Legna sat up suddenly and exclaimed, "Naïfon! What are they doing there? Why didn't they wait for our arrival?"

Läken's eyes began to tear and he said in a small, uncharacteristic voice, "Because they didn't expect your arrival. They thought they had sent you straight to your deaths."

Legna's eyes hardened. Her village had not believed she could save them, and that hurt her. "How many," she said. "How many are left in Engjëll?"

"Ten men," Läken breathed. "Two are dead, one…One has been captured. Our king. King Zemër has been captured, and the rest of the men have left to find him. Except for—"

The door banged open and there, in the doorway, stood Garren.

"Garren," Legna murmured, old, foreign emotions flooding her.

"Legna!" Garren rushed forward, kneeling next to the bed and stroking the hair from Legna's eyes. "You look…amazing. Older." He looked into her eyes. "Wiser."

She averted her eyes from his. He leaned in for a kiss, but she pulled back from him. "Garren, I can't—"

A hurt look in his eyes, his eyebrows bunched together as he studied her. "Legna, what happened out there? Don't you love me anymore?"

"I do, Garren. I just can't give you the love you seek." Her head began to pound, and she felt nauseous.

Garren drew his hand back like he had been burned. "What? But you said you loved me…" His voice trailed off as he stared forlornly at the ground.

"I didn't know what love was then," Legna said. She felt like a monster, a heartless beast no better than the Demons she killed.

Suddenly, a subdued look entered Garren's eyes. He nodded, a smile gracing his lips. "I understand," he said. "Now that I think of it, I don't know if what I felt was love either." He smiled nostalgically. "Just a childish crush." He looked into her eyes, a surprising glow of respect radiating from him. "I hope you do find true love, Legna. If anyone deserves it, it's you." He kissed her cheek gently and then strode from the room.

Tears filled her eyes as she watched him go, and she almost cried out to him to tell him to stay.

But then Traven pushed past him into the room, and her breath was swept away. His face was clean, tan, and perfect. His red hair had darkened—something that she had not noticed in their travels, and his green eyes glowed with happiness.

Silence hung in the air as they locked eyes, unsure of what to do or say.

Läken broke the silence. "Well do something, boy! You thought the girl was dead! What's wrong with your head?"

Traven took the advice and surged forward, wrapping Legna in his strong arms and lifting her from the bed, spinning her in joy.

"You're alive." He breathed. "I thought I had lost you, but here you are."

She began to cry, burying her face in his shoulder. "I'm sorry I left you." She sobbed. "I'm sorry."

"Legna," he set her down on her feet and supported her still weak body. "You did what you had to do." He caressed her cheek and leaned down to kiss her.

She met his kiss and laughed as her father said, "What in all of Mëkator did I miss on that quest? Is that why you turned down Garren?"

Traven stared at her in amazement. "You turned down Garren? For me?"

She nodded, the meaning of it dawning on her also. "Yes. I suppose that is what I did."

Läken looked Traven up and down. "You take care of my daughter, boy. I still have a decent sword arm if you take my meaning." Traven's eyes widened in fear and he let go of Legna. Läken laughed. "I'm just joking, Traven, don't worry. I know you'll be good for her."

His eyes smiled as his mouth remained a straight line, adding a light-hearted air to his stern expression.

"Do you feel well enough to go for a walk?" Traven asked Legna, offering her his hand.

"I think I can manage." She took his hand, intertwining her fingers with his. They sauntered out of the room into the kitchen and through the door, out into the eerily empty village.

"It's strange to have no one here, isn't it?" Traven said, his eyes wandering around the vacant houses. "Your father said the rest of the village should begin on their journey home soon."

Legna did not answer. They walked on in silence, thoughts churning endlessly through her head. "What happens now?" Legna said suddenly, cutting the silence in two. "We didn't finish what we were sent to do, Traven."

He looked at her, puzzled. "What do you mean? We completed the quest. We saved Engjëll. That was our goal."

She shook her head. "We saved Engjëll for the time. But Traven … Korrtar isn't dead. I didn't kill her. She escaped."

He let go of her hand in shock. "You mean she's still in Mëkator? She's still alive?"

"I don't know where she—" a flash in front of them cut Legna off, and they watched as their High King materialized before their eyes.

They both dropped to their knees, and Legna winced as she fought the urge to faint from the sudden movement.

"Rise and take comfort," Aryanis said. "Your quest would not have been finished even if you had defeated Korrtar. Each lifetime is a quest. From the minute anything is born, it is destined to be a hero of some kind. It will have smaller adventures in its lifetime that will help the quest along. But at the end of its life, that is when its quest is completed." He smiled and placed a hand on Legna's shoulder. "You have done what you set out to do. You did not know it at first, but your goal was not to kill Korrtar but to weaken her."

Legna thought about this. She had killed Korrtar's prince. Was that all she was needed for?

"Your thoughts are correct, child," Aryanis said. "Your mission was to kill her new prince. She had poured much of her power and will into this Demon, a convert you uncovered. Zemëroj, your former heir to the Engjëllen throne."

"But my King," Traven breathed. "Where is Korrtar now?"

Aryanis drew himself to his full height and exhaled in an emotion Legna could not decipher. "She has been banished from this world. She no longer presides in Mëkator." Legna began to smile before Aryanis help up a hand to tell her he was not finished.

"She now dwells in Giza. And is already beginning to wreak havoc on the citizens of that world. Now, her Demons roam free across Zerúa, slowly making their way to join their queen in Giza. Zerúans are still falling to dark thoughts, still building her army. They are only scattered for the time being. No, our work is not finished, but you have made a huge victory today. Go, celebrate, worry not about the future, but of the present. That is what is important for now." Aryanis closed his eyes and mumbled a few words to himself, and the village was brought to life. Engjëllens with startled looks on their faces lined the streets; their fright evolving to joy in seconds.

A great cheer erupted from the crowd as all eyes fell on Legna and Traven, welcoming them home and sweeping them away.

# EPILOGUE

Days after their return, the fame and attention from the adventure faded and the village began to flow as it did before. A search party was sent out for Zemër, which had not yet returned. Legna wandered the village vacantly, thinking to herself. She had changed since she had last been in Engjëll. She was withdrawn and brooding, not quite as open and friendly as she had been before. She may have saved everyone else, but her mind was still not quite right from her traumatic battle with Zemëroj. She still had not told anyone of the exact details, not even Traven or her father.

She stopped to lean against a wall, watching the busy village bustle about in such joy. *They were so oblivious to the horrors that were truly out there*, she thought. The sound of galloping hooves attracted her attention to the main path into the town square. An old elf, riding a unicorn made her grin for the first time in a while.

"Absom!" she called as she strode through the watching crowd. She still had quite a large group of fans, no matter how much she showed she did not enjoy the attention.

"Forget something?" he asked with a smile, dismounting Vella. "She showed up at my doors days after you left."

"We ran into some trouble with some Orcs and a dragon, and she escaped for her own safety."

"Well, I see you came out in one piece. What about mentally? Are you doing all right?"

Legna rubbed Vella's neck. "Actually, Absom, do you have the time for a walk in Kaparan Meadow? I need to get some things off my mind."

"I was thinking about staying in Engjëll for a little while more. I have time for my favorite little hero." He hugged her tightly, surprising her but still comforting her. "I knew you would do it," he whispered. He pulled back and said, "Now, would you mind escorting an old man through the village?" He offered her his arm.

She took it, and they started through the village slowly, not in any rush. They indulged in small talk, with nothing too important to talk about for once. As soon as they had left the village and entered the meadow, Legna decided she could not withhold what she had to say any longer.

"My battle with the Demon prince was...disturbing," she said quietly.

Absom nodded. "The creatures are fairly perturbing."

"Korrtar...she just played with me. She tried to just break down my will."

"That's typical. What was her scheme this time?"

Legna sat down in the grass, Absom sitting with her. She picked up a wish flower, blowing the puffy seeds from the stem and watching them float away. She imagined the seeds as her problems, falling to the breeze and being carried away.

She proceeded to tell Absom everything—about the castle, the battle, and Korrtar. Absom nodded, listening intently. At the part where she killed Traven, she began to cry, unable to continue.

"Hey, come here," Absom said gently. He put his arm around her and held her close. "At least you didn't have to kill me, eh?"

She laughed through her tears. "I don't think I could have done that."

She tried to continue, but Absom stopped her. "You don't have to tell me the rest. I understand what happened. Don't worry, I understand how hard that was, killing the likeness of the ones you most loved. You've done something incredible, something the most famous of heroes could not accomplish. You've set aside your feelings for what needed to be done. That does not make you a monster. That makes you a hero. Only a true hero could sacrifice everything to save what they love. You were even willing to sacrifice your own life. That's commitment. I couldn't have done it."

Legna looked up into Absom's kind grey eyes. "I'm going to get that book for you, Absom. I'm going to Pâne."

A smile graced his wise face. "All in good time, my dear. But it would be much appreciated." He stood, offering her his hand, and she took it, pulling herself up.

"I think I'll stay in Engjëll for a little longer than I intended. I haven't been here in ages, and it's still as charming as ever. It's a nice change from a big city like Mär-Lïnna, don't you say?"

Legna found herself agreeing, and she marveled at the fact that she knew what Mär-Lïnna was like. She had never before dreamed she would know so much about the world. The ring Bella had given Legna glinted on her finger, bright and beautiful.

She had much more to learn, but for now she was happy just to be a small town girl again, with no troubles and a normal life.

A thump sounded behind them and they turned to see Aspör, as fearsome and marvelous as ever.

*Well, almost a normal life,* she thought to herself. She gestured to Aspör and said to Absom, "Shall we?" Absom nodded and allowed her to help him onto the dragon's back.

Legna paused and stroked Aspör's nose, and Aspör nuzzled her in return. "It's good to be home," she said.

She climbed onto his back, and they took off, watching the meadow shrink below them until it was just a phantasmagoria of colors, like a kaleidoscopic sea.

While she enjoyed her adventure, she was ready for a little bit of a calm life.

For the moment.

# AFTERWORD

There were many people who inspired this book. My brother, Matt, an extraordinary person and one that spent countless hours discussing the fine points of my writing. I'll never forget the night we talked for three hours about how Zemëroj's transformation should take place.

My parents, of course, inspired the characters Läken and Zopporah. My mother has always wanted me to be more girly. Instead of enjoying video games and superhero movies, she's always wanted me to like things like baking and dresses. Although we are different—she likes pink, and I like blue—she still loves me and accepts me as I am. My father has always encouraged my tomboyish personality and sparked my interest in things of that sort at an early stage, just like Legna and her father, and we've gotten in some mischief together because of it that inspired some things in this book.

My friends were a huge supporter for this. I'll never forget when I first let the news out into the open. They immediately began fighting over who would receive the first copy and asking for characters written in their image. I would print out chapters at a time and bring them into school for whoever wanted to read them, and I would usually have people asking for it first thing in the morning.

How did I think of this book, you ask? Well, like every great thing. It literally started with a dream. Asleep one night, I had a dream of a village with houses made out of trees. As I walked around the village, I noticed that a small waterfall pouring out of one of the houses was made entirely of green sludge. I ran to what seemed to be the hub of the village, a gigantic oak tree with a ton of space inside. Everyone seemed to be gathered there, for something. As I burst in, all eyes focused on me. A grand looking man stood with a crown and blonde hair, and he asked me what was wrong. I told them about the water, and he immediately said we needed a hero. My crazy dream-self jumped at the chance, and as he said yes, a demon with fangs jumped from inside his body, and turning to look me in the eyes, as at this point, I was watching myself in the third person, ripped my vision to shreds. When I told my parents, they said it was interesting and that I should write a story about it. So I did, and this is what happened. So there you have it, always listen to your dreams.

A word on my age. I don't want to use this as a way to brag or be prideful. I want to inspire people, to say you are never too young to do what you love. I was fourteen when I published this because I had a dream and a God-given talent, and I wanted something done about it. Never ever let someone tell you that you cannot do something because you're a kid because that is ridiculous. Children have the youngest, most vibrant mind with none of the weight of growing up. Just because I published a book does not make me above anyone. I still attend high school, I still have to turn in homework like everyone else, and I still watch television and have pop culture obsessions just like any other fourteen-year-old. Everyone is ordinary in some ways and exceptional in others. It's just up to you to let your exceptional side shine through. I don't want to be too sappy with that, I just wanted to use it as a chance to show young people how to follow their dreams.

It isn't very important to me that my book becomes a bestseller, or a classic. I just want to make people happy with my masterpiece. That in itself is the greatest reward.

*Lamtumirë*, friends, until our next adventure.

CPSIA information can be obtained at www.ICGtesting.com
Printed in the USA
BVOW11s0553210415

396969BV00012B/97/P

9 781630 632502